CU00802584

David Burnell was born and

at Cambridge University, taugnt the subject in West Africa and came across Operational Research as a useful application. He returned to study this at Lancaster and then spent his professional career applying the subject to management problems in the Health Service, coal mining and latterly the water industry. On "retiring" he completed a PhD at Lancaster on the deeper meaning of data from London's water meters.

He and his wife live in Berkshire but own a small holiday cottage in North Cornwall. They have four grown-up children.

David is now hard at work on further books in the "Cornish Conundrum" series.

Other Cornish Conundrums by David Burnell

Doom Watch: *"Cornwall and its richly storied coast has a new writer to celebrate in David Burnell. His crafty plotting and engaging characters are sure to please crime fiction fans."* Peter Lovesey

Slate Expectations: *"combines an interesting view of an often overlooked side of Cornish history with an engaging pair of sleuths who follow the trail from past misdeeds to present murder."* Carola Dunn

"This book has an original atmospheric setting, which is sure to put Delabole on the map. A many-stranded story keeps the reader guessing, with intriguing local history colouring events up to the present day." Rebecca Tope

Looe's Connections: *"History, legend, and myth mixed with a modern technical conundrum make this an intriguing mystery."* Carola Dunn

"A super holiday read set in a super holiday location!" Judith Cutler

Peter Lovesey *is a winner of the CWA Cartier Diamond Dagger.*

Carola Dunn *is author of Daisy Dalrymple and Cornish mysteries.*

Rebecca Tope *writes the Cotswold and West Country Mysteries.*

Judith Cutler *is author of several crime series, most recently featuring Detective Superintendant Fran Harman.*

Ann Granger *(see rear cover) is the author of several crime series, including the Campbell and Carter mysteries.*

TUNNEL VISION

A Cornish Conundrum

David Burnell

SKEIN BOOKS

TUNNEL VISION

First published by Skein Books, April 2016.
Caversham, Reading

This book, although set in a real location, is entirely a work of fiction. No character is based on any real person, living or dead and any resemblance is purely coincidental.

ISBN-13: 978-1477568156
ISBN-10: 1477568158

I am grateful to Dr Chris Scruby for taking and fine-tuning the front cover photograph and my wife, Marion, for the photo of me shown at the back.

**To Myfanwy Giddings,
1945 – 2015**

A good friend over many years,
and an avid pursuer of my English infelicities;
with thanks for all your encouragements.

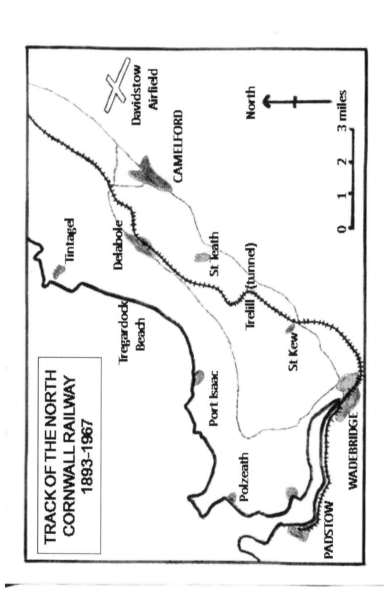

TRACK OF THE NORTH
CORNWALL RAILWAY
1893–1967

Davidstow
Airfield

CAMELFORD

Tintagel

Delabole

St Teath

Trelill (tunnel)

Tregardock
Beach

St Kew

Port Isaac

Polzeath

PADSTOW

WADEBRIDGE

North

0   1   2   3 miles

CHAPTER 1

North Cornwall May 1990

Trudy Simmons stumbled over the half-buried branch but managed, somehow, to keep her balance. Now she'd dropped even further behind. 'Wait for me,' she pleaded.

Her boyfriend, Gus, glanced back. In the fields beyond, the May full moon was beaming down. Here in the woods its light was mottled by the trees shaking in the gusty breeze. His girl – dark haired and dressed, inevitably, in gothic black - was almost invisible. 'Best slow up lads.'

Nigel, the leader of the expedition, shook his head in frustration. A mixed party hadn't been his idea in the first place. Trudy had sidled in once it was clear her boyfriend was going anyway. The fourth member of the party, Jack, was unaware of the delay and could just be seen marching on ahead.

With a struggle Nigel managed to reunite the party. 'On a night hike it's important we stick together,' he urged. 'I don't know what's ahead: I didn't get much further this afternoon.'

Slower now, slightly chastened, they headed on. Then their progress came to an abrupt halt at a barbed-wire fence.

'They obviously don't want us to go any further,' said Jack.

'But look what's beyond,' Nigel urged. 'Can't you see? That massive black void. You know, this could be the start of the old railway tunnel.'

3

'Hey, that'd be more interesting than a track through the woods,' said Gus. 'Pity we haven't got a torch.'

'But I have,' said Nigel.

What a surprise, thought Trudy. But, if she had to choose between waiting here alone or staying with them and going in, then "There is No Alternative", as the Prime Minister kept saying.

Carefully, Nigel stood on one wire to hold it down while Gus pulled up the other. They all wriggled through the gap between the two.

The tunnel had a weathered stone entrance then disappeared into deep blackness.

'D'you reckon it's safe?' asked Trudy. She was easily the youngest but someone had to be the voice of caution.

In response Nigel shone his torch onto the roof. He'd expected to see a hewn-out rocky surface but it was all smooth brickwork; he couldn't see any gaps. Shining further ahead the tunnel led away from them on a steady, left-hand curve. There seemed to be small alcoves set into the right hand wall every thirty yards. But now they were inside he could see no other obstacles.

'We'll take it slowly, guys, stick together in the middle. It's probably safe but I don't want any of us to touch the walls. Some of those bricks might be loose – or covered in mould. And if the roof looks suspect I promise we won't go any further.'

More subdued now the group headed forward. They were all in their teens. None would admit to being frightened by the dark but even so the long-abandoned tunnel was intimidating.

The way under foot was damp and slippery. The railway track had long since been removed but instead there had built up a covering of dank mud. Trudy skidded a couple of time, almost fell over but Gus managed to steady her.

Then she walked into a dangling spider's web. Her face twitched as the light thread caught on her nose. 'Aaa,' she screamed.

'It's alright,' advised her boyfriend. 'At least it's not rats.'

'Or bats,' added Jack. It was hardly an encouragement but he seemed to be relishing the challenge. Slowly, reluctantly, the group struggled on.

'How far d'you reckon it goes?' asked Trudy. It was already much further than she'd expected, her fears were mounting. Ahead she could hear a peculiar intermittent jolt – it sounded like the ghost of an old steam train.

'It's a quarter of a mile,' replied Nigel. She recalled he'd had the advantage of a preview of the route on the map.

Jack had been counting paces. 'I reckon we've done two hundred yards. There's no light ahead – or behind for that matter.'

Trudy had another problem, though. 'Guys, I'm sorry, I need the toilet.'

'Knew that second pint of cider was a mistake,' said Gus.

'I'd ordered it before I knew we were going anywhere,' she protested.

The four came to a halt and paused for deliberation.

'We'll just go on to the next alcove,' suggested Nigel. 'You wait here and then you can go over by the side once we're well ahead.'

'You're not leaving me behind in the dark,' said Trudy fearfully. 'How about . . . how about giving me the torch and you guys going on?'

'No way. I'm not moving forward without a torch,' replied

Nigel.

'Hey, I'm confused. Which way is forward?' asked Gus. Now they'd stopped he had a point. Every direction was inky black.

'We can't get lost,' asserted the confident Jack.

'Not unless there's a fork in the tunnel,' commented Gus. Trudy's fear level rose even higher, accentuating the signal from her bladder.

'Somewhere in my rucksack I've got a compass,' asserted Nigel.

'But will it work underground?' challenged Jack.

By now Trudy was desperate. This was the sort of verbal ping pong she knew boys enjoyed; it might last for some time. She stretched forward and grabbed Nigel's torch out of his hand then headed for the nearest alcove. The lads continued to argue.

To her surprise the alcove she'd chosen had a long, vertical crack, about a foot wide, in the rear. The girl decided she'd prefer to relieve herself in complete privacy and hardly hesitating, eased her way through into some sort of cave.

The lads were deep into discussion when, without warning, there was a loud scream, a sharp bang from something metal hitting the ground and then pitch darkness.

Silence.

'Trudy, are you OK?' called her boyfriend nervously. 'Trudy?'

A few seconds later he felt Trudy's hand as she struggled towards them and thrust herself into his arms. For a while she shuddered uncontrollably, unable to speak, while Gus whispered meaningless encouragements into her ear.

At last she pulled herself together. 'There was a c- cave at the back of the alcove,' she stuttered. 'I was just coming out when I shone the torch around and I saw it. There . . . there's a skeleton in there, lying next to the back wall.'

It was half an hour later when the group emerged from the tunnel, all badly shaken.

The resourceful Jack had managed to use the light from his cigarette lighter to find the alcove and then to peer into the cave. By some miracle he'd been able to spot the torch but it no longer worked: the bulb must have smashed as it fell on the hard floor. He'd also picked up a small metal object. He didn't try very hard, though, to see the bundle of bones that Trudy had reported.

It was time to retreat. Holding hands, Trudy in the middle and the outer two aligning themselves by the brick walls, the four had made their way slowly out through the coal-black passage.

The need to focus and stay vertical dominated any urge to chat.

The fact that the tunnel deviated slowly to the right gave them some confidence they were heading back the way they'd come. But it was a relief when the darkness became less absolute and then, finally, they emerged into the light of the filtered moon.

There was just enough light to see the barbed wire and ease through it. They were still a mile from Nigel's car and it was well after midnight when they reached it. By this time Trudy was shivering with shock and they agreed the priority was to take her home as soon as possible.

Next day was Sunday. Nigel called each of them and attempted to organise a meeting to decide what to do next. His instinct had been, and still was, to call the police - but he realised that it was not just his decision.

His friends were active young people, even busier than he was. Two of them were about to battle with A-levels. It was the following Friday – almost a week later - before they could all manage to meet together.

Nigel had managed to find a room for them to talk in private, behind the main bar at the Red Lion at St Kew. This was the pub they had set out from the previous Saturday and was one of their regular haunts.

After Nigel had come back with a tray of drinks analysis could began.

'I assume none of us has talked to anyone about what happened last week?' he asked; and took their silence as assent.

'The big question is, what should we do about it?'

'Surely we've got to tell the police?' asked Gus.

'We might. But before we get to that,' said Jack, 'I'd like Trudy to tell us exactly what she saw.'

Trudy was not bursting to speak but she could see she had no choice.

'I've been thinking about it all week,' she began. 'Hardly slept a wink. I only saw the bones for a few seconds, mind. I was so shocked I dropped the torch then I had to get away. I was terrified. It was pitch black by then, of course. I struggled to squeeze out and back to the rest of you.'

'Trudy, are you certain it was a skeleton?' asked Jack. 'Not just an arrangement of stones, say, that happened to look a bit like one?'

'I've seen a skeleton in the school biology lab, Jack. I know what one looks like. And this looked just like it, except it was lying down. I'm almost certain that's what I saw.'

'The thing is,' said Jack, 'I glanced at it too. It looked to me like a bundle of bones but I'm not certain they were human remains. It might have been a long-dead sheep.'

'I can tell a sheep from a human, Jack. It wasn't a sheep.'

'So did you see any signs of clothing – boots, say?'

'I was only looking for a few seconds. I didn't see anything except bones.'

'But that's much more likely to mean it was a sheep.'

There was silence at this impasse. Nigel and Gus had no facts to add.

'Suppose it was human, was there anything to suggest foul play?' asked Jack.

It was an odd question but Trudy did not hesitate. 'I didn't see any bullet hole in the skull, Jack – if that's what you mean. The bones were just lying peacefully beside the wall. But I didn't stop to look carefully.'

There was silence. Trudy was convinced and convincing. But they all remembered how tense she was, even before she saw the bones. Being certain did not guarantee she was correct. Jack had seen something too – and he was not convinced at all.

'I've been doing some research in Wadebridge Library,' said Gus. 'The books I've read suggest that in this country it takes at least a decade for a body to decompose into a skeleton. This chap – or woman - must have been lying there for years and years. It can't be anyone who disappeared recently – it's not anyone we've heard of. But we still need to tell the police.'

'We would, Gus, if we were certain it was a human and if there'd been foul play. And no doubt the police will then ask us why we didn't tell them earlier. The thing that worries me,' said Jack, with a sigh, 'is that we shouldn't have been there in the first place. Do you remember the barbed wire? Once we

9

climbed through we were technically trespassing.'

'So?' asked Nigel. He'd climbed through barbed wire fences before.

'Well, if the police were feeling generous they might not bother with that, just be pleased we've reported something. Or . . . they might decide to make examples of us – say, give each of us a caution.'

'What would than mean?' asked Trudy. It sounded ominous. She'd never been in any trouble with the police and she didn't want to start now.

Jack shrugged. 'Probably nothing. But technically it counts as a criminal offence. Now it may be alright for you lot but I'm trying to study law so it might affect things badly for me. What do we lose by not saying anything?'

The argument had raged for some time. Nigel had suggested alerting the police anonymously from a public phone box in Wadebridge. 'After all, they can go and look, same as we did.'

But the Red Lion was the nearest pub to the tunnel and they'd made no effort to keep their voices down as they planned the walk. There was a real risk, said Jack, that any police inquiries would learn about their hike from one of the Red Lion regulars.

'If they do, not reporting it will land us in even more trouble,' warned Gus gloomily.

'If it turns out it was only a sheep we might be done for wasting police time,' mused Nigel. He did not know, it was only a fear but it still raised alarms.

'I'm starting my A-levels next week,' said Trudy. 'I'm behind in my studies already - this week's been a disaster. I can do without any more distractions.'

'We didn't leave anything there,' Jack had concluded. 'I'm pretty sure we left no trace at all. If was a crime, it's certainly a very old one. The police are very busy these days. It probably won't get much attention anyway.'

Jack was the oldest of the group and not easy to dissuade. In the end it was his view against Trudy's. And they needed an agreed message before they could report anything. Eventually, with some misgivings, they all agreed to say nothing. The bones would remain undisturbed in the tunnel for many years.

But not for ever.

CHAPTER 2

May 2011

The ultimatum from Robbie Glendenning's latest girl-friend had not come like a bolt from the blue.

He'd known for some time that Cynthia was unsettled – for starters, she said, he needed to lose weight and his hair was a complete mess; and she didn't like the way he kept being called away by his job at short notice. But after their latest missed date her dissatisfaction was complete. 'You've got to choose,' she'd said haughtily, 'between your job and me.'

Well he wasn't changing the job. It'd taken him fifteen years to rise to the position of West Country reporter-at-large with a major national broadsheet and he wasn't dropping the post without a fight.

He was relatively senior. Maybe he could get the paper to give him agreed days off? He wasn't the only one that could write up a story. Though he was one of the few that could progress from local details to the wider questions for society at large.

But all that was for later. The first challenge which confronted him, as he arrived late at work just before ten, came from the office manager. 'Your editor wants to see you at eleven,' she said. 'He's coming down specially from London.'

His boss travelling to Bristol was so rare, Robbie didn't know what to expect. Was he in trouble? Had his casual expense claims caught up with him at last? Or was there some dreadful job that he would find harder to refuse if asked face to face? Did they want him to transfer to China? Or Myanmar?

Whatever it was, he had just an hour's grace. The journalist did his best to tidy his desk and refresh his mind on his most recent stories – after all, there was a good chance his editor hadn't given them that much attention.

It would be useful to have one or two forthcoming projects already in the pipeline – except that he was still waiting for various whispers to emerge. Well-signposted events like those on BBC news were all very well but the nature of the best news was that it was impossible to predict.

Just before eleven Robbie headed to the suite used by senior staff on the top floor. He felt bleak: it was just the sort of day when both lifts would be out of action. Sure enough he had to toil up five floors to reach his destination.

'Malcolm Saltburn wants to see me,' he puffed to the gate-keeper as he reached the editor's lair.

'Best get your breath back,' she advised, 'I'll let him know you're here.'

A couple of minutes later he was invited in. His editor was not alone; a smartly-dressed man in his fifties, eyes startling blue and hair beginning to grey, turned from enjoying the Bristol skyline to face him.

If this was the latest Human Relation then they'd gone in for an upgrade. He'd not met this man before – though he looked the type that you might see on Newsnight.

'Morning, Robbie. Thought it was time I came to see you.' His boss looked cheerful enough, anyway. Maybe he wasn't heading for a rollicking after all.

His boss turned to the man beside him. 'Let me introduce

you. Robbie, this is Sir Edmund Gibson. He's an old friend of mine, very active in the energy conservation movement.'

Maybe that was where he'd seen him, mused Robbie: addressing a renewable energy rally?

'Edmund,' he continued, 'this is Robbie Glendenning. He's our top man in the West. Writes all sorts of stories, even manages to make some of them eye-catching to folks in the rest of the country.'

It was probably intended as a compliment. Robbie wasn't going to argue.

'Edmund and I happened to meet at the opera a couple of evenings ago. He was telling me a really interesting story that might be about to develop down here. I thought I'd bring it your attention.'

'It's always good to have advance warning,' said Robbie. He took out his notebook and turned to the next blank page.

'Let's sit over here,' said Malcolm, pointing to some chairs round the coffee table. 'I'll order the coffee.'

A few minutes later they were ready to begin.

'I should start by telling you that I own a cottage in Cornwall at a place called Treligga.' Sir Edmund looked at the journalist to see if the name made any impression but could see it didn't.

'Don't worry, no one's ever heard of it,' he continued. 'But that doesn't matter. For a weekend retreat I want somewhere off the beaten track. It's near Delabole, with a fabulous view across to Port Isaac.'

'I know Delabole, Sir Edmund. You have to drive through it to get from Camelford to the coast.'

'That's the one. Well, my wife and I don't let our cottage out but we do encourage our friends and family to use it when we're not there. That's how Rowena was there last week.'

14

Robbie made a guess. 'She's your daughter?'

'Indeed. She's a free-spirited young lady – between our-selves, she's more like me than my wife. Plenty of enterprise. She'd been staying in Treligga on her own, which is why she found herself in the Bettle and Chisel.'

'The pub in Delabole?' Only a guess but it didn't sound like there'd be any inn in Treligga.

'That's right.' Sir Edmund turned to Malcolm. 'Your man certainly knows his territory.'

'He's not bad. But maybe you'd better get on with the story.'

'OK. Well, you'll need to meet Rowena for the full story but the edited highlights go like this.' Sir Edmund paused to assem-ble his material.

'It all started with the Liberal Democrats. In this one-sided coalition they're desperate to find things that don't cost very much but that will do something – anything - for climate change.'

Robbie had his own view on gesture politics but kept them to himself. 'So is there some new government initiative that affects Cornwall?'

Sir Edmund looked slightly disappointed that the journalist did not already know what it was. 'I guess I've got inside infor-mation. The whole thing was originally my idea.'

'You'll have to tell him, Edmund. None of us can keep track of all these initiatives – until they go wrong, of course.'

The tycoon continued. 'This one was government funding for a competition to find the most climate-sensitive scheme to attract new visitors to Cornwall. It was to be announced and promoted by the local Council. They'd just heard about it in Delabole when Rowena dropped by.'

Sir Edmund spoke as though Rowena was a rare customer.

15

The journalist made a note that he'd need to check that out.

'And were they . . . enthusiastic?' He'd been about to say 'ecstatic' but irony wasn't appropriate: the man was a friend of his boss.

'Not to start with. Till Rowena let slip it was funded by the government rather than the local Council. That boosted their interest. Everyone prefers to spend someone else's money rather than their own. So somehow or other they started to think of various ideas.'

'What Sir Edmund wondered, Robbie, was if our newspaper might cover one or two of these as they're pushed forward?'

Time down in North Cornwall in May: subtle flowers in the hedgerows, golden sands by the shore. Idyllic, thought Robbie. It would be a sharp riposte to Cynthia. Maybe not such a bad day after all.

Then his natural pessimism returned. Best to find out what the ideas were. He didn't want a month lurking on a windy foreshore in his swimming trunks.

Sir Edmund sensed the journalist needed more. 'One of the more interesting ideas is to develop a new cycle trail along the old railway line near Delabole.'

Before Robbie could work out a response his boss had cut in. 'The North Cornwall Line? That used to go through Camelford and Delabole?'

'Hey, you've actually been on it?' asked his friend.

'My family used to go on holiday in Padstow in the early sixties. We hadn't got a car; I was about seven. The best bit was the journey through Cornwall and down to the coast. Wow. To make that a cycle trail.' He felt silent, dreaming.

Robbie felt the pair needed a dose of reality. 'There already is a cycle trail. It runs along the Camel Estuary from Wadebridge to Padstow – the Camel Trail. Do tourists need any more?'

'That's one of the questions the scheme's got to answer,' replied Sir Edmund. 'To make the case properly requires a lot of work.'

There was silence for a moment.

'If you don't fancy it, Robbie, I might go myself,' said the editor. 'A short sabbatical – back to my roots or something.'

Robbie was not a railway fanatic but it could keep him away from Bristol.

'No, no, I'll take it,' he said. 'It's got potential. Some of what I'm doing here can be delegated, I'll continue the rest over the internet. It's not like the Australian bush. I can be in Delabole by the end of the week.'

He turned to the tycoon. 'Sir Edmund, could you give me the details of your cottage in Treligga, please – and also your daughter's phone number?'

CHAPTER 3

"I still have no peace. It was someone local. You and I might not have known who it was but my parents might – or yours. Not someone well-known or there would have been a rumpus. But still a human being. And if we wilfully hide the truth are we not accessories to whatever happened?" G.

As Robbie drove down to North Cornwall, he thought wistfully once again of George Gilbert.

He'd met George in Looe over a year ago and the two had helped solve a complex murder. George was some sort of business analyst – she'd called herself an "industrial mathematician". They'd become friends over a stressful week; she was the only person he'd met in recent years that he felt instinctively comfortable with. She hadn't tried to push him around, had accepted his foibles, but she also appreciated his strengths.

In turn he had a great deal of respect for her sharpness and wit. With her petite figure, cheerful face and dark curly hair, she was also very attractive.

So what had gone wrong? He wished he knew. They'd exchanged mobile numbers in Looe and kept in touch for several months. Each had demanding jobs which meant they travelled about a great deal. There'd only been a few times when their itineraries could be made to intersect.

Robbie had learned that George had been widowed two or three years earlier. That must affect her attitude to men. But he'd been on his own for a long time and been content to let a new relationship grow slowly.

He had been busy with a project in Falmouth and not managed to call her for two or three weeks. Then out of the blue his paper had asked him to do a six-month exchange with a journalist from Australia. He had tried to ring George to tell her he would be out of the country but not got through. Calls from the other side of the world had been equally unproductive. His new employer had given him an email which, it turned out, had taken his personal emails as spam. And when back from Australia he couldn't get through at all.

Maybe, he mused, George had become impatient with waiting? He'd had many romantic reverses; he put this one down as the latest – and saddest - of a long line.

What brought George to mind was that he knew she had a holiday cottage around Tintagel. If he had kept in touch and the place was empty it might have provided him with accommodation – even a good reason to meet.

As it was he'd booked in at the Bettle and Chisel in Delabole. The place had good ratings and was the epicentre of bids for what he'd nicknamed the "Green Tourist" competition. Staying there would put him on the spot to find out what was going on.

The journalist reached Delabole on Friday afternoon. The Bettle and Chisel was halfway along the main street. He booked in and claimed his guestroom. It was modestly sized but clean and tidy, with a good internet link; it would do fine.

Robbie had an appointment with Rowena for that evening but at six o'clock the pub was quiet. A chance to ask the landlord about last Friday's discussion. As he listened he marked the end of the relationship with Cynthia by ordering a large steak and chips.

The landlord, Jim, was happy to recall the evening, especially once Robbie had explained he was a journalist sent to cover developments.

'That's great. Rowena said her father might be able to win high-level support. Any publicity would be welcome.'

'At this stage, Jim, I hardly know anything. Could you tell me how it all happened?' He took out his notebook.

'Well, it all started from an article in the local paper. Cornwall Council was offering an award, it said, for the best new scheme to attract tourists in an environmentally sensitive way – whatever that means.'

Robbie could guess but didn't want to interrupt. He encouraged the landlord to continue.

'The immediate controversy was around the size of the award – a quarter of a million pounds to make the winning entry a reality. Some folk were glad to have more money to raise the tourist profile; others were indignant that "our rates were going to fund something else that was non-essential." But most realised that tourists generated much of the income in the summer months and knew we'd be worse off without them.

'Then Rowena let slip that the funding came from National Government. I don't know how she knew – is she some sort of civil servant? People were much keener to get their hands on the funds once they knew it came from somewhere else.

'After a while I saw the chance for a pub quiz to identify the best local scheme for Delabole to work on. So I offered a free round of drinks to the table producing the best scheme by nine o'clock.'

'Generous,' said Robbie diplomatically.

'Made business sense,' replied the landlord. 'I sold far more beer during the evening than usual. Folk drink more when they're trying to collaborate. It's a form of mental lubrication.'

That was one way of describing it. 'So what kinds of schemes did they come up with?'

'Can't remember them all. But I know what was handed in for the voting.'

'Go on then, give us a flavour.'

'Well, one of the schemes came from some older farmers. One – he was called Archie - started talking about the Court-room Experience at Bodmin. D'you know it?'

'No.' Robbie's job didn't give him much time for tourist activity.

'It's based on a murder that took place on Bodmin Moor in 1895. Actors re-enact the trial. Then the really cunning thing is that the audience act as the jury and give a verdict. That usually shows most people would regard what happened long ago as a miscarriage of justice.

'Another farmer was upset when he realised Bodmin was making money out of a crime that happened round here and asked whether there wasn't another crime that we could make into a tourist attraction.'

'They couldn't put on another Courtroom Experience. For a start you've no courtroom.'

'No. But could they offer something as good if they could find an unsolved crime and challenge tourists to resolve it?'

'Sounds intriguing,' commented Robbie, 'though how would they make the idea "environmentally sensitive"?'

'They had some idea of locating it in a building on the local Wind Farm.'

'OK, that's one scheme. What else was there?' Robbie knew

from Sir Edmund that one scheme was linked to the old railway line but he wanted to hear how it had arisen.

'A second scheme came from two older ladies, talking about famous people from these parts. One of them started on about Robert Stephen Hawker, the Victorian vicar from Morwenstow. Have you heard of him?'

'I've heard of Morwenstow. But I know nothing about the vicar.'

'Well, neither did her friend. She thought she was talking about Stephen Hawking, the "Brief History of Time" man from Cambridge.'

Robbie smiled. 'Not two men you'd usually confuse.'

'No. Hawker the vicar built a hut and devoted his time to watching for shipwrecks. When they happened his church helped the wrecks' survivors.'

'How on earth was that a tourist attraction?'

'It was ingenious. Their scheme involved listing famous people from North Cornwall and finding their graves in local churchyards. Entrants had a questionnaire to be answered from the words on the graves. A completed questionnaire won them a cream tea.'

Promising. Robbie could see a connection between tourists and cream teas, though not much of a link with green energy.

'But the best scheme came from the table Rowena was on, next to the farmers. It was mostly younger folk but there was one older man who started reminiscing about the railway. It stopped here, you know, on its way to Padstow. He thought building a new railway would help with climate change and also be attractive to tourists. But his table told him you couldn't do that for quarter of a million pounds.

'Then one of them remembered that the far end of the line

had been converted into a cycle trail – the Camel Trail.'

'I've heard of that,' said Robbie smugly, 'I've even cycled it. It runs alongside the Camel from Wadebridge to Padstow. So how did this work?'

'One of the lads, Nathan, lives in Delabole and works in Wadebridge. He's a solicitor. He said it was a pity the Camel Trail didn't run as far as Delabole so he could cycle to work in safety. That made them ponder the chance of extending the Camel Trail up to Delabole. That's what their scheme was aiming for.'

Robbie had no idea what this might involve but he knew Rowena was in the group behind it. He hoped she'd fill him in later on.

'So what happened when it came to the vote?'

'We were very democratic. In the end it was a dead heat between the old-crime scheme and the extended cycle trail. They were amused when they saw I'd have to provide two tables' worth of free drinks.

'But I take the long view. They'll be back to develop their schemes. No more free drinks from now on. Now, can I interest you in our locally-brewed cider?'

After supper Robbie set out to meet Rowena Gibson. Once he'd reached Treligga he saw the Gibsons had picked their location well. The view over the bay was enriched by the evening sun setting over the Atlantic. He wasn't surprised Sir Edmund found a regular excuse to come down here for the weekend.

The tycoon's holiday home was a traditional, white-painted cottage with a huge window overlooking the coast. An attractive woman, presumably Rowena, was making the most of the evening sun. As she rose from her sun lounger he saw she was generously built, with eyes a sparkling green and was endowed with auburn, shoulder length hair. He guessed she was aged around thirty.

She smiled as she saw him pushing open the gate.

'Hi,' she greeted, 'you must be Robbie. I'm Rowena. Thank you for taking an interest in our project. Come in, I'll get you a drink. It's been a lovely day but it'll cool quickly.'

Robbie followed her in and sat on a couch facing the large window. Lack of funds hadn't constrained furnishings here. He was examining the nearby wall painting when Rowena returned.

'That's by Helen Setteringham,' she informed him, 'she's an impressionist from Boscastle, paints in unusually vivid colours. That's our nearest beach, Tregardock. Have you ever been there?'

'I've never heard of it,' he confessed. 'It looks enchanting. I'll try to look while I'm down here.'

But he wasn't here to review paintings. He turned back, extracted his notebook and took his coffee. Rowena perched on the easy chair alongside, legs tucked beneath her.

'Your Dad told me something,' he told her, 'but it was all third hand. It would help if you told me the story from an insider's viewpoint.'

Rowena needed no further urging. 'I keep up with local events: I want to belong. People who own holiday cottages should put down roots. There's a footpath to the Bettle over the fields, I quite often drop in for a drink. It was pure chance I was there last week when the scheme was being talked about.'

Rowena went on to outline how the landlord had provoked a discussion so heated it had led on to the quiz. When she had finished there was a pause.

24

'So the end result,' said Robbie, 'is a group trying to turn more of the railway into a cycle trail? Isn't the Camel Trail enough?'

'The Camel Trail is very popular. This extension would put Delabole on the tourist map. That's why the locals got excited.'

'But . . . it'll never win?'

'Well . . . it would help tackle climate change. I've no idea whether the prize money would cover the costs.'

'Can you show me where it would go?' Robbie had brought a map of Bodmin Moor and opened it on the coffee table.

'You also need Wadebridge and Port Isaac.' Rowena slipped out and returned with a second map, which she laid on the coffee table.

Together they arranged the maps and pored over them. Robbie got a whiff of fine fragrance. He forced himself to focus on the maps rather than her cleavage.

'Where's Camelford?' he asked as he started to follow the old route.

'Next map.' Rowena fetched a third and they laid all three out on the floor.

'Plenty of curves,' she observed. Robbie was more aware of his companion's generous curves as she knelt on the floor facing him.

Willing himself to concentrate, he asked, 'When was the line built?'

'Late nineteenth century. It shut in the 1960s, way before my lifetime.'

But only just before his, reflected Robbie sadly. Now, half a century later, someone was itching to restore it.

'I'd appreciate help on contacts,' he said. 'Mind you, before I do I'd like to spend a day looking at the thing on the ground.'

He pointed at the maps. 'On all this maze of roads there must be places where I could see something.'

Something unusual caught his eye. 'And what happens here? It looks like the line disappears.'

'That's the Trelill tunnel. It goes right under the village: the only tunnel on the line. Look, would you like some help map-reading? I'm around for another couple of weeks. Would you like me to come with you?'

It was an offer Robbie found hard to resist.

CHAPTER 4

"As long as no-one knows, we are safe; even if the bones are redis-covered. My worry is my lost card. I couldn't find it after that night. But it could be anywhere. I got a new one but, if it still exists, the old one has my name plastered across it." N.

Robbie Glendenning stood at the entrance of Western Supplies: where might they keep hard hats?

He had no idea what reconnoitring the railway line with Rowena might entail but a tunnel had been mentioned. He hoped the local builders' merchant would stock safety helmets.

It was an unusual store to say the least. The slate floor was uneven and the aisles were laid out seemingly at random. Most of the things you could ever want would be here somewhere: the challenge was to find them.

This Saturday morning hardly anyone was trying. The only other customer was a tall man with frameless glasses, dressed incongruously in a smart suit and tie, who was scratching his head and looking harassed.

'Have you seen the hard hats?' Robbie asked him.

'Is that a new film?' the man replied distractedly, his eyes still scouring shelves. 'The nearest cinema's over Bude way. We don't go very often.'

Robbie wondered how often he went shopping. 'What are you after?' he asked with a grin.

The man held up a rectangular piece of plastic. 'The outside cover of my kitchen ventilator blew off. This is the bit I've got left. My wife insisted I came in to find one to replace it.'

'You're looking very smart for Saturday morning.' Robbie didn't usually comment on appearances but the man looked oddly out of place.

'Oh. I'm on my way to work. I'm the local doctor.'

He turned from the shelves and looked directly at Robbie. 'I've not met you before, have I? What brings you here?'

'I'm a journalist and, as I said, I'm after a hard hat. A friend's taking me to explore the old railway.'

'Good luck. You'll need heavy-duty gloves as well. Ah.' The doctor had spotted a shelf of kitchen items across the aisle. Among them was a piece of white plastic. 'That might do. Eureka.'

Five minutes later, helmet and gloves found, Robbie caught up with the doctor at the till. Bar codes had not yet reached this part of Cornwall and the shopkeeper was trying to find the price of the plastic from a battered catalogue.

The doctor kept looking at his watch. He was obviously running late.

'That'll be £6.26, Dr Southgate.'

Quickly the doctor took out his wallet and proffered a card. The shopkeeper looked at it dismissively.

'Don't do credit cards in 'ere, Doctor. Or credit of any sort.'

The doctor started feeling in his pockets. 'Blast, my change is in my other suit. Can I take it and pay you on Monday?'

Robbie could see the answer was going to be no and felt a wave of sympathy with a fellow professional.

'Look, I'm staying round the corner at the Bettle. I'll pay when I buy my helmet - you could drop the money round, say, this evening. My name's Glendenning, by the way, Robbie

Glendenning.'

The doctor was sure they'd never met but the name seemed familiar. For now he was in too much of a hurry to take it further. 'I'm Brian Southgate. That's very kind of you. I'll be there round about seven.'

An hour later Robbie drove to Treligga to pick up Rowena. It was such a glorious day that he had his Stag's roof folded back and the seats open to the skies. His guide came to the door in shorts and a strappy top, with her hair tied in a ponytail.

'I've planned a route that criss-crosses the old line,' she announced. 'It's not far but by the time we've walked back at each bridge it'll take most of the day.'

Rowena first directed them to the Delabole slate quarry. 'In its time the biggest man-made hole in Europe,' she told him. 'And the first major producer in Cornwall to use the railway.'

'Right. Where did the line run?'

'Over there. We can walk a bit of it if you like?'

Robbie nodded. Rowena led them past the fire station and onto a level pathway. 'Dark cinders,' she observed. 'Steam trains once ran here.'

At the north end of the village there was a kissing gate. 'It's only two miles to Camelford,' she said. But Robbie had seen enough and suggested they returned to his car. He was starting to feel hungry.

'There's a good pub in St Teath,' suggested Rowena, 'it's not far. We can see a bit more of the railway on the way.'

The pair drove off. The road ran alongside a cutting and then crossed over a bridge.

'Stop here a minute, please,' she instructed.

Robbie pulled into a gateway and the two walked back to the

bridge. The structure was sound but beneath was a swathe of nettles and brambles.

'We're not going down there today,' he declared. 'Your legs would need more protection. My, it would take some effort to clear that lot.'

Rowena seemed disappointed. 'Well, so far today we've seen one clear route and one obstructed. We'll need to see more to make a proper assessment.'

The White Hart bar in St Teath was almost empty.

'Hi, Rowena,' the barman greeted her. Robbie wondered if being known in every pub in the area was what his companion meant by "good local contacts". Wisely he kept the thought to himself.

Robbie squinted at the menu then ordered two ploughmen's plus cider for himself and white wine for Rowena.

'Pity there's no one else here,' he ventured.

'That's because all the customers are outside.'

Robbie had hoped to use the lunchtime to question Rowena about local folk linked to the railway. However, by the time he followed her out Rowena was being hugged by a fellow-customer.

'Hi Owen,' she responded, pulling over a chair. Robbie dutifully sat down beside her. How did she know him: weather-beaten and twice her age? Then he had a thought. If Owen had lived here all his life he would have vivid railway memories. This might be a useful encounter after all.

'Owen, this is a friend, Robbie Glendenning. Robbie, this is Owen Harris. Robbie's covering all our schemes for the Carbon Tourist Award.'

Robbie was puzzled at the way his newspaper connection

was downplayed but he didn't want to argue. Were they wary of national publicity?

'How's your scheme going?' asked Rowena. Robbie remembered the restored railway trail was only one of the ideas to come out of the pub quiz.

'First meeting last Monday,' said Owen. 'Got our committee, I was elected chairman. We're meeting again next Monday. Come if you like, m'dear - or your friend.'

'I'm away sailing,' confessed Rowena. 'Are you free, Robbie?'

'Not made any plans yet,' said Robbie cautiously. He turned to Owen. 'What does your scheme do?'

'We want to match the Courtroom Experience at Bodmin. That's based on a killing on Bodmin Moor. We want to find another old crime and then encourage visitors to solve it.'

'You mean a murder?'

'Ideally one with no known killer. We've got some ideas on ways to add in clues but we first need the basics. Trouble is it's a low crime area.'

Robbie mused for a moment. 'Why not get the Bodmin police to help? Get someone over to talk about the crimes they haven't solved.'

'That's an idea.' Owen turned to Rowena. 'Your man's already making an impact. Do come along on Monday – help us make further progress.'

It was nearly three o'clock before Robbie and Rowena made their way out of the White Hart.

'That cider's strong,' the journalist commented with a hiccup.

'Quantity's the problem. That third pint of Rattlers was a

mistake.'

'I was trying to be sociable. You saw - twice I asked for a half.'

'Yes, but sending back a pint glass to be half-filled was asking for trouble. You're not safe to drive.'

On either count she was probably right.

'OK. Owen doesn't deal in halves.' Robbie hiccupped again. 'Look, is there anyone we could see before I have to drive again?'

'The local shop's been here forever. The shopkeeper might give us names of contacts.'

Rowena greeted the shopkeeper, a man with bushy eyebrows and flashing eyes. He seemed pleased to see her. Were there any local tradesmen, mused Robbie, that his companion did not know?

Rowena introduced Robbie, 'My friend is down to cover a scheme for a new cycle trail on the old North Cornwall Line.'

'I'm interested in hearing about ways the line impacted on local life. Are there any incidents you can remember?'

The storekeeper's eyes gleamed. 'Well, just after the war, there was an accident with a runaway goods wagon from De-labole.'

Robbie nodded in encouragement.

'A wagon got loose, see. It careered down the track, faster and faster, until it caught up a goods train ahead of it. The wagon smashed into the back and blocked the line for days.'

Robbie could imagine that to any child a train crash would be exciting.

'I was at school,' Graham went on. 'We had the afternoon off to go and look - it was spectacular. They needed a big crane to put some wagons back on the rails, and take away the rest.

Best event of my school days.'

Robbie wondered how many other wagons had got loose over the years. What speed might the wagon have reached if it hadn't caught up the train? Might it even have come off the rails?

By the time they'd finished with Graham and got names of more contacts it was half past four. 'Have we still time to look at the tunnel?' asked Robbie.

'Trelill's not far. We could go and check on access. Is it another thicket of nettles?' Rowena glanced down at her bare legs and sandals. 'If it is I'd need to wear something more substantial.

'Even if we can get to it we haven't time to explore it today.' She gave him a brilliant smile. 'I could come with you next week though, if you wanted?'

CHAPTER 5

"When the trail was mooted I'd forgotten it included the tunnel. Never crossed my mind someone would go and look in it. Then I decided it wouldn't win anyway. But, you know, it's the only scheme that might affect carbon emissions. What should we do?" G.

Robbie Glendenning took his drink into the Bettle lounge and looked around for company. He had waited in vain for the doctor to return with his £6.26. It was annoying but he must have simply forgotten.

Robbie spotted a burly man with curly hair and beard, in his early thirties and drinking on his own. He headed over to his table. 'Hi, can I join you?'

'Sure. The name's Mick. You new around here?'

'I'm Robbie, got here yesterday. I'm a journalist, down to cover the "Green Tourist" Award.'

The man looked puzzled.

'It covers a wide range of schemes,' explained Robbie, 'like the one aiming to turn the old railway line into a cycle trail.'

'Oh, that - didn't recognise the official name. It'd be good for Delabole.'

'Yes. I was being shown some of it this afternoon. It looked viable, anyway.'

The man seemed to perk up. 'Hey, have you actually walked through the tunnel? I'm the one supposed to be checking that.'

'Sorry, no. My friend and I looked down on the entrance. But she wasn't dressed for brambles so we didn't get any further. I've no ideas if it's safe. I guess that might be the scheme's showstopper.'

Mick mused. 'My Dad was always fearful of that tunnel. He told me, over and over again, not to go anywhere near it. But I was here when the bids began. I'm an engineer, see. I thought this cycle trail was an excuse to see it for myself.'

It started to dawn on Robbie that the trail would need tighter inspection than a few glimpses from Rowena.

'Don't let me stop you, Mick. In fact it would be great to come with you. When are you planning to go?'

Three days later, Tuesday, Robbie parked his car in Trelill and awaited his new companion.

Remembering the brambles on his previous visit, he was dressed for a scramble and carrying his new helmet. After so much talk he looked forward to seeing the inside of the tunnel.

Trelill was perched on top of the hillside within which the trains had once run. Had the villagers been able to hear the noise beneath? That would be very irritating. He wondered, too, if there had been any trains at night. It was a different world then – even though it was only fifty years earlier.

While he waited, Robbie reflected on the campaign meeting he'd attended in St Teath the evening before with an Inspector from Bodmin Police. Robbie had got to the White Hart early and had eaten his meal in the corner, well away from the bar. He'd been in a prime position to take notes quietly.

The speaker, a lean-framed man with glasses and a rather gloomy outlook, had been introduced by Owen as Inspector

Lambourn. Robbie regretted his advice that had inflicted him on the meeting.

Lambourn had been asked to speak on crimes in North Cornwall. 'Serious crime is unusual in this area,' he had begun, 'unsolved crime, well, it's almost unknown.' Despite persistent questions he'd come up with no specific examples where the campaign could start work.

Deflated, they had tried to make use of his expertise. 'What action would the police take,' asked a Doom Bar, 'if a body was found, say, in a cave on the coast?'

Lambourn had been dismissive. 'That would never happen. A high tide would surge into the cave and drag the body out to sea.'

'But suppose it didn't?' asked the Doom Bar.

'Or what if the body was found in a golf bunker?' added a Rattlers.

Eventually the penny had dropped. His audience wanted to know the police procedures when a body was found. 'For example,' asked Owen, 'how would the person be identified?'

The Inspector was more comfortable with this. 'We have a Missing Persons Register to track anyone reported missing. That'd give us a list to work from.'

'How far back does it go?' asked a Lemon Shandy.

'And how long's it been computerised?' asked a Chardonnay.

'We've got every disappearance since the 1990s on the system. Many are reported missing but most turn up again. You'd need a lot more facts before you took an inquiry any further.'

A new line of questioning was needed.

'So what could you learn from a body - or even a skeleton?' asked the Doom Bar.

'Could you find how long it had been there?' the Chardonnay wondered.

'It's hard to be precise on date of death without some additional data,' answered the policeman.

'But you'd get the DNA at any rate, even from a skeleton?'

'We could. Though we'd need a reason before we incurred the expense.' And Lambourn warned, 'DNA would only help identify a skeleton if there was a matching sample on police records from when they'd been alive.'

The Rattler pounced. 'So it'd be easier to identify the skeleton of a common criminal than an honest citizen?' This question had led to a fierce debate.

Finally the Inspector had stepped in. 'This is one reason,' he said, 'why some us think we should hold the DNA of every citizen. But there are also good arguments against.'

The meeting had gone on for some time and broken up in disarray.

The toot of a horn brought Robbie out of his reverie. Mick had driven up in a white van. He recalled the man was an engineer. This visit was no doubt being squeezed in between appointments.

'I talked to the people that own the north end of the tunnel,' Mick explained. 'It's OK for us to go in and have a look. As far as they know, no-one's been inside for years. The best way in is down here.'

He had already taken two high-visibility jackets and a torch from his van. Now he reached for an extendable metal pole – presumably to test the brickwork.

Robbie followed him past a few cottages then down towards a cutting. He took pictures of the stone-clad entrance as it came into view.

They had to battle with brambles to get on to the railway track. Rowena might have struggled. There was barbed wire flung across the entrance but it was possible to wriggle round it.

'Not that secure,' laughed Mick, as they stepped inside.

The engineer shone his torch around them. The tunnel was lined with soot-darkened bricks; they couldn't spot any missing. He poked one or two with his stick but they stayed firmly in position.

Robbie noted the ground was mostly covered with cinders.

'I can't test every brick,' said the engineer. 'We'll walk through slowly and give the roof a visual inspection. Prod a bit more if it looks dodgy.'

The tunnel was on a slow right hand curve. After fifty yards the entrance was out of sight. When Mick stopped and turned off the torch it was intensely dark.

The only sound was from dripping water, some way ahead. 'We'll need to check that's not doing any long-term damage,' the engineer observed.

Mick was concentrating hard, examining the brickwork overhead. Robbie left him to focus. To his eyes the surface looked in good condition.

Every thirty yards there were alcoves. Robbie guessed these must have been for railway staff to shelter as trains went past. That wouldn't be too pleasant. They'd have to cope with billows of smoke and steam as well as the clanking of pistons and the groans of the carriage connections. No lights in the early days.

'I reckon we're halfway,' said Mick, pausing for a moment. 'That dripping noise comes from somewhere round here.'

'Am I cracking up?' asked Robbie. 'I can feel a breeze. Why

on earth should that be? I didn't notice anything near the entrance.'

'You're not going mad; I can feel it as well. Hey, look over there,' said Mick, as he flashed his torch around, 'there's a gap at the back of that alcove. And some sort of hollow beyond – it's not just solid rock. That'll be where the breeze comes from.'

The pair went over. There was a gap in the alcove bricks, about a foot wide, running from floor to ceiling. Standing next to it, they could feel a breeze blowing into the tunnel and hear the sound of dripping water beyond.

'I think we'd better have a look inside,' proposed Mick. It would be a squeeze but they were both intrigued: why should there be a void in mid-tunnel?

Robbie held the torch as Mick took the lead and wormed his way through, then reached back for the torch. The journalist wished now that he'd brought his own. He squeezed after the engineer into the void beyond.

Mick was first and foremost trying to assess the risk of roof fall, so his torch started by pointing upwards. As the beam passed slowly over the surface, they could see that the roof was no longer brick-lined; but though far from being even it looked quite robust.

On the far side they could see something that looked like the bottom of a chute. It was here water was dripping down. Robbie took another photograph.

'The bottom of an old ventilation shaft,' said the engineer. 'I bet the water's running down from an opening on the surface, somewhere in Trelill. And that's where the draught comes from too.'

Finally Mick let the torch pass slowly over the floor of the cavern. And at the far side, the final part of the cavern to be exposed, they saw lying, in gruesome glory, a bare, pale-boned, full-sized skeleton.

Afterwards Robbie marvelled that they had kept so calm. It helped that they were practical men who could support one another - and that they had a good torch.

For a short while action took over from feelings. They were both shocked, of course; but they had come for an inspection. It helped that they were looking out for things that had gone wrong.

Phones would not work inside the tunnel. They were aware they had a responsibility to report their finding to the authorities; but a few minutes delay would not make any difference.

Robbie did his best to assemble a photographic record from all angles. At Mick's suggestion he placed the engineer's rod beside the body as a measuring stick. They might not know who it was but they could still assess their height.

Whilst he was doing this, Mick passed the torch slowly and carefully over the floor of the cavern. There were no signs of remnants of clothes or other objects which might give a clue to the skeleton's identity. The floor was damp and slightly muddy from the rain dripping down. There was also a dank smell, which neither man could identify, coming from the floor near the narrow entrance.

After quarter of an hour they'd done all they could. With some difficulty they squeezed back through the narrow aperture and into the main tunnel.

'Whew. For a horrible minute I thought we were going to end up stuck in there,' confessed Robbie.

'Yes, I could see you struggling. I was wishing I'd gone first. You might have blocked the entrance with me trapped inside.'

'Like Winnie the Pooh, over-eating when he went to visit Rabbit?'

Low-grade gallows humour but it was a way for them to handle the tension.

'Now, Robbie, forwards or back? I guess we're about half way.'

'We'll keep walking. You can inspect and I'll pace how far we are to the entrance. I mean, we don't know how many more skeletons we might find.'

Mick was equally shaken. 'To be honest, I don't give a damn about the state of the tunnel. But "I've started so I'll finish", as they say on television.'

CHAPTER 6

"Right now all we can do is hope for the best. For all we know the bones might have been removed in the years we were away. Or disposed of quietly at any other time over the last twenty years." N.

Although Robbie had conducted many interviews with victims and bystanders, he had never been interviewed directly by the police following the discovery of a body. This was the first time, though, that he had been the finder.

He reassured himself that the experience would be good to look back on. Later he was amazed at his naivety.

Mick had asserted that the police only needed to see one of them and rushed off to his next appointment. Later, Robbie conjectured that his colleague had greater experience of the local police and how they could drag things out.

Good citizen Glendenning had called Bodmin Police once the pair had returned to their vehicles, while Mick had driven away.

'So you've found a skeleton, sir. Inside a railway tunnel. But not on an operating line.' The desk sergeant had been confronted that morning with a suspected bomb alert at Bodmin Parkway. A set of bones sounded light by comparison. 'Stay in Trelill, please. I'll get someone over to check.'

The intervening hour had given Robbie time to reflect on his discovery and the next steps in the investigation. Identifying a long-dead skeleton might prove a challenge, he hadn't noticed any clothes. How good was forensic science at dating bones? Could they tell how long ago he (or she?) had died?

Trelill was off the beaten track. One or two tractors went by but there were no bystanders to chat with. Eventually a police car arrived and two officers got out. Robbie introduced himself and pointed out where he had forced a way down to the tunnel.

'Wait here please, sir,' he was told.

A further hour went by. Robbie was starting to regret having been a good citizen. Inevitably the returning police made no comment on their findings.

'Right, sir. Our Inspector says he'd like to interview you in Bodmin.'

Robbie was about to protest, then realised that being awkward might arouse suspicion. Mick had claimed he'd had permission to explore the tunnel; but then Mick was no longer with him.

Three quarters of an hour later the journalist was in Bodmin, ensconced in a cramped interview room with a uniformed Inspector.

It was the same man he'd seen in St Teath the night before. Was this a chance to share ideas about the case with a senior policeman? Lambourn looked like he had other problems on his mind. Robbie concluded that his rank probably reflected years in service rather than innate wisdom.

The basic facts of the interview – names, date and time - were intoned into the recorder and the questioning began.

'So, Mr Glendenning, what were you doing in the tunnel in the first place?'

'I'm staying in Delabole, helping with schemes for the Green Tourist Award. One is after a new cycle trail all the way up to

Delabole. So before we got any further someone needed to check that the tunnel itself was safe.'

'Ah, so you're a structural engineer?'

'No, but I was with an experienced engineer, Mick. He had to rush off to another appointment.'

'Hm. So can you tell me his full name and address, please?'

'I met him in the Bettle and Chisel. I'm sure he's local. I think the name was painted on his van.' The journalist screwed up his eyes in concentration. 'It was something like Hutching. But I'm sorry, we didn't swap addresses.'

The policeman mused for a moment and then took up another strand of complaint.

'So the Green Tourist Award allows you to trespass where you like?'

'Mick said he had permission for us to go down to the tunnel.'

'And now he's disappeared. How very convenient.'

Robbie could see he was on shaky ground. It would be best to remain silent.

After a pause the Inspector continued. 'My men tell me the skeleton wasn't just dumped in the tunnel. It was hidden well away, inside a cave. They say someone walking straight through would never have seen it. So how did you two vigilantes come across it?'

Robbie didn't like to be termed a vigilante but decided not to argue. 'We were trying to inspect the tunnel. There was a draught from one of the alcoves down the side, from some sort of ventilator shaft. We squeezed in to have a look and then we saw the skeleton. It was a shock to us both. Of course, we didn't touch anything.'

'Thank heavens for that. No doubt there are fingerprints

everywhere.'

The comment was laced in sarcasm. With a less hostile Inspector Robbie would have asked a question or two about forensics and skeleton dating; but with this man it would be a waste of time.

'So after a few moments we moved on,' the journalist continued. 'As soon as we were out of the tunnel and back on the road we rang in to report to the police. And I've been waiting for your men to turn up and then complete their checks, or travelling to talk to you, ever since.'

The policeman could see this was an unsatisfactory interview on both sides. It was important he didn't overreact. At this stage there was no reason to suppose anything more than natural death had occurred, many years before. Though the reports from his men suggested it had happened in a peculiar location. However, even if there was something more sinister, there was no way this man could have anything to do with a death from decades earlier.

'We will be making enquiries sir,' he announced portentously. 'In the fullness of time we may need the support of the general public in North Cornwall. But early on there is a lot to be done using our own records plus forensic analysis. It would really help if we didn't have to do that in the glare of media publicity.'

The Inspector paused to look the journalist in the eye and then continued. 'So I'm asking you, sir, as a responsible citizen, not to say anything about this find to anyone for at least a week. We don't want some bloody newshound chasing around, misrepresenting facts and disturbing everybody. It might all be completely innocent. Can I have your assurance on that, sir?'

Put like that, Robbie couldn't see how he could refuse.

'What about Mick?' he asked.

'Don't worry about him, sir. I'm sure we can find him. And when we do we'll be sure to put him under the same embargo.'

As he drove back towards Delabole, Robbie felt a mixture of emotions. The interview had not gone as he'd hoped. The only plus was that he'd left his camera in his car, so no question of photographic evidence had been raised. No doubt the police would have taken pictures of their own.

On the down side, he'd been treated not as a good citizen but almost as a troublemaker. If this was typical of the way crime reports were handled by the local police then it was no wonder reported crime rates came out so low.

In truth, he didn't have much confidence in Lambourn's insights. The fact that despite his concerns about the press the man hadn't even found out Robbie was a roving journalist was hardly a mark of competence.

The trouble was, he was being asked to neglect an event that to a journalist would be his bread and butter. Finding out more was exactly what his newspaper paid him for.

As he pondered this he realised that studying the case for a cycle trail might in all conscience overlap with the kind of enquiries he would have made on the skeleton in the tunnel. Had he not set himself, a couple of days ago, to understand the social impact of the railway?

Then he began to smile. One hidden benefit of the embargo was that, for the time being, he could do so without any competition from media rivals.

Once he reached Delabole Robbie checked in the bar for Mick but the engineer wasn't there. 'He's only here once or twice a week,' Jim told him. 'Depends on where his work takes him.'

The enquiry sparked a reminder. The landlord continued, 'But if you're after company this evening there was a phone call for you from Brian Southgate.'

He scrabbled through various messages on the reception desk. Finally the relevant one was found and handed over.

'Great,' said Robbie. The doctor had invited him to supper. He'd get his £6.26 back after all. Quickly he rang to confirm he could come and then headed upstairs for a shower. The day might end better than it had begun.

Something about the doctor's distracted manner in Western Supplies had made him suspect the man might not be teetotal.

It was worth taking a chance, anyway. The journalist dropped into the Spar and bought one of their more expensive red wines. Then he set out on the short journey to the Southgates.

'Good evening, Robbie. Welcome. Do come in. Before we go any further, here's the money you lent me the other day.' So that was alright then.

He led the journalist through into a well-upholstered lounge. Robbie was expecting to meet his wife but there was no-one else there.

'Is your wife not in?'

'She was, on the evening I first invited you.' Brian noticed the surprised look on his visitor's face and grinned.

'Don't tell me you've only just got the message. I rang on Saturday, the day we met in Western Supplies.' He shook his head. 'Those guys at the Bettle need a full-time receptionist if they're going to have roving journalists staying there. Still, you're here now – and just as welcome. But I'm afraid it's

Alice's regular evening out with her family.'

It was an awkward situation but the doctor did not seem in the least embarrassed. 'Another Cornish foible. Fortunately there's plenty of food left. Alice cooked a huge casserole which we've been eating for days.'

Belatedly, Robbie remembered his purchase. 'I hope it's OK, I brought some wine with me,' he said, as he handed over the Merlot.

'Excellent. I've got a bottle too. Two should see us through the evening. Which one shall we open first?'

A few minutes later, drinks poured, Robbie voiced a concern. 'Brian, can I ask: what made you think I was a roving reporter?'

'I think we have a mutual friend. She's often down here – she has a little cottage in Treknow. She mentioned your name last year - told us all about you. She seemed to like you.'

Robbie was stunned. 'You don't mean George Gilbert? How on earth do you know George Gilbert?'

'I was a close friend of her late husband, Mark. But she implied that the friendship had fizzled out. You hadn't returned her phone calls.'

'Brian, it wasn't like that. I was sent to Australia for six months at two days' notice. I tried to phone but I couldn't get through. When I got back I tried again but she'd changed her number. I had to assume that she'd given up on me and up-dated her phone.'

'So this is turning into an evening of late connections,' said Brian, grinning from ear to ear. 'Would you like her new number?'

For a few minutes the prospect of a reunion with George derailed Robbie's other concerns. As he thought about her and their disrupted friendship many questions had to be asked. Was she well? Still living in London as a business analyst? Most serious of all, was there a significant other in her life?

As Robbie voiced his worries Brian grinned. He didn't often have the chance to play cupid.

'How about this? I'll ring George later and tell her I've met you in Delabole. If she sounds like she cares I could offer her your number. If for some reason she's "moved on" then I'll let you know. But I'm hoping something can be worked out for both of you.'

In the circumstances Robbie would have been happy with dry biscuits. But Alice's chicken casserole was delicious.

As the pair made the most of it, along with the Merlot, Brian remarked, 'You'd better tell me what you're doing here. If the conversation with George goes as we hope then I'll need to be up to speed.'

So Robbie explained about the Green Tourist Award and his consequent deployment to Delabole. 'I expect to be here for another couple of weeks.'

To his surprise, Brian had heard of the Award too. 'What a coincidence. That's what Alice has taken on. They called on her last weekend and asked her to be the cycle trail bid chairman.'

'Is that because of her role as the doctor's wife?'

Brian roared with laughter until he almost choked. 'Doctors don't have that much status anymore. No, it's her role in the village that's done the trick. She's head teacher at the local primary school. And very efficient too.'

'Sounds like I'll need to come here again to interview her.'

'She won't be late home. Half nine, maybe. But don't expect an easy interview.'

CHAPTER 7

Wednesday morning and Robbie awoke alert, almost excited. Last night's conversation with Brian had left him feeling there was hope that George Gilbert was not lost altogether. True, there was no hard evidence but he trusted Brian to call her and pass on his number. For a few minutes the anticipation took precedence over any thoughts about the skeleton.

Alice had returned home soon after nine. Robbie's first impression had been of a tall, slim woman, almost brusque. Even off duty she was tidily dressed in a turquoise cashmere jumper and dark trousers, a scarf nonchalantly knotted around her neck. Their conversation had been short. Alice had refused to answer any questions about the bid itself. 'Our next meeting's Friday, Robbie – eight pm in the Bettle and Chisel. Come and see for yourself.'

She had, though, given him some background on why she had taken on the project. He'd been surprised to learn that the head teacher was less fired up by "Green Issues" than by her interest in the local railway.

'For many years it was the main point at which the outside world impacted. I mean, you could stand on Delabole station and catch a train direct to London. The children at my school did all sorts of projects about it.'

'Even after it was dismantled?'

Alice shrugged. 'That didn't help. But when I took over as head six years ago, I saw it was the most natural way of connecting our pupils with the world outside. Especially when I discovered the Archive.'

Alice could not have guessed how the phrase would capture the interest of the history graduate. 'Was that some sort of historical treasure trove?'

'It was more a social commentary. It went right back to the coming of the railway. After the official opening every child had to produce an account of the day. Then – and this is the magical part – one of the teachers used this raw material to produce an overall story. It was even displayed on Open Day. The whole village was behind it.'

'Amazing. Did this happen very often?'

'The success of the first year made folk hungry for more. The head was always being asked about it. So, of course, next year it had to be repeated. There was plenty to report: the railway was still being built.'

'Were there accounts every year, then?'

'Not in the war years. And recession years were pretty thin. It all depended on what material the kids had to hand. One or two engine drivers lived locally. If any of their children came to the school you can bet they were well grilled.'

'So this treasure . . . is it kept at your school?'

Alice looked slightly downcast. 'It was - till the most recent inspection. But our Railway Archive wasn't a standard item. The Inspector didn't like it, treated it like something from the Middle Ages.'

A look of horror shot across Robbie's face. 'It's not . . . it's not been lost?'

'Don't be silly. I just had to move it off site. Fortunately the

51

head teacher in post when the railway was running, Miss Trevelyan, still lives in the village. She's a reliable librarian. I can get you an interview with her if you'd like?'

This morning Robbie faced a conflict between the story he was supposed to be following, the Green Tourist Award, and the story he longed to chase, the skeleton. But how? He would need skill to work round the police embargo. The local news carried no mention of any find so far.

Given names and addresses he could talk to ex-railwaymen about how the railway was run. That might narrow the dates when the person could have died. The question was, where could he start?

Then he remembered Mick, the one person he could talk to about the skeleton. He rushed downstairs to find the landlord.

'I'd like to get hold of a chap called Mick,' he began. 'He was here on Saturday. Local engineer, I believe.'

'That'd be Mick Hucknall, he's one of our regulars. His work takes him all over North Cornwall. He might not be here for a week.'

That was a blow. 'What kind of work does he do?'

'Stoves and heating control systems. He's on commission, of course.'

Robbie mused for a moment. 'So he must advertise some-where?'

'Local paper, I should think.' The landlord reached behind the bar. 'Here's this week's Gazette. Take a look for yourself.'

Robbie seized the newspaper. 'There's a "Trevor Hucknall" offering stove maintenance in Camelford,' he reported doubt-fully.

'That's his Dad,' the landlord replied. 'But it's Mick that's got the energy; he does all the chasing. It's thanks to him they're still in business.'

One phone call and a short journey later, Robbie was navigating the industrial estate in Camelford, looking for Hucknall Stoves. On entering he found himself in a room cluttered with wood-burning stoves. A homely looking, plump woman was at the reception desk.

'Good morning,' he began. 'I'm trying to catch up on an acquaintance of mine by the name of Mick Hucknall.'

'That'd be our son. He does all the site visits these days.'

'Sounds like him. I'm told he fine tunes stoves.'

'That's Mick. He's out today, I'm afraid. Over in Bodmin. Probably be there all day. He should be back this evening. Can I give him a message?'

As he drafted the message Robbie recalled the embargo: no mention of the tunnel. He wrote, "Police ok. Like to catch up asap. Robbie"

The journalist was about to leave when an older man, dressed in crumpled overalls, appeared from the rear workshop. The woman turned to him.

'Ah, Trevor. This man was after our Mick. I've taken a message.'

Trevor frowned. 'He's not in trouble, I hope?'

'Nothing like that,' Robbie reassured him. 'Just give him the message.'

Trevor seized the page and examined it carefully. Then he sniffed and headed back for his workshop.

Robbie felt anything but welcome and slipped quickly back to his car.

As he headed back towards Delabole his phone rang. Perhaps this was George? Quickly he pulled into a gateway.

'Robbie Glendenning.'

He felt a tad disappointed. It was not George but Rowena.

'Robbie, would you like to come for a swim on Tregardock Beach? It's the last chance before I go on my sailing course.'

Robbie was not often invited to swim on a secluded beach with a pretty girl. He tried not to sound too enthusiastic. Half an hour later, after picking up swimming gear from the Bettle, he arrived in Treligga.

'We can walk from here,' his new friend asserted. The pair took a footpath across the sloping fields. After half a mile the track joined a gorse-surrounded path which led down towards the cliffs. The beach stretched out below. It was low tide and there was plenty of deserted sand.

A path zigzagged down the hillside, the final stage a twenty-foot scramble using a rope. This was not a beach for tourists.

Rowena was used to it. Robbie tried to look nonchalant as he followed, taking the weight on his arms. He just wished he was lighter.

Robbie had swimming trunks under his shorts. He didn't like to think what Rowena had in mind. Was he to see more of the curves? But as he prepared to swim he noted Rowena peeling off her sundress to reveal a sparse bikini.

The pair headed down to the sea. Rowena ran ahead, drawn on by the surging waves and the frothing surf. Robbie gritted his teeth as he followed her into the cold waves.

Half an hour later Rowena noticed Robbie's shivers. 'It's not that warm,' she admitted, 'Let's go back to the beach.' She produced a Frisbee. Every missed catch meant an energetic chase. By the time Robbie had lumbered after it for the umpteenth time he was feeling almost warm.

Eventually they settled down out of the wind. Robbie slipped on his clothes. Rowena lay beside him, her almost-naked body absorbing the hazy sunshine.

'What a way to spend a working Wednesday,' said Robbie. Then his phone rang. It was Alice Southgate.

'I got hold of Miss Trevelyan. She'd love to talk to you about the Railway Archive - this afternoon, if that's convenient?'

The intrusion of work seemed to challenge the familiarity between himself and Rowena. Perhaps it was as well.

'I've an interview this afternoon,' he explained. 'What time will you set off for your sailing?'

'My gosh, it's one o'clock,' Rowena exclaimed. 'We'd best be heading back.'

From the sublime to the ridiculous, thought Robbie. This morning he had been on the beach with a gorgeous thirty something, this afternoon he had to interview someone who must be at least eighty.

Miss Trevelyan's bungalow was on the edge of Delabole. The former head teacher had been keeping watch and opened the door to greet him.

'Mr Glendenning, how good of you to come. I loved your coverage of last year's General Election. You're obviously someone who gets on well with people. I've got some cake for later, but would you like to start with tea or coffee or with a cold drink?'

Robbie felt ashamed. Miss Trevelyan was still young at heart. She had a cheerful face, curly grey hair and a firm, upright stance. This might be a fun interview after all.

He followed her inside and found himself in a comfortable lounge. There were many photographs and other treasures adorning the walls.

'I'm so pleased someone's taking an interest in the North Cornwall Railway,' she explained, once Robbie had been supplied with an ice-cold bottle of ginger beer while his hostess enjoyed a glass of lemonade. 'You know, it was magical to have a railway line going right through the village – just like a film set. It was less than fifty years ago. In those days we'd have heard trains passing at the bottom of that field two or three times during the course of this interview.'

Robbie let her reminisce. She was an ideal witness, crisp and clear. She must have been an inspiring teacher.

'Could I ask some questions about you?' he asked, once there was a lull in the conversation. 'For example, have you always lived around here? How long were you linked with the school? When did you retire as head teacher?'

'I thought you were going to ask how long I'd been linked with the railway. That's a more interesting question. As far as teaching's concerned, I became a teacher here in 1955 and head in 1965. I retired in 1989. I've lived around here, apart from time at College, all my life. And I hope for a few more years yet.'

'So what are your links with the railway?'

'My grandfather was a Railway Director. He was a businessman in Padstow; he got onto the Board to make sure the line went on after Delabole.'

'Surely it wouldn't terminate here? It's hardly a tourist centre. There's no beach unless you rock-climb down to Tregardock.'

Miss Trevelyan wrinkled her nose with a smile. Obviously she'd climbed down to Tregardock Beach many times in her

56

younger days.

'But you're making the common mistake of thinking of the railway as being mainly for passengers. For most of its life freight was at least as important.'

Robbie thought for a moment. Miss Trevelyan watched him struggling. She still had a teacher's knack for making her pupils interpolate as much as they could from what they actually knew.

'Is this something to do with slate?' he hazarded.

'Yes, that's right. The local Slate Quarry was big even in the nineteenth century. The folk that ran it were desperate for a railway to take their output up to the rest of the country.

'Do you know,' she went on, 'before the railway they used to heave their slate down the coast to Port Gaverne – next to Port Isaac - and send it off in small boats. In those days packing boats was a woman's job.'

She sniffed in disgust. 'I'm glad I didn't have to do it. No, without my grandfather, the North Cornwall line might never have got as far as Padstow.'

This was a more vivid history than Robbie dared dream of. He had hoped to find firsthand accounts of recent history – it was, after all, only fifty years earlier. But a direct connection with the railway's beginnings was remarkable.

He must learn all he could. 'How well did you know your grandfather?'

'He was quite rich. He ended up with a big house near St Kew, down towards Wadebridge. I was born in 1929 and we had a cottage on his estate. When the depression came my father lost his job as a fisherman, left home to look for work and never came back. Two years later my mother died of tuberculosis. I was brought up in my grandfather's house by my aunt. She was a widow, her husband had been killed in the Great

War.'

She paused to compose herself; these were sad memories. 'So I spent most of my childhood with my grandfather. I took the name Trevelyan. We got on well; the railway was always one thing he was happy to talk about. I often used to ask him about it. If he didn't know he would find someone who did.'

'That's why, when I became a teacher here, I was so keen to pass on my interest. I'd had a diary since I learnt to write so I'd already got notes from my grandfather. As a teacher I could see that the history of the local railway had potential. It could give my pupils a pride in local events and Cornish enterprise.

'There was already a tradition that every summer the top class would research some aspect of the railway. We made good use of the children's families' memories and personal history, as well as talking to the passengers and railway workers round about. Then I'd take the raw material the youngsters brought in and pull them into a coherent account, all typed up for the Open Day. It was very popular.'

'And what happened once the Open Day was over?' Robbie held his breath: this was usually the point where a line of en-quiry petered out.

'I kept them. In the end there were over fifty folders. I was only there for ten years while the railway was running. But I augmented the earlier files from my own diaries. When I retired it stayed in the school.

'Then Mrs Southgate found them. Once she realised what they were she asked me if I'd look after them. So now they're all here.

'Would you like to see them straight away - or after we've had some cake?'

CHAPTER 8

I t was early evening when Robbie's phone rang again. This time it was George Gilbert.

'Hi Robbie, is this a convenient time to talk?'

'George!' For a second, frustrated emotions got the better of him. It didn't help that the call came as he had just taken a mouthful of Bettle beef and ale pie.

He started to choke. A fellow diner from the next table saw his distress, stood up and gave him a couple of hearty thumps on the back.

Meanwhile the call continued. 'Robbie! Robbie? Are you OK – it sounds like someone is beating you up?' It wasn't the best way to resume a friendship.

The journalist swallowed hard, waved away his helper and shut his eyes.

'George, I'm just having my evening meal at the Bettle and Chisel. Can I ring you back in half an hour? This isn't the best place for a private conversation.'

'Fine, I'm in all evening.' He noted her mobile, landline and address; he wasn't intending to lose contact again.

Twenty minutes later Robbie had persuaded the bar-girl to let him take his Eton Mess and a second pint of cider back to his room. He settled himself and then returned the call.

'Hi George. Thank you so much for ringing.'

'Hey, Robbie, it's good to talk again. I kept wondering why

you'd stopped calling. After a few months I gave up. Then I upgraded my phone and had to change my number. Honestly, I wasn't trying to lose you.' She sounded distraught.

'It was my newspaper, George. They suddenly needed me in Australia – a six-month swap with a guy on the Sydney Herald. It had been talked about for weeks then the whole thing was brought forward. His father in the UK went from being sick to being critically ill. My exchange had to be here but he was under pressure back there. They needed an experienced journalist to take over his story.'

The journalist sighed. 'They gave me an air ticket and forty eight hours to pack. I tried ringing you but I could never get through.'

'Maybe I was on a project too. They send me all over the country. I turn off my personal mobile while I'm working, so I can be out of touch too.' She laughed. 'You wouldn't think it would be so easy to lose a connection.'

'Or simulate a disappearance. I might have been kidnapped and held to ransom. But I didn't expect you'd come tramping the outback to find me.'

'I had no idea that was where you'd gone.'

It had just been a series of unfortunate accidents. Suddenly the urge to share yesterday's discovery of the skeleton in the tunnel became overwhelming. It was hard work keeping it to himself. And it was a murder that had started their friendship in Looe. That showed him George was well able to keep a secret.

'Actually, George, I've just come across a real disappearance. But the police had told me to keep it quiet until they're ready to handle the publicity.'

'Then you must. But if you ever want to chew over the outline with someone I'm all ears. And if there's any background I can help with I've plenty of time at the moment.'

'Why? Hey, you've not been laid off, have you?'

'No, it's nothing like that - they're short of senior analysts like me. No, it's my poor Polly.'

Robbie remembered, with a struggle, that Polly was George's only child. He'd never met her. By now she must be in her late teens.

'So what's happened to her?'

'Well, she was on a gap year before starting at Uni. Working in a remote clinic in Sierra Leone. She got a bug the doctors couldn't diagnose. She lost all her energy, became listless and lifeless. So, two weeks ago, they sent her home for rest and treatment. I'm confined to the house looking after her.'

'Sounds nasty. Do they know what it might be?'

'It's not Ebola, they say. Fortunately. But it might be something similar. That's why I'm in here as chief medical officer and nurse. The medics are waiting on test results. Only a week, they told me. Huh. That was ten days ago. I may be in here for some time.'

Robbie could see why George had plenty of time. For an hour the pair shared stories of their last year, the people they'd each come across and some of their foibles. There were plenty of laughs. It was almost as if the gap in their friendship had never occurred.

Robbie knew he had to do something with this new resource.

'I'd really like to share my most recent find. But the police have told me I mustn't tell anyone. Mind, if you were to make intelligent guesses and I told you which ones were wrong, you could glean enough for us to have a discussion. But I could tell the police, in all honesty, that I hadn't told anyone anything.'

'Freedom of Information doesn't work in industry, Robbie. Lots of time we're working with conjectures. I can be useful even without all the facts. I'd love to have something new to get my teeth into – something beyond Polly's illness. It's like . . . well, it's like being in a continuous episode of Casualty. Why not tell me all that you can?'

'OK, we'll see how it goes. Did Brian tell you why I'm down here?'

'The Green Tourist Award? Trying to extend the Camel Trail up to Delabole? His wife chairs the bid, he tells me. Have you met her?'

'Late one evening, after a meal with Brian. I'll have a longer chat after Friday's campaign meeting. The find's nothing directly to do with her.'

'So it's something to do with the bid? Or the topic? Relating, maybe, to the challenges of developing a new cycle trail?'

'You're getting warm. So far I've been looking at sections of the old railway. If you look carefully you can see the whole line on Explorer maps. I'm interested in the bit from Delabole to Wadebridge.'

'Wait a minute. I've got that map here. I'll ring you back when I've found it.'

Robbie took the opportunity to stretch his legs. Ten minutes later his friend called again.

'I've found the map covering Bodmin Moor. There's a dismantled railway line winding across it. There's one place it disappears. Is that a tunnel?'

'The only one on the line. That would be a key part of a new cycle trail. Someone would need to check it was safe.'

'Sounds like a job for Robbie Glendenning.'

'True. With a local heating engineer I met in the bar.'

'Hm. So is that where the incident arose?'

Robbie smiled. 'I'm horribly predictable.'

'What sort of find, I wonder.' She paused for thought. 'Was it someone you met in the tunnel?'

'No. There was barbed wire at both ends, though hardly Colditz calibre.'

'So if it wasn't someone you met was it something you found?'

'Keep going.'

'You talked earlier about a disappearance. So . . . might we be talking about a body?'

'Not that young.'

'Oh.' George paused to think. 'You mean . . . a skeleton?'

'Well done. Any guess on where it might have been found?'

'You say it was inside the tunnel. If you two could slip in then so could anyone else. A skeleton would have been there for a long time, so it couldn't have been that obvious. I dunno. Maybe some sort of cave?'

'It was. I think we've enough data now for a conversation. You could keep on guessing but I haven't much more to add. There were no signs of violence and no trace of clothing. So what do we think?'

George took a moment to respond. 'Well, here are some questions for starters. First, can Forensics date this skeleton so we know how long it's been there? Hey, could Brian Southgate tell us how modern-day Forensics works?'

'What dates should we be interested in?'

'You say this is on an old railway line. So was the railway running when the corpse arrived? A train timetable might even show when.'

'Also, George, accurate dating might help work out who the victim was. There must be records of locals who've gone missing. Any filtering would help trim down the list. Right now it could be any time in the last century.'

'Hey, it could be one of the tunnel's builders. If the cave was well-hidden the poor bloke might have been left there. There used to be lots of deaths in construction. No Health and Safety in those days.'

'He was found in a cave, you say?' she went on. 'Odd it was inside the hill. Was it natural? The chances of the tunnel intersecting it are minimal.'

'It wasn't really a cave. More an odd-shaped void.'

There was a pause and then George picked up another point. 'Whoever it was, the lack of clothing is peculiar. There'd be something left, whatever the material – at least from the shoes. Doesn't that make accidental death unlikely?'

'It might. I can imagine a tramp on a cold winter's day, after the line was shut, wandering into the tunnel to die. Maybe even finding a cave to end his life. But surely he'd be wearing something?'

'And if there was someone with him - or if someone found him - surely they wouldn't take away the clothing? But on the other hand, if it was just a place to hide a victim then it's not very convenient, is it?'

Having someone to argue with was certainly beneficial. Even speaking of the skeleton as a victim raised a whole forest of further questions.

A new thought came. 'Last week, George, I heard about one accident. A slate wagon got loose at Delabole and ran down the track. It only stopped when it hit a goods train. There was a massive smash. But suppose that happened again, with someone in the wagon. Might it derail inside the tunnel?'

'You mean, if someone was killed inside the tunnel they might be shoved away inside the cave. That'd be one reason for a body being there. That's one thing I can work on, Robbie. We could see if the idea is viable.'

'Anything you could find about train times might be relevant as well. How fast did they travel? Can you get hold of any old schedules?'

They agreed to talk again the following evening. Having an investigative partner – even one 250 miles away – made Robbie feel a great deal better.

CHAPTER 9

Robbie was surprised to see it was only ten o'clock. Before he went to sleep he must start on the Archive. The old lady had recorded the loan in her notebook but he'd only been lent it for two weeks.

He had borrowed the whole Archive. Which bits might relate to the skeleton? Why was the tunnel built, for a start? How come there a cave inside?

Robbie opened the first box, labelled 1893-5, and began to read.

'The most memorable day in Delabole's history', claimed Sir Anthony Aristotle, as he looked around complacently. As far as the eye could see there were people, locals in their Sunday best as well as many from further afield. Excitement was in the air.

'You can be very proud,' said his daughter Emmeline. 'You've got the line to Delabole. We'll be the capital of North Cornwall.'

It was October 19th 1893. The crowd was gathered in Delabole station, milling around the first passenger train ever to arrive. For many it was the first train they had ever seen.

Some were strolling along the platform; many of the rest, especially the younger element, were at track level, examining the new structures. The engine turntable – to be used next day to turn the engine, so it could return to London – was a particular source of delight.

A few had started up the track towards Camelford. There would be no more traffic this day. The only train, engine steaming and carriages gleaming, was the harbinger of the slowly-expanding North Cornwall Railway. This celebration was to mark its arrival at Delabole.

Sir Anthony was manager of the local Slate Quarry, where some geological quirk had left a massive amount of high-quality slate. With the growth of Victorian towns there was a huge market for slate and the coming of the railway gave the Quarry far better access. Sir Anthony might soon be a very wealthy man.

The North Cornwall Railway was controlled by local committees. John Trevelyan, a neighbour of Sir Anthony, joined him as he surveyed the scene.

'Good turnout sir, I warrant more than a thousand. They're pleased to have contact with the outside world. At least until they learn what the outside world is like. But it'll be good for your business. Have we finalised the route to Wadebridge?'

Sir Anthony wasn't much interested. 'All my slate will go east up the line,' he replied. 'What do I gain from a link to Wadebridge?'

'Lower shipment costs, sir. Two-way traffic. Delabole has the best slate in the country, but it's not a place folk want to visit. Whereas Padstow, on the coast, has vast scope for visitor expansion.'

'You think visitors will want to come to Cornwall?' Sir Anthony looked scornful.

Trevelyan gestured over towards Wadebridge. 'The cost of extending the line is not large.'

'Cornish landscape doesn't lend itself to railways. To reach

Padstow you've first got to reach Wadebridge. That means a tunnel
or a viaduct.'

'The consulting engineers know that, Sir Anthony. All they
want is a decision on whether to dig one or build the other.'

'One day soon, John, we'll tell them. For today let's just celebrate the line reaching Delabole.'

Robbie noted the name Trevelyan. Was this Miss Trevelyan's
grandfather?. For now he picked up another extract.

*The controversy over route persisted. The inhabitants of Trelill
had been alarmed at the prospect of a tunnel beneath their homes.
What was the risk of collapse? And even if the tunnel was built,
how much noise would there be from trains beneath their cottages
night and day?*

*The tunnel would mean a detour. By now Sir Anthony knew the
line could not end at Delabole. He'd also seen the chance for profit
from a direct-route viaduct, constructed over many towers of slate.*

*The debate had raged. Eventually a geologist had declared the
tunnel was the cheaper option. But to placate Trelill it would be dug
only with pickaxes.*

*The work started in October 1894. With a single-track line only
a few men could dig at once. Once inside the tunnel the width
slowed progress. The new Ordnance Survey Map had the tunnel
twelve hundred feet long: at the rate they were digging it could take
a year to complete.*

*Should they use dynamite? John Trevelyan insisted their solemn
pledge be honoured. In the end it was decided to dig from both ends.*

It was known where the track should emerge but the maps were not accurate enough to guarantee the two tunnels would meet. But the teams must surely hear each other?

The work continued. Both tunnels reached three hundred foot into the hillside. Setting the direction was complicated by the bend and it would be easy to veer off course.

March arrived. The two tunnels were each six hundred feet long. Had they dug off course? How accurate were the maps? An error of a few feet could mean the tunnels would not meet at all.

By mid March they still hadn't met. The surveyor ordered long drills then drilled out from the southern tunnel in all directions. The lamp was doused - but still nothing could be seen. In desperation he sent for a "shrieker" which could exude a high-pitched note for several hours. He started this inside the northern tunnel then made his way over to the southern end. He and the two supervisors listened hard.

'I can't hear anything,' said the older supervisor despondently.

'But I can,' said the surveyor. 'It's very high-pitched. You two are old. Your hearing's probably reduced with age.'

He started pacing. 'It's loudest here.' He was thirty feet from the end.

Another hole was drilled. Then, as they took out the drill, the shrill noise became audible to all and they gave a massive cheer. Within hours the tunnels had been joined.

The committee demanded a walk through - there was credit from being one of the first. Though it had taken months to dig, the walk took only a few minutes. John Trevelyan commended the supervisors heartily.

Sir Anthony, still smarting from the rejection of the viaduct, was outspoken in his criticism. 'It's not exactly smooth, is it?'

A brick lining was suggested. Bricks were not cheap and skill was needed to make a rounded roof-arch but the cost was small in comparison to the overall construction costs. A stone entrance was added at each end.

By May 1895 the North Cornwall Railway reached from Launceston to Wadebridge. Four years later it had been extended to Padstow. Passengers could now travel 260 miles from London Waterloo directly to the North Cornwall coast in little more than seven hours.

An era of prosperity had begun for this most remote of English counties.

A useful read, thought Robbie. The extract had given him some background for the Green Tourist cycle trail as well as the hiding place for the skeleton.

There'd been plenty of controversy over the tunnel. Could the overlapping tunnels account for the wedge-shaped void where he'd found the skeleton?

No mention yet of a ventilation shaft. Maybe in later documents . . . but it was too late for any more this evening. Robbie decided to call it a day.

CHAPTER 10

Friday evening, Robbie recalled, as he set off for breakfast, was the next meeting of the cycle trail campaign. He had every intention of attending. At least he could report that without running into the embargo.

What difference would a skeleton make once it was announced? (There was nothing yet on the local news.) The cycle trail had to go through the tunnel, which Mick had found structurally sound. But the project could be disrupted, if not destroyed, by the discovery of a long dead body along the way.

There were two possibilities. The news might raise awareness and hence aid publicity. Or it could make the Council far more reluctant to pick the idea at all. Much would depend on the alternatives they could choose from.

But a mystery skeleton was exactly what one other bid had been looking for. If the police didn't make much progress with it, would this give scope for the public to contribute? The risk of the public being more successful might even make the police take the case more seriously.

So the evening was spoken for; what could he do with the rest of the day?

If she wasn't away sailing, Robbie might have called on Rowena Gibson. She must have more useful contacts. However, she would want to know exactly what he had been doing and she'd probably extract mention of the skeleton.

And once she knew, from what he'd seen of her social

network, the rest of Delabole would know within the hour. Even when she was back it would be safest to keep out of her way until he was able to speak more freely.

There must be other aspects of railway memories. How were trains controlled on a single track line; how was it maintained? The memories might help make sense of how the body could have got there and also enliven the cycle trail bid. As he ate his breakfast, Robbie looked through his notebook for any names he'd been given earlier.

Later the journalist drove to St Kew to visit Harold Shoesmith, one time signalman on the North Cornwall Railway. Harold, elderly and now almost blind, was looked after by his daughter Della.

It was Della that had answered his call. 'Dad has good days and not-so-good days. He's been a bit seedy recently but today it looks like he's fine. Strike while the iron's hot: come this morning if you can. Say about eleven?'

Robbie found their cottage without difficulty. Della was a cheerful woman in her fifties; she greeted him warmly. It must be hard work, he thought, looking after someone so old.

Robbie followed her in. The former signalman heard him enter and stood up to greet him; Robbie shook his hand warmly. He was small in stature but with a ruddy, well-seasoned face that proclaimed a continuing interaction with the wider world. 'I'm afraid I can't see like I used to,' he wheezed. 'But being blind don't make me senile.'

Robbie accepted the offer of a cup of tea and settled himself in a rocking chair. He explained to Harold how he was working with a group in Delabole to try and develop a cycle path along the old railway line as far as Wadebridge. 'I'm after some historical perspective: how the line was really run.'

Robbie could see from the way his face perked up that mention of the North Cornwall Railway had sparked the old man's interest.

'I joined the railway straight after the Second World War,' the old man began. 'I'd served in the Signals Corps in North Africa and then in Italy. When I wuz back, trying to work out what to do, training up for the signals seemed a good line to take. I wuz brought up around here, see; so once I'd qualified I wuz pleased to be asked to run the St Kew signal box – especially as a cottage came with the job.'

He started waving his hand. Robbie wondered if he wanted water, then realised with a shock that he was talking about the cottage they were sitting in.

'So the line ran close to this cottage?'

'Right beside us – just over there.' He pointed towards the window overlooking the back garden.

Robbie suddenly realised that this would mean the cycle trail, if it ever happened, would pass the man's back garden. How would he feel about that, he wondered. Maybe being blind would have its compensation.

The journalist decided not to pursue the issue at this point. His goal today was to learn more about past operations.

'Wasn't St Kew a small station to have its own signal box?'

'Well, the railway wuz only single line, see. Trains could only pass at the stations where the track doubled out. It wuz vital they never met in between.'

'And that never happened – over the whole seventy year life of the railway?'

'Just the once – long before my time. In 1896, over near Otterham. It wuz winter and raining like hell. A goods train which wuz travelling in reverse back toward Launceston tried to stop in one of the two tracks at the station. But with the slippery track and limited brakes the goods train skidded onto the single line. A passenger train wuz coming the other way. It couldn't stop – ran straight into the back of it.'

'How dreadful – were many killed?' asked the journalist.

'Nah – the steam engine ploughed through the wagons and derailed most of 'em. Its own carriages stayed on the line. Took a bit of sorting out, I guess. But see, that's what these petrolheads forget: railways are a very safe means of transport. Not many accidents of any sort in my day. No, not many.'

The old man gave a sigh. For a moment Robbie thought he had dozed off. But it was just a natural pause in his reminiscences.

'So how did you control a single track railway?' he asked, once the old man was alert again.

'Ah. There wuz what we called a "token" – a circular metal hoop with an 'andle. A train couldn't start on the next section until the driver had the token. Once it reached the next station it wuz handed in to the signal box there. Then reissued to a train coming the other way. Very simple but effective.'

Robbie thought for a moment. 'That's fine as long as trains alternated. But that couldn't always happen, I mean, what if a train was late? There must times when two or even more trains travelled one way before one came back. What happened then?'

'Ah, I never said there wuz only one token, did I? Each box had several tokens. If a second train came after the first, the box ahead would be warned. It wouldn't issue any returning token until the second one had got there as well.'

'So you'd to watch for trains leaving the section as much as entering it?'

'Oh yes. You couldn't go to sleep on the job. See, there were only half a dozen passenger trains each way each day - less on Sundays. That might not sound much. But there were also plenty of goods trains running up and down.'

Robbie remembered Miss Trevelyan had talked about the importance of goods traffic. With sequential interviews you could take what you learned from one interview onto the next. 'You mean the slate trains from Delabole?'

'And the fish from Padstow, the cattle from Wadebridge and the building materials for pretty much everywhere. Plus rabbits, fuel and china clay. Just after the war the roads weren't geared up for high volumes of heavy goods; they had to come by train. Some, like the slate, were regular hauls and were scheduled.

'But the real challenge wuz hybrid trains, with both passengers and goods. Sometimes a train would have to wait while the extra freight wagons were added. Or wait again, two stations further on, while they were taken off.'

'Didn't the passenger find that very irritating? I know I would.'

'No, passengers just accepted the delay: it was how life was. People had more time than they do today. Seemed a lot happier for it, I'd say.'

Harold looked alert. It was time to move onto a trickier topic. This could be the only time he would question a witness who had once enjoyed daily contact with the railway.

'Were there ever problems with vandals on this part of the line?'

For the first time Harold looked troubled. Maybe he had unhappy memories. But natural courtesy towards his interviewer kept him going.

'Usually it wuz fine. The railway had been here for a long

time. Kids studied it at school – travelled on it in the holidays. It wuz part of the landscape.'

'But . . .'

'The only trouble I can remember was with some lads from the Children's Home in St Kew. That was in the early sixties.'

Robbie tried to hide his excitement. He'd never heard mention of a Children's Home, least of all one with a link to the railway.

'So what happened?'

'Well, there wuz rumours in St Kew that it wasn't the happiest of Homes. Course, the kids in there were orphans, came from a broken family or one that couldn't cope with them. Maybe foster parents who couldn't cope with them either. They hadn't had the best of starts to life.'

'Useful background, Harold. But what took place that affected the railway?'

'It only happened once. Maybe there wuz some trouble at the Home to make 'em protest? The first I heard wuz from the driver of a goods train that had just passed through the tunnel. Talked to him as I took his token. He wuz looking very shaken. Someone had tried to drop a rock on his engine as it came out the tunnel. I mean, that could have been very nasty.'

'It certainly could – he might have been killed. What did you do?'

'It wuz the last train of the day. I got my wife to cover for me in the signal box – in case there wuz a call from up or down the line – and set out up the track. It's two miles from here to Trelill, took me half an hour.'

'What did you find?'

'Whoever had dropped the rock didn't know, of course, that it wuz the last train. They were still hanging about over the tunnel entrance.'

'But didn't they see you walking up the track?'

The signalman gave a sigh. 'I'm not a complete idiot, Mr Glendenning. I knew the terrain. At this end there's a wood, runs right up to the tunnel. Once I got near I slipped into the trees and crept up as quiet as I could.'

There was a pause but it was just another of Harold's recovery breaks. After a minute he continued. 'I could see the trouble came from three lads – teenagers, all fairly big. They'd built up a pile of rocks above the tunnel, right over the track. They wuz waiting for another train they could bombard.'

'So what did you do?'

'Well, for quite a while I did nothing. I mean, what could I do? There wuz three of 'em - I couldn't handle 'em all. But if they saw me and scarpered I'd never know who they were. Maybe if they knew they'd been seen that would stop 'em doing it again – but maybe it wouldn't.'

'So you waited. Could you see their faces?'

'Yup. They weren't wearing masks - and I'd good eyesight in those days. Kids didn't dye their hair or any of that nonsense. After maybe half an hour they must have decided there wuz no more trains coming.'

'So did you try to follow them?'

'Huh. Wasn't a matter of following. They came down the slope and started towards me - walking past me along the track. Chatting away, jaunty as anything. I stood still as a mouse till they wuz past me, then followed 'em carefully.'

'Great. Did you manage to find out where they came from?'

'I did. The St Kew Children's Home was close to the track, see. Once they got near they slipped off and shinned over the wall.'

Another recovery pause and then Harold continued.

'I decided I'd report the matter to the manager at the Home. See if he could sort it out. If he did nothing – or if it happened again - then I'd be straight to the police. But maybe they would have ways of getting through to the lads that were more direct and more effective. That seemed to deal with it, anyway.'

There was a pause. Harold seemed to have run out of steam. Della must have been waiting for a suitable point to bring out the tea. Now she entered with a tray in her hands. There was a pause while she poured a mug for each of them. 'It's easier for my Dad not to bother with saucers,' she explained.

Robbie was pleased to see that the old man could apparently cope with chocolate digestives.

During the tea-taking the journalist remembered that George had talked about finding train schedules on the internet. But was there not a clash between the idea of published schedules and the local improvisation, with goods wagons being added or removed, which Harold had just outlined?

'How did the official schedules match what you described earlier?'

'They worked for the main express trains from London – like the Atlantic Coast Express. You've heard of that?'

Robbie nodded then realised his silent agreement would not be seen. 'That was the through train from Waterloo to Padstow?'

'That's right. Those folk wanted a timetable and we had to make sure it wuz followed. Of course, there wuz still delays. That's the nature of a railway. Bad weather didn't start in the twenty first century, you know.'

'But you've no record of what times the trains actually ran?'

Robbie had asked not expecting for a moment a positive

answer. But he seemed to have struck a bell.

The old man beamed and turned towards his daughter. 'Della, I told you my notebooks would be wanted one day. Fetch 'em out please. They're in that box at the back of my wardrobe.'

CHAPTER 11

*"It may be alright but we have to keep in touch. There's a meeting, I
think, today. I've decided to attend. See you there?" G.*

Friday evening was the first working meeting of the North
Cornwall cycle trail campaign. As the meeting was at the
Bettle and Chisel, Robbie could combine attendance with a
leisurely evening meal.

What kinds of people would give up time for this? His trip
with Rowena had shown him how much work was needed if
the trail was ever to be restored.

Whatever else, the campaigners were in good heart. There
were a dozen present, Mick Hucknall wasn't among them. Alice
was there too, though only sipping lemonade. She'd nodded to
Robbie on arrival but he sensed he was to remain in the background. Press coverage might cramp their style.

He could see why they'd wanted Alice as chair. Her skills as
a head teacher were subtle but strategic: she could keep control
without putting anyone down too hard. Once the meeting
opened she asked for a Minute Secretary to track their deci-
sions. A tiny woman called Jess agreed to fulfil this role.

Item one was the legal obstacles in setting up the old railway
route as a cycleway. Nathan Selvey, a fit-looking solicitor who,
Robbie remembered, hoped to cycle to work in Wadebridge,
reported his initial findings.

'So what constitutes a Right of Way? My first thought was

that any public railway line must be one. If people could go along inside a train they could surely go along on a bicycle? And once established, it's forever – even if a farmer tries to seal it off.'

'Or puts a bull in the field,' voiced someone on the next table. It sounded like the voice of bitter experience.

'But it depends on how the land was closed. If it "reverted to the original owner" there'd be no ongoing Right. In that case the battle's much harder.'

There was a murmur of dismay. Were they to be thwarted before they could even begin? Nathan seized the chance to start his beer, then resumed.

'From the Land Registry I've got a list: thirty landowners who together own all the land used by the railway between here and Wadebridge.' He handed over the paper to Jess. 'The key question is their attitudes to the cycle trail. There are broadly three possibilities.'

Nathan had another swig. There was quiet. This was serious stuff.

'Some will be in favour. Maybe they or their children like cycling. If so the easiest option is a "permissive footpath" across their land. The trail will still need to be cleared – gorse removed and so on - and fences built. That might take some time but it's not a show-stopper.'

'I'm sure there'd be plenty of volunteers,' observed Alice. Nathan nodded his appreciation and then continued.

'The second group will be those with no interest in cycling but who might cooperate, given financial incentives.'

'You mean they're open to a bribe?' asked the man who had fallen foul of a bull. Nathan gave an ambiguous shrug.

'The last group are those who'll do their best to block it.

81

They might own pedigree cows, say, and not want them disturbed. We'd need Council support to take them on. And it could take a while.'

Nathan took another swig. Setting the world to rights was thirsty work.

'At this stage I've no idea how the thirty divide up. I'd say the whole scheme is only viable if half are with us. We might handle one or two who are hostile, but not more.'

'Even two would be a handful,' muttered the bull expert. Robbie wondered how many bulls he'd encountered on his epic walk.

'So that's who they are: how could we categorise them?' asked Alice.

'The first step's a letter, to find where each one stands.'

'OK. That's what we'll do. Now let's move on,' said the chair. She knew the value of short meetings.

'Item two is the impact of the cycle trail on tourist numbers. Jill, you've being giving this some thought?'

Jill Frewer worked in the Tintagel Visitor Centre and conducted surveys on many aspects of tourism.

'We could learn so much from just one or two surveys.'

'But wouldn't that be expensive?'

'Not if we used volunteers.'

Alice looked round. 'How many could give an afternoon to helping with a survey?'

Half a dozen hands went up. 'That's plenty,' said Jill. 'Jess, get their names.'

Jill went on to explain, 'One question is for those already on the Camel Trail, whether they'd want to do more. Is there a market for our extension?'

'Is not the key question whether more trails will boost

tourist numbers?' Alice was sharp, Robbie had to admit.

'The Council 'd like to know that,' admitted Jill. 'But I don't know what sort of survey would help find it out. You'd never tell for sure.'

Jill paused but no-one wanted to argue.

'There's another question,' she continued. 'Among non-cyclists, what might make them do a cycle trail; and would a second trail help?'

'Sample some hotel and holiday-cottage owners?' asked Nathan.

'Hey, that's an idea. I could slip it in with the regular questions.'

The chair sensed interest in surveys was waning. 'Right. Item three is the cost of restoration. I asked Mick Hucknall to assess the work needed.'

Robbie couldn't see him. The engineer still hadn't replied to his message.

'He can't be here,' said Alice, 'but he sent me a note.' She pulled it out and began to read.

' "Looked at the bridges. The road bridges are fine. The only one missing is at St Kew. That might need a pedestrian crossing." '

'There'd be plenty of complaints about traffic lights in the middle of nowhere.' The bull specialist was quick to detect trouble.

'But if there were complaints, the Council might install a footbridge - if the trail proved popular,' suggested Nathan. 'Might not be too expensive.'

Had the solicitor studied politics during his legal training? thought Robbie.

'Mick also says, "The biggest unknown is the Trelill tunnel."'

'Even the odd brick falling down could be lethal,' asserted the bull expert.

Alice continued, 'Mick concludes, "I'll inspect the tunnel next week." And that was written . . . the day before yesterday.'

A smart way of gaining time, thought Robbie. No doubt the police embargo was weighing on him too.

They were almost at the end. Alice observed, 'Lastly we must consider publicity. We'll need to be able to show it's got local support.' Nods of agreement from around the bar.

'I'd be happy to help pull material together.' This was Geri Turner, a serious-looking, dark-haired woman in her thirties. A few more offered their support.

'Well, Geri,' said Alice, 'looks like you've got helpers. If anyone has photos of the route, please send copies to Geri.'

'Great! Well, is there any other business?' Alice looked around her but there were no takers. 'Then I declare the meeting closed.'

Robbie introduced himself to everyone who had spoken. When the hubbub had died down he retired to his room to ring George Gilbert.

George sounded pleased to hear him. 'No obvious change in Polly's condition,' she said, 'so I'm still stuck in London. Tell me what you've been doing, Robbie. It's deadly dull here.'

Robbie started with the encounter with the signalman. 'He spoke of a dozen trains a day, plus goods trains. It'd not be easy to slip casually into the tunnel.'

'But what about at night? Did trains run then?'

'Don't think so. Have you managed to find any timetables?'

'One or two. There's plenty on the internet about rolling stock and one or two schedules. Let me see . . . no, the ones

I've found have no trains at night. I'll keep looking.'

Robbie went on to tell her about the incident of vandalism from the local Children's Home. 'So that's a few youngsters on the edge of the law, living locally and with a good understanding of the railway.'

'How are you going to take that any further?'

'Don't know yet. I don't even know when it all happened. Or where - I had a look for the Children's Home on my way home but I couldn't find it.'

'Someone must remember. The Home must have had local impact.'

It was something to work on. They talked on but had no insights.

'I've not got very far with the maths of loose wagons,' said George as they drew to a close. 'Polly's awake most of the day. I'm busy running around after her. Poor kid - she's just so inert.'

'It's great to have help, George, but your key task is with your daughter. I'll give you another call tomorrow. Right now I've got to read the Archive.'

CHAPTER 12

In fact I've two primary sources to look at, thought Robbie, as he remembered the signalman's notebooks. A quick glance showed they were much weaker on narrative than Miss Trevelyan's Archive though stronger on detail.

Each notebook dealt with a different year that Harold had worked as signalman, from 1948 until 1966. Each day listed times and cargo of the trains passing St Kew, with comments on why they were late.

Too much detail for this time of night. He'd read one incident from the Archive before he went to sleep. Last night he'd been in the nineteenth century; tonight he picked a story from the folder for 1922.

Hyacinth Trevelyan tells of a first class rail journey to Exeter.

I'd decided to travel from St Kew up to the prosperous city of Exeter. There were clothes shops there stocking modern, post-war designs. Though the North Cornwall Railway had been making this journey possible for thirty years it was still a source of wonder and pleasure.

Strictly speaking, a train journey wasn't necessary. My father was a wealthy man. After spending the Great War improving the design of radios he had celebrated peace by taking ownership of an expensive Morgan.

I'd learned how to drive and could use this when required. A license was issued to anyone who applied; I could drive anything from a motor mower to a large tractor. But what to do if the vehicle broke down was a worry. And a good reason to travel by train.

My train was due to leave St Kew at nine-thirty. It was a quiet station – the village itself was a mile away – but there were half a dozen others already waiting to travel.

Every station on the line looked the same. Father had been on the committee when the line was designed and had said they must not waste money on differential designs. As a result none of them had a footbridge.

My platform was on the far side. I crossed over via the small width of filled-in track. My fellow-passengers were mostly business men. My train, when it finally rattled into view, was pulled by a Beattie tank engine, short enough to handle the bends on the North Cornwall line.

The last two carriages did not even fit onto the platform. I would have to make allowance when choosing a carriage for my return journey. I was the only one from St Kew travelling first class; and was indeed the only passenger in my compartment.

There was the sound of a whistle then a jolt and the train started to move. The slow, regular rhythm of the pistons started to increase in tempo.

It was strikingly warm. I lowered the carriage window and looked out across the Amble valley; the sea was beyond the horizon. The route to Launceston was a steady climb to a height of nearly a thousand feet.

The engine gave a sharp whistle. Then, before I could work out *why, the train flashed into Trelill tunnel. Immediately the compartment filled with dense smoke. Instinctively I closed my eyes and reached down for the strap controlling the window, desperate to pull it closed. But it was pitch black and I struggled in vain.*

The crisis did not last long. A minute later the train came out into the daylight. I stopped coughing and breathed a sigh of relief. I was so cross I had forgotten about the tunnel and the need to keep all carriage windows closed until we were through it. Father had even reminded me about it over breakfast. It was, after all, the only tunnel on the line.

There was plenty of smoke inside the carriage but with the window open it was starting to dissipate.

Then I glanced at my face in the mirror. It was covered with smut. And my fashionably smart bonnet, which had started the day a picturesque pale blue, was now a dirty grey. But before I could do anything about it the train was pulling into Port Isaac Road.

This station was less used than St Kew: few were waiting. With a bit of luck none would be travelling first class. Then my carriage door was pulled open by a porter and an elegantly-clad lady climbed in. With a shock I recognised her. It was Emmeline Aristotle, the daughter of the recently-retired manager of Delabole Slate Quarry.

'My father always said that tunnel was a mistake,' began Emmeline, as she took the seat opposite, noted the residue and deduced the cause of my discomfort. 'He did his best, you know, to persuade the committee to build a viaduct instead, but your father blocked it.'

Until I could wash I was in a weak position. But, like my father, I did not like to lose an argument. 'You may be right, Emmeline. Of course there were a dozen on the committee, not just your father and mine. My father never discussed the details of the railway with me. Mind, I'm much younger than you so I was told very little.'

This was a good line of argument and it hit home. Emmeline was over fifty whereas I was still the right side of forty. She struggled to restore the focus of attention onto the tunnel.

'What I don't understand is why they didn't build in ventilation, for example, a shaft going up through the hillside. That would reduce the smoke's impact. You'd be better off keeping the carriage window shut, of course, but you might not look like a chimney sweep if you left it open.'

I giggled. There was no point in taking myself too seriously: right now I did look peculiar. Just because our fathers had argued was no reason for us to do so.

'Well maybe that could still be done. They did a lot of digging under trenches during the war. It's nearly thirty years since they built the tunnel. There've been massive engineering developments since then - and plenty of new explosives. They would never build a railway tunnel without ventilation if they were starting today.'

I had an exhilarating day in Exeter, during which I had bought two new outfits as well as a replacement bonnet. That evening, back in St Kew, I accosted father on the subject of tunnel ventilation.

'Do you know, that's not a bad idea,' he observed. 'I'm not on the committee any more but I know someone who is. I've got a business associate over in Plymouth. He could probably organise it.'

My wise father pondered the practicalities. 'It could be done on successive Sundays – there are no trains then, are there? There were plenty of passengers today? There must be the funds to de-

velop the line further.'

As he read, a smile of satisfaction played across Robbie's face. This was progress indeed! By pure chance he had landed on an article linked to the tunnel's ventilation shaft. It seemed it was built around 1923.

It would not be possible for a shaft to be drilled into the odd-shaped void without anyone noticing a body lying on the far side. That must set an earlier limit on the date when the skeleton arrived.

This was the only account he had come across of someone travelling the line. It gave other details which he would only appreciate with time.

CHAPTER 13

The metal ventilation shaft had been the object of Robbie's subconscious wanderings. He was not usually a worrier – didn't often dream around his problems. His routine was to work hard and then sleep soundly. But this time there was an elusive thought bugging him as he got up.

Was it a mere coincidence that the ventilation shaft ended only a few yards from where the body lay; or was there some other explanation?

It was as a sausage was delivered to his plate from the grill that a further thought occurred. So far he had presumed that the dead person had walked into the tunnel alive (if the death was an accident or suicide) or had been dragged in (if it was something worse). Both theories had plenty of difficulties.

But was it possible that the person had got there by being posted, alive or dead, down the metal shaft?

It was a daft idea. He wished he'd examined the tunnel shaft more carefully. Was there any sort of grill over the bottom? When he had seen it, the discovery of the skeleton had, inevitably, taken all his attention.

Perhaps the heating engineer would remember more? Then he recalled Mick Hucknall hadn't been back in touch. The man was almost acting as if he hadn't been there – some bizarre form of avoidance. He wondered what he could do. There was little point in leaving a second message at the same office in Camelford. In any case, today was Saturday. The place might well be closed.

Robbie mused on how the question could be taken further. Could he go back to the tunnel and take a second look? But now the police had been alerted, the tunnel was probably closed off.

Had the shaft been clogged, anyway? He replayed events in his mind. Then he remembered the draught of air which had drawn Mick and him into the void. That must have come from somewhere - which implied the shaft was open and came out somewhere else. Where was the top? It must be somewhere in Trelill, half way between the two tunnel exits.

The shaft probably ended in someone's garden.

But he could hardly conduct a house-to-house search to find it – at least not while the skeleton was under a police embargo.

One lesson Robbie had learned over his years as a journalist was to make the most of the sources he had already. In this case the source was the spritely Miss Trevelyan. It might be worth another conversation with her.

He could start by checking out her relationship with the Hyacinth Trevelyan that he'd read about the night before.

When the journalist phoned her after breakfast, Miss Trevelyan was happy to see him again. 'I'm not expecting any visitors today. Why not come for coffee later this morning?'

It was Saturday and he'd hoped to have a few hours off; but for someone who was retired, one day was probably much like another.

'I haven't got very far yet, but I've been enjoying the Archive,' Robbie began, as he took a mug of coffee from the old lady and placed it on the side table.

She smiled. 'I thought you might.'

'One thing I wanted to ask you is, how are you related to Hyacinth Trevelyan? I read that she was a daughter of John Trevelyan, one of the Railway Directors, but I wasn't sure - it might be a common local name.'

'That's easy, Robbie. Hyacinth was my mother's only sister, my aunt. And she was the lady that brought me up after my mother died.'

So that question was answered.

'I was reading a story about Hyacinth last night, you see. The time she forgot to close the carriage window and got covered in soot as it went through the tunnel.'

The old lady laughed. 'Hyacinth could usually see the funny side of things, even when she was the victim. Didn't take herself too seriously, which I think is a wise attitude. We had many a laugh together. I was very fortunate to have her as my surrogate mother.'

'It'll probably tell me somewhere later on, but could I ask, when did John Trevelyan, your grandfather, die?'

'Just after the war - 1946. He was well into his eighties. I was in my late teens, still living at home. I helped nurse him at the end. Mind, he'd stopped having anything to do with the railway long before then.'

'In the story I was reading, which was set in 1922, he was talking about putting a ventilation shaft into the tunnel. To reduce the impact of the smoke, you see – if anyone else was daft enough to leave the window open.' He smiled as he spoke, to show he was teasing.

'Oh yes, I know about that. That must have been the last time he had much influence. My "mum" told me about it. In fact my grandfather showed it me.'

Robbie took a sip of his coffee. 'When you say "showed

you", you mean he took you into the tunnel?'

'Don't be silly, Mr Glendenning. There were trains every day except during the war. I meant he showed me where the shaft came out in Trelill.'

'You don't remember where that was, exactly?' Robbie tried to pop the question casually but this was really why he'd come.

'Course I do. It was in the garden of Mr and Mrs Shawcross. Their daughter, Elsie, was a friend of mine. I was brought up in St Kew, not far away. A two mile walk to see a friend was nothing in those days. She still lives there, actually. We phone each other from time to time.'

Older people didn't move about like today's youngsters. Robbie wondered if he dared take this further. But first he had another topic to clarify.

'Yesterday I went to see someone else you might know,' he said. 'He lives in St Kew itself.'

For a moment he'd intrigued the old teacher. 'Hm, who can that be?' she mused.

She looked hard at Robbie. 'You're busy trying to find details of life on the old railway, aren't you? So was it someone who had direct dealings with the railway when it ran?'

'It was. The local signalman, in fact: Harold Shoesmith. He's going blind, I'm afraid, but he'd very good recall of how the line worked – especially the finer details of running a single track line.'

'Oh, I knew Harold well. He's in good health, I hope?'

'He looks healthy enough, anyway. He lent me his notes from his time as a signalman – with train times and holdup details. So now I've got two primary sources for my potted railway history.'

'Yes, we often asked Harold to talk to us for the school

projects.'

'One thing he told me about was vandalism on the line. Did that make your Archive?'

'I don't think so. What happened?'

'It was to do with some lads from the Children's Home in St Kew. I looked for the place on my way home but couldn't find it.'

'No, it's gone now.' Miss Trevelyan looked sad. Robbie's instinct registered that there was more to be uncovered here.

'Can you tell me anything about it?' he asked gently.

'How much d'you want to know? Before it became a Home, in the 1950s, it was the house I was brought up in. Once my grandfather died, and later my "mum", the place had to be sold. The Council bought it for social work. I don't suppose they changed it much. Probably did little more than block off the cellar.'

'So when did it stop being a Children's Home?'

'Let me see. The late 1970s, I think. There were always rumours of things not quite right, if you know what I mean. I don't know anything explicit, I'm afraid. Nothing was ever formally proved but I guess the Council decided not to take any more risks.'

It was some progress but it didn't sound like Miss Trevelyan could take the trail much further.

As the conversation drew to a close Robbie went back to the ventilation shaft. 'I wouldn't mind seeing it, you know. It's probably the only part of the railway that's still standing. Maybe, next time you're talking to Elsie, you could see if she was willing to let someone come and have a look at it.'

Miss Trevelyan looked excited. 'You could take me with you. I'd love to see her again. I'll give her a ring this afternoon.'

CHAPTER 14

By Monday Robbie was starting to feel hemmed in by the embargo. It was a good job he was from a responsible newspaper and not the tabloid press. But a week was a long time for the police to consult old records and to make secret enquiries.

He suspected their main challenge was caution on how the discovery, once announced, would be received by the media. Inspector Lambourn was not the most media-savvy policeman he'd ever come across. Maybe they were looking for someone better to handle the case?

Or were they trying to concoct a story that would mean they didn't need to do any investigation at all?

Looking through his notes, Robbie saw the name and number of another local "from a railway family". Looking at the work they'd been doing – he'd been a "lineman", whatever that was - he saw the visit might provide more information that would advance the skeleton enquiry.

After breakfast he rang the number to make an appointment. He was discouraged to learn the man had died a decade earlier.

'But I looked after Dad for many years,' he was told. 'He was always talking about his work and its foibles, at least till his final years. If you're trying to learn about life on the railway, I'd be happy to tell you what I can remember.'

Mrs Betsy Chalkpit turned out to be a tall, sprightly woman in her seventies. She was the daughter of the man Robbie had been hoping to interview.

'My Dad was one of the "Permanent Way Maintenance Gang" on the North Cornwall Railway between Delabole and Wadebridge.'

Robbie spotted at once that this included the Trelill tunnel. So the man had done maintenance on the piece of track running past the cave inside. He might yet learn something of value.

Robbie explained the admittable reason for his interest in the old railway. Betsy had heard about the bid for the Green Tourist Award from village gossip. This made her keen to help if she could.

She made them each a cup of coffee and the pair sat down.

'So your Dad was a linesman?' Robbie began.

'No, a linesman is someone who runs up and down the pitch and occasionally waves his flag,' she replied. 'Clogs up the process when you think you've scored. No, a lineman is a vital part of railway safety. At least that's what my Dad was taught and believed for many years.'

'I'm so sorry, he was a lineman. I'm still getting my terms sorted out. Can you tell me what a lineman used to do?'

'I'm hazy about the early days, before I was born, but I can give you an eye-witness account from the early 1960s. I was just twenty. My Dad used to hire me in the summer holidays, when his colleagues were taking their annual leave. That was also the time of year when the railway was at its busiest.'

Robbie remembered his editor talking about his own experience of the North Cornwall Railway. 'I suppose there'd be lots of passengers coming to Padstow for their summer holidays?'

'That's right. The rest of the gang were doubtful about a girl helping them – this was before Women's Lib - but my Dad was glad to have someone he could trust. He said it was better than having some school-leaver foisted on him who knew little and cared less. From my point of view it was good to have some spending money of my own.'

'So what did linemen actually do?'

'In my Dad's case they worked as a gang of four, with my father in charge. They had a motorised trolley; their job was to survey the line.'

'By which you mean . . . ?'

'They had to look for loose fittings that needed banging back into place, for cracked rails that needed replacing, and for points into the sidings to make sure they couldn't jam. They also had to make sure the signal connections kept working.'

'Hm. Sounds a lot to watch out for. How far did they cover each day?'

'Dad's gang was responsible for the fifteen miles of track from Delabole to Wadebridge. Then there were another two miles of sidings at various stations. They would inspect about three miles each day, so each part of the line got looked at once a week.'

Robbie did some arithmetic. 'You mean they didn't work on Sundays?'

'Not usually. But they - we - might if there was an emergency.'

This was important, thought Robbie. Someone who studied the gang's progress would be able to slip into the tunnel without meeting them. But it would take some research: they would need to be local.

'The trolley ran along the track? What happened when a

train came along?'

'Well, the signalmen knew which part of the line we were on each day – Dad made sure of that. And they made sure all the train drivers knew as well. The train drivers had to pick up a token from the signalman for the next section of track before they could go on to it.'

Robbie understood that bit from his interview with Harold. 'But just knowing your gang was somewhere ahead of them couldn't be all that was needed? The trains still had to run. What happened when they caught you up?'

'The gang could get the trolley off the track pretty quickly once they had to. A jack was part of the equipment. One of the gang watched out for trains and made sure we were off in time.' Betsy smiled. 'That was usually the work I did.'

For a fleeting second Robbie was taken back to the book called the Railway Children. What if, just for once, the signalman forgot to give the warning? He tried to imagine a young Betsy, running along the track and waving a bright red petticoat, to try and stop an oncoming train. He shook his head and brought himself back to the present.

'Wasn't it dangerous to operate on a live railway line?'

'In theory it could be. That's why we never worked at night – or even dusk. And we didn't go out if it was foggy or when visibility was poor. That would have been dangerous.'

'With Cornish weather, that would give you plenty of time off.'

Betsy was ready with an answer. 'Overall the gang worked longer in the summer than the winter. But that was OK: rail traffic was much heavier in summer months.'

'OK, that's the logistics. But I'm still not quite clear, what did the gang actually do? For example, how much of your time were you inspecting the track as opposed to repairing it?'

'That's a good question.' Betsy paused to consider. 'I suppose that in the summer of 1960, the first year I was helping, the ratio of inspection to repair was probably 90:10. Two years later closure of the line was looming. Beeching was underway; we all knew what it would mean.'

Betsy paused for a moment. 'By 1962 there were a lot more repairs needed. The balance was more like 70:30. We probably took longer to complete each tour of our designated section as time went on.'

'I'm impressed. For events fifty years ago you've got amazing recall. But can I ask another question? If your gang didn't operate in poor visibility, how on earth did you maintain the track inside the Trelill tunnel? I mean, you can't see from one end to the other.'

'How do you know that?' Have you been there?'

Robbie took a second to answer. 'I've looked down on one entrance; and I've seen the map.' Better to not say too much. Betsy seemed satisfied, anyway.

'My Dad was always very nervous about that bit. I think he remembered the war. Fortunately the trains were on a fifteen mph speed limit there so that track wasn't buffeted as hard as the rest.'

'But it would still need checking?'

Betsy frowned as she thought about her answer. 'Well, that bit only came round once a week. When it did, we'd ride the trolley down from Delabole to one end, ease it off the rails, carry our kit with us and walk through for a manual inspection. And hope like hell there were no urgent repairs needed, so we could pass swiftly on.'

'And you never had to repair anything?'

'Work only had to be done once when I was there. It was a bit frightening. But there were alcoves to hide in when a train went by.'

Robbie had seen them. He was about to share tunnel and alcove experiences with Betsy when he remembered the embargo.

He thought back to her words. One part of Betsy's answer hinted at something unexpected. 'What did you mean, "he remembered the war"? Did something odd happen to him here then?'

'Well, you know they used the tunnel to store munitions during the Second World War?'

'No. Gracious me, no-one's told me that.' Robbie thought for a moment. Why did that make her father nervous?

'You mean he was afraid there might still be explosives left and something could set them off?'

'He would never explain. But in later life, especially when he'd had too much to drink, he often talked about "ghosts in the tunnel". It didn't make any sense: I never saw anything odd when I was helping him. I assumed it must be something to do with the munitions. I mean, there's no other reason to associate the place with death, is there?'

CHAPTER 15

For once Robbie watched the news in the residents' lounge as he had his evening meal. Had the police put out any statement about the skeleton?

But there was nothing. He felt frustrated; he didn't want to broadcast his story across the village, but still . . . It was all very well talking over the phone with George but he needed to share with someone face to face.

It was a week since he'd visited Dr Brian Southgate and shared a bottle (or two) of red wine. Maybe his wife - the redoubtable Alice - would be out again? Robbie's conscience twitched at the thought of breaking the embargo; but he could talk to the doctor in confidence: arguably it was a matter of health.

And even if the doctor's wife was in, he was inclined to tell her about the skeleton as well. She would need to know as she was involved in the cycle trail bid, so might appreciate confidential advanced notice.

A phone call told him he was in luck: Brian was in and Alice was out, visiting her family in Camelford. 'I'm on my own, Robbie, supposedly reading the latest medical journal: I'd be glad of your company.'

The journalist called in at the local Spar and bought a couple of bottles of their costliest red wine. He had never heard of the vineyard, but expensive might mean at least mean that it was fine-tasting.

Fifteen minutes later he was seated at the doctor's while his host was in the kitchen, fetching a bottle opener, two glasses and a bowl of dry-roasted peanuts.

'Something odd's happened to me, and if you don't mind I'd like to talk it over,' he began.

Brian hid his surprise; had his new friend been caught drinking and driving? He encouraged him to continue.

Robbie took a large sip of his wine – it was a reserve Merlot, most drinkable – then described his visit to the Trelill tunnel with Mick Hucknall and the discovery of the skeleton behind the fractured alcove. Before Brian could comment, he went on to his encounter with Inspector Lambourn in Bodmin and how he'd been ordered to keep the information to himself.

'It wouldn't be like this if Peter Travers was here,' was his companion's immediate observation. 'He's our regular local bobby but he's away on a course at the moment. Have some more wine.'

The pair refilled their glasses; Brian started to ponder.

'It's a while since I was at medical college, but I remember the rudiments of skeleton analysis. It doesn't arise much in normal health care but it was covered on the basic forensics course.'

Robbie was encouraged. This was what he had been missing: an intelligent conversation around his discovery.

'It should be relatively easy,' the doctor continued, 'from the width of the pelvis and the shape of the thigh bones, to say whether the body was male or female.'

'You mean the female body has to be shaped so it can give birth?'

'That's right. And the colour of the bones might tell an expert roughly how long it's been there. After several decades a

103

sort of film develops on the bones, which isn't apparent on a new skeleton.'

'That's one sort of age,' conceded the journalist. 'How about the other sort: the age the person was when they died?'

'I recall something about the texture of the bones telling roughly how old the person was. But it's not a lot to go on. Poor old Lambourn might have a case on his hands. Perhaps he's keeping quiet because he's stuck.'

Robbie hadn't expected to hear support for the Inspector. Forensics must be trickier than he'd realised.

'Well, where the skeleton was found must tell us something,' said Robbie as he took another swig. 'We know the body can't have been there for much more than a century - they didn't build the tunnel until 1894.'

'Someone's been swatting up on their history.'

'It's all in the Archive from Miss Trevelyan that your Alice put me on to.'

The journalist recalled his reading from the night before. 'And in fact they didn't put the ventilation shaft in till after the Great War. If the body was there then it would certainly have been spotted. So it's less than ninety years old. It couldn't be one of the original construction navvies.'

'I can see that the date of death is important – might be all the police have to go on,' mused the doctor. 'But why are you starting from the far end of the time frame?' He paused to draw his thoughts together.

'Isn't the most likely scenario that it's the skeleton of a tramp who wandered into the tunnel for shelter after the line closed, and died, say, of hypothermia or starvation? I mean, the railway closed half a century ago. That's plenty of time for a dead body to turn into a skeleton. Especially if the cavern was damp.'

Robbie suddenly remembered his photographs. Maybe Brian's expertise could be harnessed more precisely? 'Wait a minute.' He dashed into the porch and retrieved the camera from his jacket pocket.

'I'd almost forgotten. I've got photos. Could I download them onto your computer? It's hard to make much sense of them on the camera.'

The doctor was keen to oblige. Ten minutes later the recent contents of Robbie's camera had been transferred to his computer.

It was just as well, the journalist thought, that he hadn't taken any pictures of his swimming expedition with Rowena. That might have been a distraction.

The doctor had a large monitor and soon brought up the first skeleton picture. He flipped quickly through the rest then went back to the beginning for a more detailed look.

'Considering you were taking them by flash, in a cavern in pitch darkness, these are excellent pictures, Robbie.'

Robbie was studying them carefully as well. The pictures looked good on a big screen. They reminded him vividly of his find and his feelings. At the time, he supposed, he must have been in shock; now the sadness of the event and awful loneliness of the corpse in death were completely in focus.

Brian proceeded to spend a few minutes on each photograph of the sequence. Robbie couldn't sustain the attention and fetched and opened the second bottle. He refilled their glasses.

'Put the first one in the outside dustbin,' he was instructed.

When he came back inside Brian was ready to give him feedback.

'First point: I'm only working from the pictures, and you'd

need to have the corpse in front of you to be sure, but I reckon there's a sheen on those bones. That means it's probably been there fifty years – maybe longer.

'Secondly, it's male. Not some prostitute who'd been taken somewhere, assaulted, stripped and then killed. So that's one credible scenario we can rule out.

'Thirdly, I can't be sure, but it looks to me like the skeleton of a young man in his twenties rather than someone much older. That's surprising. So, if those forensics are accurate, where does it take us?'

Both men drank some wine and considered the options.

'Is there any way of narrowing down the time that the skeleton – he, I suppose I should say – has been there? I mean, the age of the line tells us he couldn't have been there more than a century. Could carbon dating tell us more?'

Brian laughed. 'Carbon dating is great for archaeologists. It might tell you which century a skeleton was laid down, for example if one was found in an ancient tomb. But it can't pin down which decade.'

Robbie felt slightly disappointed. Forensics would only take them so far. Other skills would be needed.

What about Brian's other points?

'OK, let's take the chap's age when he died. Not much above twenty five, you suggest. That certainly goes against the "decrepit old tramp" theory. I suppose some vagrants are young. But why on earth should someone that youthful want to end his life in a remote tunnel?'

More alcohol was consumed but no enlightenment came.

'There's just one more thing I recall,' offered the journalist after a long pause. 'It's unclear in the photos, since they're all focussed on the bones, but they've reminded me of it. That is, the skeleton was laid out alongside the far wall of the cavern. Is that likely for a natural death?'

Brian pondered. 'It's possible someone would die by chance in that position but it's pretty unlikely. I mean, someone might have a heart attack and keel over near the wall – maybe clutch it as they went down - but they wouldn't sink down neatly beside it.

'No, if I was asked by the police, I'd say the position of the skeleton points to suicide – or, of course, to murder. Perhaps that's why the police are taking so long to announce the discovery?'

CHAPTER 16

It was too late when Robbie got back to the Bettle to ring George. His head was buzzing with questions and ideas. But he and the doctor had decided he must maintain silence on the skeleton for a little longer.

The police might well need more time for their enquiries if the case was really as serious as the pair had surmised.

Alice came home later than usual, just giving them time to finish the second bottle. Robbie managed to slip away as she returned without saying anything about the skeleton. He promised, though, to attend the next meeting of the cycle trail campaign later in the week.

Time for one more account from the Archive. Betsy Chalkpit's tale of the munitions dump had caught his imagination. What did the Archive have to say about wartime?

He tracked down a folder covering 1939-45 and started to read.

The Second World War had been running for two years when the decision was made to close the North Cornwall Railway. Passenger traffic had been reducing for years; numbers in the 1930s were only a third of the peak seen a decade earlier. The country had more useful ways of deploying manpower than running half-empty trains through Cornwall.

No-one objected too loudly, although the management of De-

labole Slate Quarry realised that with no way to ship the slate, their business, already running on a shoe-string, would need to hibernate in sympathy.

The North Cornwall Railway had made one distinctive contribution to the war effort. At the start of the war several trains had arrived from London Waterloo containing children, evacuated on government orders to keep them away from the chaos of the expected bombing raids.

The children had had a mixed reception at Camelford, Wadebridge or Padstow. A few had been adopted into the extended families of Cornish farmers. They would soon join the workforce as the farms struggled with limited manpower to produce food for a starving nation. One or two had been taken under sufferance and would suffer mistreatment. Between these extremes many were merely tolerated, in the context of war, but would never become part of the community.

A few, though, would adapt so well to life in rural Cornwall that they would settle and never return to the big city.

Even though the crux of the fighting was far to the east, the war affected everything and everyone. In 1940 the German invasion had been expected any day across the English Channel; the south coast took the lion's share of whatever defences were to be found. By 1941 the threat of invasion had receded and the need to protect the whole British coastline was in focus. An armoured train was improvised - a tank engine sandwiched between two armoured carriages. This was used to patrol the track alongside the Camel estuary between Padstow and Wadebridge. No-one knew how well this contraption would perform under enemy fire.

One local change was the construction of Davidstow Airfield, close to the North Cornwall Line as it linked Camelford to Launceston. The Airfield was for the Beaufighters and Wellingtons of Coastal Command, patrolling the North Atlantic in search for German e-boats or submarines.

In World War One, Commanding Officer Bill Penistone had been a flight lieutenant in the Royal Flying Corps. By 1939 he had long retired to run a butcher's shop in Camelford. But now he'd been brought back into service: even his out-dated experience might be of some use.

At the outbreak of war his son Jimmy, just turned eighteen, had volunteered to serve in the RAF even before hostilities commenced. The lad had been accepted. Tests showed he had inherited his father's flying skills, so he was soon in training as a fighter pilot. Three months later, he had been killed over the hop fields of Kent as he flew his Spitfire in the Battle of Britain.

Jimmy was their only son; neither Bill nor his wife Martha had really got over the shock. Now he went through the motions of command but his mind was often elsewhere. It was a mercy that the planes he now had to deal with were not fighters but bombers.

One day Penistone was approached by Stores Officer Alastair McTavish. McTavish was from a younger generation, a Glaswegian, who resented being posted to the far southwest - and who had made that view plain.

'Seeking leave, sir,' he'd said on one occasion, 'to visit my family. My son's fifth birthday.'

'I'd like to visit mine, McTavish. Trouble is, he's dead. Permission denied.'

On this occasion his request was related to the airbase. 'Sir, I'm concerned about the safety of our stores. We'll be getting another delivery of depth charges next week. I'm not happy to hold them in the hanger. No enemy bombers over Cornwall so far but that could change. One bomb on the hanger and the damage would be immense. The blast could wipe out all our planes – and half our men.'

Penistone considered. Like most on the base he found McTavish annoying, but the man had a point. He'd seen ammunition dumps explode in the Great War: the effect was mayhem. 'They might,' he agreed. 'What do you require?'

'Sir,' McTavish responded, 'Somewhere well off site where our depth charges could be stored until needed.'

Penistone was baffled. Outside-the-box thinking wasn't his strong suit. Why should anyone else want depth charges stored near them, either?

Then he remembered the North Cornwall Line - and the Trelill tunnel. 'How about a railway tunnel,' he asked, 'assuming it wasn't in operational use?'

It was war-time. Though there was a forest of bureaucracy, red tape could be side-stepped by seasoned military men who knew how to wield authority. Penistone was very assertive on minimising risks for his men.

Six weeks later permission had been granted and the process begun. A special train brought explosives down from Exeter. It had stopped near the airbase, but now, after picking up McTavish and his men, it carried on.

The train pulled past silent stations at Camelford, Delabole and Port Isaac Road, until it reached the Trelill tunnel. There the platoon from the airfield, who had travelled the ten miles in the guard's van, was commanded to empty the wagons one by one and wheel the destructive cargo in huge wheelbarrows, carefully, to the far end of the tunnel.

A pair of iron gates had been hung on the entrance at the south: it was sealed. At the northern end another pair awaited installation. These contained a large doorway and a series of padlocks. Once delivery was complete, Penistone would keep all the keys on the base. They weren't planning to guard the store but would ensure no-one else had access.

The preliminary walk through the quarter-mile of pitch-black tunnel tested their nerves. The transfer began. But the jolt as the wheelbarrow passed over each sleeper was worrying. The men were used to working with stores. They knew each depth charge had a safety pin twisted to the off position. The trouble was, no-one knew how safe that really made them.

A less dangerous way to move the explosive cargo was needed.

The depth charges were cylindrical, two foot across and three foot high. 'They're smaller than the track width, sir,' said one of the men. 'Could the charges be laid on their side and rolled along inside the rails?'

They might. But no-one could be sure what the effect of rotation might be on the explosive within; and no-one was keen to try.

The engine driver paced back and forth. He had orders to return to Exeter as soon as possible: other places also needed munitions. Then he realised that, as a full-time railwayman, he had some inside knowledge.

'What you really want,' he suggested, 'is a lineman's trolley to

run along the track and take the cargo, drum by drum, to the far end.'

'Och, where do we find one of those in the middle of a war?' complained the Stores Officer.

'It'll have been left beside the track. A trolley has no other use. There has to be one somewhere between here and Delabole.'

McTavish was torn. In the end he sent a pair of soldiers in search of the alleged trolley. Meanwhile the rest of the platoon sweated away, removing the depth charges from the train, wagon by wagon, and laying them gently beside the track.

Suddenly the soldiers were seen, coming down the slope. McTavish feared they would run into the train but they stopped just in time. With help the trolley was prised off the track.

The engine driver knew what came next. Slowly he reversed his train past the trolley. Then the frame was restored and brought to the tunnel entrance.

'This trolley stays here for future use,' vowed McTavish, as the work began to move the depth charges into the tunnel.

Commander Penistone instructed the base staff on their return that Trelill tunnel munitions store was a military secret. 'We don't want the location of the store to become so well known that German sympathisers hear of it.'

So Stores Officer McTavish was surprised, when he took the next supply train to the tunnel, to find what looked like a farmer's wife armed with an antiquated shotgun sitting above the tunnel entrance.

This was meant to be a secret operation. He gave an order and

113

the woman was quickly seized. It transpired she was Mrs Lilly Poundstock, the owner of one of the cottages above the tunnel.

'We 'eard the commotion last time the train come,' she explained. 'Once you'd all gone, my daughter scrambled down to see what had 'appened. She saw them gates at both ends. Later my neighbour saw huge cans of fuel – or else it were stocks of munitions. Which is it?'

'That's a military secret, madam.'

'We've kept all this to ourselves,' she replied. 'We're not idiots. We realised it was something military and had to remain secret.

'But what would 'appen if someone less friendly fired a rocket through a gate? Ever since they built the tunnel we've been scared of explosives. Whether it was fuel or ammunition, the amount looked enough for our village to be wiped out. That's why we mounted a guard to protect it.'

McTavish had misjudged the dynamics of village life. Penistone had commanded the troops to keep quiet about the store. But it couldn't be kept quiet from everyone – not with a special train on an otherwise disused line.

It was time to seek reconciliation.

'I'm grateful for your efforts,' he responded. 'We'll bring fire-resistant material, stretch it behind the gates. That should stop people seeing inside – you're right, an incendiary attack is a real risk. OK, we'll do that. And if you see anything untoward please tell us straight away.'

Lilly Poundstock was not the only one to know about the tunnel. A supply train arriving every few months could not be kept hidden *from the local community. Or the boys on a local farm.*

Twice they saw the train come and go without learning more. The next visit happened while they were away at school. Their dad mentioned it afterwards but that was far too late.

The next occasion was in the school holidays. The lads slipped away from their weeding in the field behind the farmhouse and chased along the track.

They couldn't keep up with the train but there was no difficulty in following its route. At last, coming round a bend, they saw the train halted outside Trelill tunnel. And soldiers, unloading something – they'd no idea what – from the train.

The lads were shrewd enough not to go any closer and retreated back along the track. By the time the train returned they were well into their weeding. But now they knew where to search.

A few days later they set off again. But though they walked nonchalantly along the track, Lilly Poundstock observed them from her vantage point and quietly dropped to the trackside ready for them.

When the boys got to the gate and saw the padlocks they knew they would get no further. They had just shinned up the gate to see if they could see anything inside – there was a slight gap at the top if they could only reach high enough – when a cough made them aware they were not alone.

Turning, they saw a sturdy woman in the middle of the track, armed with a shotgun - which was pointing in their direction.

'Hello, Mrs Poundstock.' The older lad was surprised they were not alone but he'd as much right to be there as she did. 'You out looking for rabbits? Why's this blocked off? What's in 'ere?'

'Never you mind. There's a war on: lots of things you're best not to know. Now if you'll get back to your farm I'll say nowt more about it. But I'll be watching. And if I see you here again, there'll be trouble. Do we understand each another?'

The boys were in a weak position. Oddly, the woman seemed to speak with authority. Was she some part of the operation inside the tunnel?

But they didn't want their dad alerted. Quietly, they turned away and started back towards the farm.

Robbie was saturated with tunnel tales. There was more but he couldn't take it in. He put down the article, turned off his light, and went straight to sleep.

CHAPTER 17

Robbie was surprised, when settling himself for his usual breakfast next morning, to be approached by the landlord rather than the waitress.

'I've got something for you,' he murmured. 'Come and collect it after you've eaten.'

The journalist had no idea what it might be and ate less slowly than usual. Soon he was knocking at the landlord's door.

'It's this,' said Jim. He handed over a brown envelope with the words "Robbie – tubby man, tousled hair. Private" inscribed. 'It was pushed through the Bettle front door late last night.'

'Thank you,' said the journalist. He hastened back to his room. It turned out to contain a short, handwritten note from Mick.

'Robbie, I'll explain when I see you but it's a long story and I'm a mess. I'll see you tomorrow at eleven. Come to the car park in Camelford, opposite Peckish Fish and Chips, in your Stag. Park back from the road and wear something unusual. My friend will meet you. DON'T TELL ANYONE. Mick.'

It was one of the oddest notes he had ever received. In other circumstances Robbie would have suspected a joke. But Mick hadn't seemed a joker; and he'd started to wonder where the engineer was. This might be the answer. There were, though, one or two precautions he could take and he took a few minutes to prepare.

"Wear something unusual." He'd one sweater with him that he'd not worn so far: that would have to do. He discarded the tweed jacket he normally wore for interviews, retrieving his sunglasses from a side pocket. He didn't often wear them, least of all for interviews. Finally he put on his sunhat to hide his tousled hair. Long years had taught him that a comb would have little effect.

Half an hour later, just before eleven, he swung into the main Camelford car park and manoeuvred into one of the furthest spaces. He'd done his part; who would turn up to guide him?

A few moments went by. Robbie started to feel vulnerable. Then a woman in her mid thirties appeared from behind. She'd not come through the car park, he'd been watching for that. There must be a back entrance. She tapped on his side window, beckoning. For better or worse the die was cast.

The journalist got swiftly out of the car. 'Hi,' he said, 'I'm Robbie Glendenning.'

'I'm Annabel,' the woman replied. 'Mick's friend. Thank you for coming.'

Quickly she turned on her heels and headed to the far end of the car park, Robbie a few steps behind. A footpath cut through onto an estate of small bungalows, each with a tiny garden. Annabel walked to the furthest one and up the short path. 'He's in here. Please come in.'

The two entered and Annabel relocked and bolted the door. 'You'll find him in the bedroom at the back.' Then she called, 'Hi Mick, I've brought him.'

Robbie stepped down the hall and opened the door. Mick

was sitting up in the bed, looking sorry for himself. His face was heavily bandaged and bruised and his right arm was in a sling. Plasters covered his left hand. There might be injuries lower down too but the duvet covered them over.

Mick's voice was gruff but it was clear from the gleam in his eyes that he was pleased to see the journalist. 'Thanks so much for coming, Robbie.'

Robbie claimed the seat by the bed. Annabel retreated to the kitchen. 'What on earth's happened to you, Mick?'

'It's a long story, Robbie. The headline version is that I had a massive row with my Dad. He'd been drinking heavily when I got back from Bodmin – the day you called at the sales office. He gets like that from time to time. We had an argument and then we came to blows. After that the old man beat me up so badly that I had to get out the house. Annabel, bless her, is a nurse. She took pity on me and bandaged me up. I've been hiding here ever since.'

It was a good job Robbie had seen Mick in action in the tunnel and knew that he was normally level-headed. Even so it was a bizarre story.

'Can you give me the longer version, Mick. What on earth did you argue about?'

'It all started with the note you left me.'

'Eh? What was wrong with that? I tried very hard to give nothing away.'

'Trouble was, you mentioned the police. That's like a red rag to a bull with my Dad. He had to know what you and I'd been doing that involved the cops. The more I avoided explaining the madder he got. Eventually, when I was tired, I must have slipped up and mentioned the tunnel.'

'Didn't you say something last week about your Dad never

wanting you to go there?'

'Well remembered. That was the trigger: he went completely out of control. Being a friend of someone who talked to the police was bad enough, but going into the tunnel was something else altogether. He shouted and screamed, then hit me as hard as he could. I tried to reason with him but it was a waste of time. I think he might have killed me if he wasn't so drunk.'

'Crazy. Have you any idea why the tunnel gave him such bad vibes?'

'No idea at all. But he'd said it often enough, from when I was very young.'

'So it must be something that happened a long time ago. Tell me, was your Dad brought up around here?'

'He was born in Camelford in 1944. He'll be seventy soon enough – if he survives that long. As far as I know he's always lived in these parts. Mind, he had a rough childhood. His dad was killed in the war.'

'What about his mum?'

'It was tragic. His mum couldn't handle being a widow and also being solely responsible for a small child. Her husband hadn't left her much. She went to pieces – on the streets of Wadebridge. In the end she committed suicide.'

Robbie was silent. Every battle had two sides; for a moment he tried to see another point of view.

'Poor kid – your Dad, I mean. What a mess. Given that start in life it's a wonder he's done as well as he has. I mean, everyone says you're the driving force in Hucknall Stoves but your Dad must have made a big contribution to get it all started.'

'I'd say most of that's down to my Mum. She's local, too - comes from St Kew. She met Dad soon after he left school, fell for him and turned him round, basically. She's a very loving person. Somehow she managed to sidestep his problems and boost his strengths.'

Robbie remembered the friendly woman behind the counter at Hucknall Stoves. Yes, he could imagine her as a home builder and domestic anchor.

That raised another question. 'What did your Mum make of the tussle between you and your Dad?'

'It was her evening out. She wasn't there.'

'Mm. I hope she's alright. Sounds like your Dad was practically out of his mind.'

Mick could see where he was heading. 'He wouldn't go for her. Or at least, as far as I know he never has. She's seen him drunk lots of times over the years.'

Robbie took stock.

'OK, Mick, what happens now? What do you want me to do to help sort this out? If you want, I could go round to the Sales Office and check your Mum's alright? Do you want me with you when you report the assault to the police?'

'Oh, it's not a police matter, Robbie. I've had a few days to muse about it. The bandages look bad but Annabel says there's nothing broken – just lots of bruises. And once my Dad's sobered up he'll probably regret it all happened.'

Robbie wondered at the power of humans to forgive. Family bonds could be very strong. 'We do need to know, though, why the tunnel causes your Dad so much anguish. Otherwise another careless mention could make the whole bloody thing happen again.'

Talk of the tunnel reminded him of the reason he'd been trying to contact Mick in the first place. 'By the way, have the police been in touch?'

'No. Though I've not been easy to find. Why should they?'

'Well, you know you generously left me to report the skeleton? The police weren't that friendly, put me on a strict embargo not to tell anyone until they'd done some preliminary investigation. I haven't seen anything on the news so I suppose it still applies. They said they'd tell you the same. But I probably gave them the wrong surname – I'd only seen it briefly on your van.

'Sounds like the least of my problems at the moment, Robbie. Odd, though, it's the same tunnel as haunted my Dad. Wonder if there's any connection?'

CHAPTER 18

It was a pensive Robbie Glendenning who arrived back at the Bettle that afternoon.

Mick had declared in the end that Robbie had performed a useful role by coming to hear him out. 'You're not a local,' he'd explained. 'You've given me a wider perspective.' A couple more days' recovery with Annabel, he'd said, and he'd risk seeing his father again – though he'd make sure they met first in the sales office, with his mother also present. There was a lot of sorting out to be done before he could go back to work.

Robbie knew there must be more behind their argument and longed to know what it was. He was sure Mick didn't know any more. His Mum might but it was unlikely she'd talk – least of all to a journalist. So how on earth could he deepen his understanding? In the end he decided it was time to harness the resources of his newspaper's research group in London.

Fortunately the group did not ask too many questions about the topics they were asked to look into. Journalists were always following leads, sometimes little more than hunches; they didn't always lead anywhere. His broadsheet took the view that inquisitiveness was a prime virtue that had to be encouraged.

'What I'm interested in,' he began, once the opening pleasantries were over, is a Children's Home, located in St Kew from the mid 1950s until the 1970s. I'm not certain of those dates mind, but there can't have been more than one Home there around that time. I'm pretty sure it was run by the Council. The place was close by the railway line and, I think, used to belong to a businessman called John Trevelyan. I had a look for the place but I couldn't find it. It's possible the building's now been demolished.'

'OK, got that. What do you want to know?'

'Well, I've heard there were rumours of abuse in the Home. I've no idea if that's true – I doubt if anything came to court. But has anyone in more recent times tried to report trouble of that kind? One of the children, for example, claiming abuse while he lived there. More than one might help prove the case.'

'We'll do our best, Robbie – but all we can do, once we've found the name of the Home, is trawl newspaper archives. It's a long shot.'

'Still worth a try. And can you find names of the officials – say the manager of the Home or the support staff? If they're still around they might give me an interview.'

'We're talking a long time back, Robbie. Won't they all be dead?'

'If the manager was, say, forty in 1960, then he's now ninety, could be either dead or senile. But twenty-something cooks or housekeepers would only be in their seventies. The immediate problem for me is to find them.'

'OK, Robbie. We'll do our best. I presume you'd prefer a short answer within days rather than a long spiel, months down the line?'

'That's true.' The call ended and Robbie put down his phone. It was a shot in the dark but he'd got a couple of oddities – something might join up. What else could the Home have links with?

He was still musing on possibilities when his phone rang. Was this going to be George? It turned out that it was Miss

Trevelyan.

'Good afternoon, Mr Glendenning. I've got hold of Elsie.'

For a second Robbie wondered who she was talking about. Then he recalled their last conversation – this was the lady in Trelill.

'Great. And can we see her?'

'She's not very interested in the ventilation shaft but she'd love to see me. Would tomorrow afternoon fit in with your schedule?'

'That's fine, Miss Trevelyan. Shall I come for you at, say, two o'clock?'

In truth Robbie didn't have a schedule to fit in with. It was good, though, to keep all his lines of enquiry running.

Wednesday afternoon found Robbie pulling up outside Miss Trevelyan's bungalow. She was ready and waiting.

'This is exciting,' she remarked. 'I haven't seen Elsie for years. I make good use of buses but none of 'em go to Trelill. Elsie suffers from rheumatism, I don't think she drives these days.'

The old lady chattered away. An afternoon out was a treat, something to be enjoyed whatever the outcome. Robbie had hoped to ask more about her childhood home in St Kew to assist his research group but didn't feel he could interrupt the flow.

Twenty minutes later they were in Trelill. Robbie parked as before in the side road and they walked a hundred yards to Elsie's home. It was on the main road and, Robbie noted, at the centre of the village - exactly where you'd expect a ventilation shaft which connected to the tunnel below.

'Welcome, m'dear. It's been a long time. And this is your

125

friend?" Elsie was of an age with Miss Trevelyan but in a less good state of health; Robbie had noted a mobility scooter parked in her front garden.

Introductions were made. The two women could obviously talk for England. Robbie managed to give an abbreviated account of his project and then asked if he could inspect the top of the ventilation shaft in Elsie's back garden.

'If you wants. It's not much to look at, though.' She led him through the cottage and out of the back door. 'It's down there, see.' She waved at a brick construction at the bottom of her garden.

'Leave it to me,' the journalist replied. Even from this distance he could see the building was surrounded by thorns and brambles. Elsie was glad to continue talking with her old friend and the two disappeared. Robbie was pleased he'd remembered the gloves he'd bought for use inside the tunnel. This piece of research would be a bit of a struggle.

He really had no idea what to expect. What did the tops of 1920s ventilation shafts look like? Were they designed with easy access?

Access was far from easy today. A preliminary reconnoitre showed the brick hut had a barred window frame at the rear – but with no glass. Presumably this had been to allow train smoke to dissipate. The only door was firmly locked with a massive, rusty padlock. It seemed no-one had been inside for years.

He mused for a moment. That didn't prove it was always inaccessible. The skeleton, after all, was fifty years old. What had the hut been like half a century earlier? What he needed, to eliminate the idea completely, was to find that the shaft had only a narrow diameter.

With a grimace Robbie forced his way through the brambles and round the hut until he could peer through the barred window. Mercifully he'd had the foresight to bring a torch. He shone it in and squinted to make sense of the interior.

At first he could see only cobwebs then dimly it started to make sense. The metal shaft which emerged from the ground was, perhaps, eighteen inches in diameter. If it was that wide all the way down, someone slim enough might be able to slide, or be slid, down. The shaft rose to waist height and then rotated through ninety degrees, with the final exit facing the window. And looking at this more carefully, he could see that the shaft top was also barred.

The whole thing was a solid piece of engineering designed to avoid trouble for the trains below. Small rocks might fall or be pushed through the gaps between the bars – maybe that was what he'd seen on the floor of the cave far below – but certainly nothing as big as a human body. One fanciful idea to account for the human remains below could now be discounted.

The journalist took a few pictures to record his findings and then struggled back through the brambles, round the hut and up to the cottage. The old ladies were still talking fiercely but stopped when they saw him.

'Would 'ee like a cup of tea,' asked Elsie, 'we wuz waiting till you came back, see.'

His main goal achieved, Robbie was happy to spend time with Elsie and Miss Trevelyan – he gathered her first name was Grace.

'Have you lived here all your life?' he asked, once the tea had been produced.

'Eighty two years, m'dear. Grace and I went to school together in St Kew.'

127

'So you lived in this cottage throughout the war?'

The old lady nodded. 'Them wuz dark times. The army 'ad summat stored down below, see. It wuz only after Mrs Poundstock protested that they put the padlock on the hut door. And took away the key.'

An alert woman. She knew what queries the shaft hut might raise. But the extra detail only reinforced his observations.

An hour later Elsie started to look very tired. 'We'd best be going now,' said Miss Trevelyan. Her friend did not demur.

As they reached the car, it occurred to Robbie that while he had got her to these parts he could make more use of the retired head's knowledge. 'We could go back via St Kew if you like,' he offered.

'That's very kind of you. I'd love to see Harold Shoesmith if he's feeling up to it,' the lady murmured. 'We could call at the door and see how he is, anyway.'

Della was delighted to see them. 'Harold's been on good form lately,' she said, 'I think your interview last week bucked him up.'

They went inside. Robbie was happy to let the older generation chat for a while. It was as the visit was drawing to a close that he intervened.

'Harold, can I ask you just a couple more questions about your time on the railway?'

'Fire away, young man.'

'We talked about collisions on the line and you said the last one was 1896. But someone I talked to last week was telling me about a runaway wagon from Delabole that ran down the slope and caught up a goods train – caused a massive smash.'

'Yes, I remember that. Far side the tunnel from here. It's

recorded in my notebook. But that didn't involve any passenger trains.'

'What I wanted to know was, were there any other examples like that? For example, did any other runaway wagons overturn on one of the bends?'

'Not in my years, anyway.'

So the runaway wagon scenario, if it happened at all, could only have worked before the war.

'Right. The other thing was, do you remember telling me about the vandals dropping rocks onto a train?'

'I do.'

'Well, you ended the story by telling me you went to the Children's Home to report the lads to the manager. Then Della brought our teas in.'

'She's a good lass.'

'Certainly is. What I wondered was, did it work? I mean, was there any more trouble later or did the manager sort it?'

'I don't know what happened but we never 'ad more trouble on the railway. The manager made his inquiries - got a shortlist. Then he had me back, two days later, to pick out the culprits. Between us we found all three.'

'Great. Well done. I know this is a ridiculous question from something so long ago, but did you get to know their names?'

There was a pause. Robbie feared Harold was having one of his siestas.

Then a smile broke over his face. 'I can't remember their names now,' he said. 'But the manager told me what they were and I'm sure I wrote them in my notebook. You've got 'em at the moment, haven't you? Look up the names for yourself. It wuz sometime in the early sixties.'

129

CHAPTER 19

Late on Thursday morning a cautious Robbie Glendenning drove into the industrial estate in Camelford and round to Hucknall Stoves. It was time to have one serious attempt at helping resolve issues in the Hucknall household.

Once again there were no customers present. But even if there were, they'd find Mick's mother still holding the fort behind the counter.

Robbie had already had a long phone conversation with her – he now knew her as Jennie. If anything was going to be improved here it would need her input. After the last altercation Jennie was as keen as anyone to put relations in her home on a better footing.

'Hi Jennie. Is the truce still holding?'

'Just about. They're both trying their best but it's a long way back to normal relations. There's something Trevor associates with that tunnel that's beyond fear, it's an ongoing nightmare - pure terror. I've known him since I was seventeen and even I don't know what it is. So how can we help him?'

She seemed to be speaking more freely than on his last visit.

'Is your husband around at the moment?' asked Robbie.

'He's out on a job today. Mick's still not fit to work, see. So to keep the business afloat, Trevor's having to fill in, which serves him right. Make him aware how much he relies on Mick, anyway.'

'I've been making enquiries, got hold of a few facts that

might open things up a bit. What we need to contrive is a conversation with Trevor which doesn't start with him being drunk and which has other people around to discourage him from becoming violent. So I wondered, would the two of you let me take you out for a decent meal? And if so, where do you suggest?'

It was clear Jennie had not been taken out for a meal for a long time. 'That'd be lovely, Robbie. One of my friends said there was a really good restaurant in Boscastle – the Riverside, I think she called it. Her husband said they do great steaks. I know that's my Trevor's favourite.'

She took stock for a moment. 'I'll do my best to try and persuade him that we're on his side. I've already hidden away the bottles he keeps in the house. I'll let you know as soon as he comes home and I've got him agreeable.'

Robbie was encouraged to receive a call from Jennie later that afternoon. 'Trevor is willing to admit he needs help. He's agreed to come for a meal. Could we try this evening, before he loses his nerve?' Robbie had already made enquiries and made a provisional booking. 'OK. I'll pick you both up at seven.'

One of Robbie's strengths was that he was good with people. The conversation in the Stag was slightly forced but it was clear all three were trying to make this work. The staff team at the Riverside were welcoming. Soon they were seated at the end table with a view over the River Valence. The men ordered rib-eye steak and chips with brandy and peppercorn sauce, Jennie some salmon, dauphinois potatoes and salad.

As soon as the meals had been served Robbie decided it was time to begin.

'We're all agreed, Trevor - that's Jennie, Mick and I - that you have some dreadful memories associated with the Trelill tunnel. What I'd like to do is to try and help you open up these memories so we can see a way forward. I know that's hard for you but the alternative – hiding them away – is not easy either.'

Trevor cut a piece of steak as he pondered. 'That's more or less what Jennie said. OK, if it'll help put things right with Mick then I'm prepared to have a go.'

Robbie took a deep breath. 'I've been finding out a lot about the old railway, talking to those who used to work there. One of the things mentioned was vandalism by some of the lads from the Children's Home in St Kew. I was told they dropped rocks from the hillside above the tunnel onto a passing train.'

He paused to await a response.

Trevor looked shocked and then distraught. 'Bad thing to do: wasn't fair on the driver. It wasn't his fault. I tried to tell 'em they shouldn't.'

'But you admit you were around at the time?'

'I was brought up in the Home, if that's what you mean. The Laurels, they called it. It was somewhere for Social Services to put me after my mum committed suicide. I was stuck in there for nigh on ten years – till Jennie found me.' He smiled at the woman beside him. She gave his hand an encouraging squeeze.

'So even though some vandalism took place at the tunnel while you were there, that's not what has given you such terrible memories?'

'Not exactly.'

'But it was linked in some way?'

Robbie could see Trevor was starting to look agitated. He decided to work with the rumours and to put forward some intelligent guesses.

'Things weren't easy in the Laurels, I imagine?'

'Not easy at all.'

'In those days corporal punishment was normal, wasn't it?'

'That bastard Adam was the worse. Not that big but he was bloody strong. Think he'd been in the army.'

'Adam . . . Was he one of the kids in the Home?'

'Was he 'eck. He was the bloody deputy manager. His remit was to impose discipline at the Laurels – and he did it in his own special way.'

'You mean he abused you?'

'You might call it that. He bullied us – all of us. Took great pleasure in it.'

'Didn't the manager keep him in check?'

'Huh. Sundays was when it happened – almost every Sunday. That was the day the manager was off site, see, and Adam was left in charge.'

It was time for another shot in the dark. 'Was this down in the cellar?'

Trevor looked at him. 'How the hell d'you know that?'

Jennie put her hand on his arm. 'Easy, dear, Robbie's only trying to make sense of it all so he can help you.'

'Just a guess, Trevor. I know someone else who used to live there in earlier times. So what happened to you three lads after you'd dropped the rocks?'

'Adam was instructed by the manager to punish us. That made it official so he was allowed to do it during the week. He did it on the Tuesday, a week before Christmas. Took us down to the cellar, unlocked his cane and gave each of us a severe beating.'

It was time now for Robbie to take a stab in the dark. 'But this time something else happened the following weekend?'

Trevor looked at him, eyes agog. 'You know – you know

133

what happened, don't you?'

'A few bits of it, anyway. Why don't you tell us in your own words?'

'What had happened to us was the final straw. Things had been getting worse in the Laurels for ages. The rot started when Adam arrived. We'd only gone to throw rocks at the train as a form of rebellion. It was pathetic but we knew no-one would listen. We couldn't see how else to say we were desperate.'

'So emotions were running high. With Adam the focus, the one you all hated. So on that Sunday . . .'

'We'd agreed on the Tuesday evening that we'd had enough and we made a plan. Individually Adam was stronger than each one of us. But if we all acted together we knew we could handle him. So that's what we did.'

Robbie could have made many comments but judged it was better to remain silent. Trevor took a deep breath and then plunged on.

'Stage one was to make sure there would be no witnesses. Between us, over the next couple of days, we talked to all the staff and persuaded them that next Sunday would be a good time to phone in sick. They could sense something was going to happen but no-one was on Adam's side. The staff had felt the rough end of his tongue too. They knew he was a sadistic bully.'

'What were you aiming for?'

'Our first idea was retaliation. But the more we talked, the more we realised that wouldn't work. Next week Adam would still be deputy manager and he'd pick us off, one by one, deal with us even more harshly. What we really wanted was to be rid of him for good.'

'You mean to kill him?' Jennie looked horrified.

'Hell no, Jennie. We might have been bad but we weren't

evil. What we wanted to do was to humiliate him so he'd lose face - wouldn't want to stay on. Every bully is the outside face of a coward. We wanted him to know we'd all seen the coward inside. Puncture the arrogance.'

'So what happened?'

'One of the lads in the Home – one of Adam's more frequent victims - had been hankering after something special, building up tools for the job. Through some contact or other he'd acquired some handcuffs.'

Robbie managed to drain his face of emotion but he was shocked - and this would only be the start. 'How on earth did you plan to fit them on?'

'Adam had his own flat at the Laurels. It was in the stable block at the rear. We'd seen the manager driving away Saturday evening. Now Adam was the only one in authority left on site. Everything was ready.'

Trevor paused, ate another chunk of steak and then continued.

'Early that Sunday morning, long before it was light, one of us switched off the electricity fuses. The whole place was plunged into darkness. Then four of us crept into Adam's room. He was still asleep. Two of us – the heavier ones - sat on the bed squashing him down, while a third slid a bucket over his head.'

'That'd wake him up.'

'Yes. Adam did what you'd expect – first he swore, then reached up with both hands to try and pull it off. It was at that point the fourth lad in our gang slipped on the handcuffs.'

This was getting serious. 'Adam would rebel against that,' Robbie observed.

'He was livid but as yet he didn't realise the scale of the

problem. By the time he did we'd removed all his clothes and got the second pair of handcuffs on his ankles and a blindfold over his face. Now he'd started to realise there were a lot of us and only one of him. He was terrified, began to whimper.

'Next we tied a rope through the handcuffs and dragged him off the bed, into the hall and down the stairs. Then we pulled him across the gravel courtyard and down the stone steps into the cellar. We weren't too gentle. No-one had much respect for him. By now he was sobbing in fear.'

Trevor took another mouthful of his steak. Robbie and Jennie ate more as well. This was not an account to be hurried.

'The plan was to hang him up from the pipe across the ceiling. Plenty of us had suffered like that at his hands, now it was his turn. We'd found the keys in his flat. We could unlock the cane and beat him like he'd beaten us.'

'You say that was the plan,' said Robbie. 'Did something go wrong?'

'By the time we'd reached the cellar he'd stopped shrieking or making much noise. He was still breathing but he was more or less unconscious.'

Robbie swallowed hard. 'Did you intend to kill him?' He was thinking of a skeleton that he'd found not long ago, not far from the Laurels.

Trevor looked shocked. 'Not at all. The plan was to make him suffer until he begged for mercy. We didn't think that would take very long. Then we would confront him and force him to write a letter, handing in his notice with immediate effect.'

Robbie could see snags with the plan but half a century ago it might have worked. Might even have been a rough form of justice.

'We hadn't expected him to collapse before we'd started. We began to struggle with what to do next. This was outside the plan.'

Silence for a few minutes as all three ate and mused. Then Trevor resumed.

'We had to get him out of the Laurels. There'd been no witnesses. No-one except us lads had seen what had happened. If Adam disappeared - I mean just went away - then people might have their suspicions but nothing more. All we needed was a plausible reason why he would choose to go.'

'I don't suppose any of you could drive?' It was a fair guess. Robbie had already found how well-targeted guesses drove Trevor on.

'That's right - all we had was the Home's large wheelbarrow. It only needed a couple to push it, we drew lots as to who it was going be. I'd done my part by helping put on the handcuffs. To be honest I was glad to be out of it.'

'Was Adam still unconscious?'

'He was mumbling away but hardly with it. And we hadn't yet taken off the handcuffs.'

'But where would your mates take him?'

'They didn't say and we didn't ask – ever. The Home was beside the railway. We knew the time of every train. And we knew there were wagons in the sidings at St Kew. These would be hitched onto passenger trains next morning to be moved on. If Adam could be dumped naked into one of the wagons in dead of night he might wake up and find he'd travelled a very long way indeed. That would be the best we could do, anyway.'

Trevor sighed and continued. 'Our most plausible liars set to work concocting a story explaining how Adam had been called away at short notice. "A letter had come on Saturday morning," it was said, "giving him a nasty jolt." He'd announced that he had to go away over Christmas and taken the letter with him. We also worked out the quiet way we might have spent the day in his absence. Everybody had to fix their details and then we rehearsed them to make sure they hung together. It was a sort of collective alibi.'

There was a pause. Trevor seemed exhausted.

'I can see why the day left such a mark on you, darling,' said Jennie, 'but it was fifty years ago. You were young, Adam provoked you and you responded. You can't let it destroy the rest of your life. Thank you for sharing it with us.'

Robbie had been left with more critical thoughts and more searching questions. Later he would have many more. He judged, though, that now was not the time to voice them.

CHAPTER 20

It was Friday and Robbie thought he was starting to make real progress. There was plenty from the evening before for him to get his teeth into. Once breakfast was over he was in touch once more with his research group.

'Thank you, your first efforts were very helpful,' he began. 'As a result I had a good conversation with a key witness yesterday. Now I need more. My focus is a series of events that took place in the Laurels at St Kew in the early 1960s. Can you find the names of any staff working there at the time? There was a deputy manager called "Adam". My witness described him as a sadistic bully but couldn't remember his full name. I'd love to know his name and background. And can we find any trace of him later on?'

He wondered whether he should say anything to the police but judged it would be better to complete his own enquiries first. Trevor's confession had been on the basis of a background briefing and the man had not meant it to go further. The journalist wondered once again what the police were now doing.

Later that morning, as he was doing some editorial work for his newspaper over the internet, he had a call from Rowena. They hadn't spoken for a week, he'd better answer. The woman was as bouncy as ever and not unduly upset that he hadn't been in touch. 'You're here to work. Not just to potter about. But I wondered if you'd like to go for another swim at Tregardock

Beach? Low tide's about four o'clock.'

Robbie hesitated. By late afternoon he would be glad of a break. But he must make Rowena aware that he had a friend back in London. It would be a pity if she got any wrong ideas.

But Rowena wasn't taking much notice of his hesitation. She prattled on. The local garage was trying to repair her car. She sounded wistful about making the most of the good weather – at least travelling further afield than her walks to Delabole and Trebarwith Strand.

By the end of the call, Robbie found he had agreed to take her to look at Trelill tunnel after lunch before returning for a late afternoon swim at Tregardock. 'But that can't last long. I must be back for early evening, it's the next meeting of the cycle trail campaign.'

Robbie hadn't wanted to take Rowena into the tunnel at all – he resolved that he would not tell her what he and Mick had found – but he was interested to see what the police had done since his last visit. Was it festooned with crime scene tape and a police guard? The answer might tell him how seriously the police were taking his find.

Not wanting a lunchtime drink after last night's wine he skipped lunch, picked up Rowena at Treligga and drove south. She had tied back her hair and was in walking gear. Obviously she nursed hopes of stepping inside the tunnel.

'One lesson from my last visit,' he told her, 'is that it's easier to get into the tunnel from the south.'

Though he didn't know how easy that would now be.

He had looked at the map and spotted they could walk along the old railway line for a mile up to the tunnel from a road near St Kew. 'If you don't mind the walk, it'll add to what we know about cycle trail access.'

Robbie managed to avoid talking about his experience in the tunnel by telling Rowena about his other interviews from the last week. He had got beyond his companion's knowledge of folk in the area, at least in some respects.

The former railway track started on an embankment and climbed slowly through a long wood. There was the odd bramble but it was passable; they soon found themselves at the tunnel entrance. There was wire fencing that had been there for a long time but would be easy enough to slip past.

There was, though, a new notice attached to it: 'Keep Out'. So that was how the police here protected their crime scenes.

But Rowena had sniffed at the notice and had wriggled past the fencing panel while Robbie was still considering his options.

'Come on – even someone of your width should be able to follow me,' she challenged, smiling at him mischievously through the fencing.

The choice had been made. He squeezed past the fencing and joined her in the entrance.

'It's an hour to low tide,' she told him. 'Time to walk through the tunnel and back again. Then I could tell the campaign how it really felt.'

Robbie hadn't intended to walk right through. But the trip would give him chance to see if there was any further sign of police activity. He extracted his torch.

Rowena burbled away as they started the traverse. In contrast Robbie was silent, partly weighed down by the memory of his last visit. He was also trying to watch out for any fresh signs of human activity.

A few minutes later they reached the critical recess. Rowena was still talking away – Robbie wondered, later, if this was simply a way of hiding her nerves – but he came to a halt and shone his torch around.

No, there was nothing distinctive about this section of the tunnel. No signs, for example, of anything painted on the brickwork. Was that a faint arrow mark in the cinders? Maybe that was a guide to Forensics.

Rowena had seen nothing and was already ahead of him.

There had been alcoves all the way. The fractured opening at the back would only be seen by someone who was pointing their torch directly at it.

All in all, the gap could have remained hidden for a very long time.

Rowena had come to a halt and was waiting. She was taking the opportunity to point her torch around her. But before he pressed on, Robbie stepped over to the side for one last look at the cavern entrance.

There was no police tape. They must have decided that anything like that would have drawn unnecessary attention to the spot.

He didn't want to go inside the cave again. Presumably the skeleton had been removed; he'd seen more than enough last time. But as his hands grasped the entrance he noticed a rough feeling on the bricks. What on earth was it?

Quickly, he took a picture. No time for more: Rowena was walking back towards him. He quickly moved forward and away from the opening. 'Don't worry, I just wanted a record of the brickwork. Let's keep going.'

Rowena suspected nothing. She continued to chatter inconsequentially as they completed the walk through the tunnel. Once they reached the entrance they were glad to be back into daylight.

Rowena insisted that Robbie took a picture of her standing

in the tunnel opening. 'One day this might be part of the cycle trail's publicity,' she laughed.

Their return journey passed without incident. Rowena continued with her monologue, seeming to expect no reply. It was back at the tunnel's southern entrance that their troubles began.

Robbie first noticed the uniformed policeman as he slid through the fence with Rowena close behind. So there was a guard after all. He was pleased to know they were taking it all so seriously.

He was rather less pleased when the policeman asked them to accompany him to the Police Station in Bodmin. Rowena was more than indignant – practically incandescent – and that didn't help either.

'I don't understand why we need to go the Police Station,' Robbie protested, 'but, if we do, let me drive us over there in my own car. I know where the station is: I've been before. My car is parked down this track. That way we'll be able to get home again without any bother when you've finished with us.'

Robbie thought afterwards that the policeman might have allowed this if Rowena had not been so rude towards him. But the officer had been offended; this was one way of making their lives more of a misery.

Could he make a run for it? Then once at his car, drive to Bodmin in his own time. But the policeman looked fitter than he was; he didn't think he'd get that far. Of course, the policeman might not have caught them both. If Rowena had had the wit to head in the opposite direction at the same time she might have got away. But her auburn hair was distinctive and she was often in North Cornwall. He doubted she'd want to risk arrest on every future visit.

143

So in the end, reluctantly – Rowena still muttering imprecations under her breath – the pair followed the officer out through the wood, up the hillside and into the police car, which was parked in Trelill.

By now they were both angry. Robbie had some inkling of what might be the cause of their journey, but as far as Rowena was concerned they'd done no more than wander into a long-abandoned tunnel.

Neither of them spoke on the way, or as they were accompanied inside Bodmin Police Station and taken to separate interview rooms.

It was as well Robbie did not expect to be dealt with straight away. Almost an hour had elapsed before Inspector Lambourn joined him in the interview room. The journalist hoped that this meant he'd already questioned Rowena. At least she could make a start on finding a taxi back to Delabole.

Inspector Lambourn looked disgruntled. Their previous meeting could hardly be described as a "bundle of fun"; but that was a carnival compared to the present occasion.

Robbie gave his name and current address. There was no point in bothering the police in Cornwall with an address in Bristol. He wondered whether it would help or hinder his cause to explain that he was a journalist with a major national newspaper. For the moment the question was not raised.

Instead Lambourn began with a question which seemed completely irrelevant. 'Where did you eat on Monday evening?'

Robbie wondered if he was going crackers. He thought back. He'd eaten in several places over the last week.

'Can I consult my diary, please?' The Inspector nodded, reluctantly.

Robbie reached in his fleece pocket. Now he was glad that he wrote down his appointments carefully as a basis for expense claims. He flipped through the pages. There it was: St Teath. For the moment he couldn't think why on earth he should eat there.

He looked up. 'According to my diary, I ate at the White Hart Inn in St Teath. My diary doesn't record what I ate but I can tell you it cost me £14.75.'

But the Inspector wasn't interested in his personal finances.

'Why did you eat there, Mr Glendenning, rather than where you were staying - the Bettle and Chisel in Delabole?'

Why indeed? For a moment Robbie had no idea; was he allowed to say "Pass"? There must be some reason to drive out of Delabole. He normally tried not to combine drinking and driving. Then he remembered.

'It was the inaugural meeting of the group that was bidding to put together an entry for the Green Tourist Award. I'd met Owen Harris, the man heading it up, over the weekend and he invited me along. I kept on the sidelines. I was only there as an observer.'

More details came flooding back. He looked at the long face of the policeman. 'You were there too. I heard your talk – about old crimes - it was very interesting.'

For a second the policeman seemed pleased that he had been deemed a success. Robbie still had no idea where all this was leading, but the policeman did.

'So you'll remember me saying that there wasn't much unsolved crime in the area?'

'I recall you saying that this was – always had been - a low-crime area. You were very proud of that record. It's such a beautiful area, you implied, that even criminals get distracted. I think it rather mucked up the group's plans though.'

'And then, within 24 hours, you produced for me a possible incident that might form the basis of the group's bid.'

Robbie had not connected the two events before. 'I suppose, looking back, it was a bit of a coincidence.'

Lambourn banged his fist on the table. 'It was a hell of a coincidence, sir. But, I can tell you, as a policeman, I don't like coincidences. There's normally some reason why a coincidence happened – and my job is to find it.'

There was silence in the interview room. Then the policeman resumed.

'So you admit you were at that meeting at the invitation of Harris? What was the deal you offered him?'

'Deal? Deal? I'm sorry, I don't understand.'

'How much did he agree to pay you to arrange a suitably old skeleton in a suitably remote location?'

Robbie didn't answer for a moment. His eyes bulged at the inanity of the question. Finally, angrily, he put his thoughts into words.

'Are you accusing me, Inspector, of putting that skeleton there myself – and then pretending to find it, as a basis for Harris's Award bid? That's the daftest thing I've ever heard.'

'I'm not accusing you, Mr Glendenning. Not yet, anyway. I'm simply asking the question. It's the coincidence of timing, you see. That Award is worth winning: a quarter of a million pounds is well worth having. But for that bid to win it needs a body. And you're the common link between the two.'

Robbie was silent. He'd gathered from recent conversations with Brian that Lambourn was an inert policeman, the sleeper of Bodmin Police Station, the man who rejected, nay ridiculed, even the concept of crime. And now the man appeared to be

trying to implicate him in finding an old skeleton, hauling it –
goodness only knows how - into a remote tunnel and then
expecting the police to treat it as a serious crime.

He had been wondering all week what the police had made
of the skeleton. Was it an inconvenience or a virtually insoluble
crime?

It had never crossed his mind that they might regard it as
some form of macabre joke.

Lambourn continued, 'Of course, I was aware of the coincidence when you first reported the skeleton. That's why I gave
you a hard time. I recognised you from the meeting the night
before. I don't want to insult you, and I wouldn't claim I'm
much to look at, but a face like yours is not easy to forget.

'But today – today when I saw you on the CCTV we'd
arranged to cover the entrance to the tunnel – then I thought
this was a coincidence too far.

'Tell me, why did you come back to the tunnel this second –
or was it third - time?'

An idea seemed to strike the policeman. 'Ah, I know - had
you got more clues to plant? Or had you something else to
make our detective work more challenging and to liven up the
bid?'

CHAPTER 21

Alice Southgate had not been too alarmed, when she called the second meeting of the cycle trail campaign together in the Bettle, to see Robbie Glendenning was not present. She twisted round to see through the doorway into the further bar: but no, he wasn't there either.

He was, after all, an outsider so she couldn't expect him to turn up on time. He was a journalist, probably drinking with one of his "sources". Alice had come across two expensive wine bottles in her dustbin recently and had guessed how her husband and Robbie had fuelled their discussions the evening before.

For the moment she called those present to order and presented her draft agenda. Jess then read out the minutes of last week's meeting and these were agreed.

Item one was progress or otherwise in discussions with the landowners who owned the land that the trail would pass over.

Nathan gave his report. His letters had been sent out to the landowners last weekend, delivered by hand to highlight their urgency.

He had received written replies from six and oral responses from a dozen more: he would prompt the rest that weekend. Since so many had already replied, that should drag a response from the rest by the next meeting.

'And the replies so far, what did they say?' asked a cider drinker.

'Well, let's assume those who haven't replied yet match those who have. On that basis I'd say it's looking good.

'Twelve – that's two-thirds - are fully in favour. They buy the argument that a new cycle trail would be popular with tourists and hence good for the area. They'd be happy to create permissive footpaths over the parts of their land covered by the trail, if and when it was all going ahead.'

There was a murmur of satisfaction. This was better than they had hoped.

Nathan continued, 'Five more said they'd be willing to negotiate some sort of deal with the Council to allow it to go ahead. They're not mad cyclists or climate fanatics but they're not latter-day Luddites either. They'd be willing to move with the times if that was the way the times were moving.'

Jess looked up from her laptop. 'Any idea how much this might cost?'

'Not yet. And we won't until the whole scheme's been approved. If we won the Green Award, of course, there'd be a quarter of million pounds to put toward it. The important thing is that these guys won't try to block it.'

Alice had been keeping careful count of the numbers. 'So that leaves just one, you're saying, who is seriously hostile?'

Nathan nodded. 'I won't tell you the name at this stage, if you don't mind. This correspondence is confidential; I can tell you overall results, but these people have some right of privacy. But you might not be too surprised.'

Alice was intrigued but knew Nathan was being wise. They had to apply their finite collective energy where it was most needed. Timing their battles was important.

She glanced down at her agenda and then around the room.

'The next possible showstopper is the state of the Trelill

149

tunnel. If work was needed to restore it that could cost millions; the scheme would become unworkable. But for the moment Mick doesn't seem to be with us.'

She laughed, 'I hope he's not got lost in the tunnel. In the meantime, let's have Jill tell us about her surveys.'

The manager of the Tourist Centre had made good use of her volunteers. 'We finalised the questionnaire on Saturday. My volunteers stood by the end of the Camel Trail at Padstow all Sunday afternoon. Fortunately the weather was sunny. In the end we had nearly 250 sets of answers. We put these into the software we use on other surveys and I've got the results here. That's a respectable size for a survey, by the way.'

Jill was sounding defensive. Alice saw she must commend her efforts. 'It's amazing to have the result within a week of commissioning. Well done – to you and your volunteers. So what does it tell us?'

'This survey was addressed to our natural supporters - people who already like and use cycle trails. But it's encouraging, nonetheless. The headline number is that 75% would be interested in doing another cycle trail. Maybe not in the same holiday, as they'd already done the Camel Trail. But it would give them something to come back for next time. They would be even keener if there were more facilities in Delabole – cream tea shops and so on.'

The results prompted some debate. Alice let the discussion run in the hope of seeing Mick arrive. In the end she moved the meeting on to publicity.

Geri spoke for the publicity group. They'd had a few pictures but needed more. 'The trouble is the new trail's had no visitors so there's been no cause to take photos. But we've walked bits of it and we know where better shots could be taken. If it's fine tomorrow we hope to widen the coverage.'

'By next week,' she promised, 'we'll have some sort of brochure – that's not too late, is it?'

The meeting was almost over when Rowena Gibson stormed in. She looked extremely angry.

'I've got an item for "Any Other Business",' she claimed, once that item was announced. 'I'm not sure if it's relevant - but it concerns Robbie Glendenning.'

'We were expecting him,' responded Alice, 'so it's certainly relevant. We wanted to know what he and Mick had made of Trelill tunnel. Has something happened to him?'

So Rowena gave them a dramatic account of her trip with Robbie that afternoon to the Trelill tunnel. Then she told how the pair had been accosted on their way out and taken by police car to Bodmin Police Station.

'First they left me to smoulder in an interview room. Then they kept asking me what I was doing in there and what I had seen. Over and over again. I explained about the cycle trail and said we'd come to see if it would be practical. And I told them that since the tunnel was pitch black I'd seen nothing. They let me out after an hour, but then it took ages for me to find a taxi back. I came here as soon as I'd had something to eat.'

'Can someone get Rowena a drink, please,' asked Alice. A half of cider was quickly produced.

'I asked about Robbie, of course,' she went on, 'but they said he was still to be interviewed. So as far as I know he's still in Bodmin nick, answering their damn-fool questions. Goodness only knows what they think he's done. But I thought I'd better come and tell you.'

There were shouts of amazement. No-one was on the side

of the police. 'It's bloody Bodmin, trying to sabotage our scheme,' pronounced the cider drinker.

Once the meeting had been declared closed, Geri sidled up to Alice as she sat quietly enjoying her lemonade and lime in the corner. The head teacher shuffled along to make room on the bench beside her.

Geri looked worried – almost guilty. Alice knew that look: it was a grown-up version of the expression as she saw on the faces of her pupils, when they'd been caught in a major misdemeanour. Her work for the day wasn't yet over.

She turned towards her. 'Geri, are you worried about something? You look really upset. What's bothering you? Do you want to talk about it? Look, no-one can hear us in this corner. What's up?'

Geri paused, battling between a long-lasting vow of silence and an immediate need to share. 'It might be nothing. It was something that happened to me a long time ago – in that wretched tunnel, as a matter of fact.'

To Alice this made no sense. For as long as she'd known her Geri had been sensible. 'I'm sorry, I don't understand.'

'Well, can I ask, do you think that it's something that's been found inside there that's put Robbie into all this trouble?'

CHAPTER 22

Meanwhile Robbie Glendenning was making no progress at all in his efforts to convince Inspector Lambourn that he was not an instigator of crime. Why couldn't the man see that it really all was just a horrible coincidence?

He was sure now that the policeman was not simply going through his procedures. Bizarrely, the man was convinced that Robbie had planted the skeleton inside the tunnel; then pretended to re-discover it as the starting point for a mystery-murder bid.

At some point early in the interview the policeman had asked to see his camera. Robbie wondered how the police even knew he had a camera.

Then he remembered the photo he had taken of Rowena in the tunnel entrance. If the police had arranged a security camera at one end of the tunnel they would have one at the other end as well. They must have seen him taking the picture – the only one he'd taken that day.

The camera had been taken away and he presumed the pictures had been downloaded. Any doubt was removed when a constable came in with a bundle of photos, culminating with his picture of Rowena at the tunnel entrance.

He had started to protest about an invasion of privacy but Lambourn wasn't interested. However important it wasn't really the nub of their disagreement.

'Sir, why did you take all these pictures of the skeleton?'

'I wanted to be sure good pictures were taken before the body was removed.'

'So you assumed the police would not do so?'

For the moment Robbie had no answer.

'Have you shown them to Harris?'

'I haven't shown them to anyone - or tried to get them published.' As he said this, Robbie remembered Brian downloading them onto his computer the evening before. But that was a private viewing so didn't need to be mentioned.

'And what on earth is this?' The policeman shoved the picture he had taken of the brick edge in the narrow opening in front of him.

It looked pretty obscure. Even by flash it was only black cloth on smoky brick in a pitch-back tunnel. Robbie was tempted to say it was a candidate starter picture for University Challenge, but held back: the policeman didn't seem to have a sense of humour.

'It's the one thing I learned, going back in the tunnel today. I didn't go in to the cavern where the skeleton was found – I hadn't said anything about it to Rowena, as I hope you've discovered. But I stood trying to work out how easy it would be to miss the entrance gap if you were walking through. To be honest I was wondering if a gang of maintenance men would notice the gap as they carried out their work.

'And then I observed something odd about the bricks at the edge of the opening. It felt – well, it felt almost like a piece of cloth. I've no idea what it means but I can't believe it was part of the original design.'

The policeman eyed him suspiciously. For someone trying to protest his innocence he'd got a bizarre approach. He'd never seen anything like it in all his years in the force. Being hoisted by his own petard hardly covered it.

'And did you glue the cloth on yourself? It'd make a hell of a complication for your mystery.'

'No, no. For goodness sake, I'm trying to help you. I haven't done anything to make it harder. It's hard enough already.'

At this point Lambourn suggested they might both benefit from a break. The truth was, he'd run out of questions but not out of suspicion. A quarter of an hour on his own might give Glendenning time to come to his senses.

Robbie wondered, as he sat in silence, whether it would be helpful to tell the policeman about his profession. He was, after all, a senior journalist on a major newspaper. Why not get Lambourn to ring up his editor in London?

The editor could confirm that Robbie had a legitimate interest in the cycle trail and hence the tunnel and wasn't some maniac trying to ensnare the police.

But what would it do for his standing in the newspaper if he had to be bailed out from a Police Station in darkest Cornwall? There was some aura in newspaper circles in being freed from Baghdad or Beirut; but Bodmin? He would never live it down.

He glanced at his watch. It was now early Friday evening. By now his editor would have left the office. He might have gone home or out for a meal. He might have taken his wife to the theatre. No doubt he could be found but only with much difficulty – and at some future risk to Glendenning's career. A night in Bodmin Police Station might be the less bad option.

Having concluded that there was no 'get out of jail' card to hand, he buckled down to proving that he wasn't responsible for introducing the skeleton in the first place.

When Lambourn came back he seemed more amenable to letting the journalist talk. Robbie took the chance to launch into his latest line of defence.

'Look, because of a coincidence of timing you think I had something to do with putting the skeleton in that cavern. But don't you see, even if for some obscure reason I'd wanted to – which I didn't – it would be practically impossible.'

Robbie drew a deep breath. The policeman watched with interest. For once he would have something to tell his fellow officers at their next review.

Robbie continued. 'First of all, where on earth would I get a skeleton? Because this is a real one – not just plastic, like medical students use these days. I mean, are you thinking I'm a grave-robber as well?

'Secondly, how could I move the skeleton without it just falling apart? I didn't touch it, but it looked pretty delicate when I saw it on Tuesday.

'And thirdly, even if I could get hold of a full set of bones and could wrap it in bubble-wrap inside a coffin, how would I, on my own, get this coffin out of the car, down the embankment, through the fence, along the tunnel – and finally, through a one foot wide opening into the cavern. What sort of magic wheelbarrow are we talking about?'

Lambourn glowered back. 'No-one has said that you produced this whole display entirely on your own. I don't know yet: maybe Miss Gibson helped you. She's a good friend of Owen Harris, I believe? Or what about this Mick Hutching? He disappeared pretty quick after you alerted us. We haven't managed to track him down yet.'

Robbie never knew where the interview might have gone next. He'd fired his last shots and they'd been taken as blanks.

But at that moment a constable appeared and whispered into Lambourn's ear. 'Excuse me a minute,' the Inspector said and strode out.

It was in fact nearly an hour before the Inspector reappeared. But clearly he had learned something in the meantime which had changed his perspective on the problem and on his prisoner.

'Right sir,' he said, 'I don't think we need to take this any further. You can have your camera back and then you can leave. One of your friends is waiting outside to take you home.

'No doubt we'll meet again. I hope that next time it will be in less contentious circumstances.'

CHAPTER 23

A few minutes later a bemused Robbie Glendenning found himself in the Police Station reception, being greeted by Alice Southgate. Fearsome she might be, but that didn't matter as long as she was fearsome on his behalf. Even in a police station she looked well in control.

Alongside her was a woman of a similar age. He recognised her vaguely then remembered she was in charge of the publicity for the cycle trail campaign. This was the person to whom he'd been emailing his pictures of the trail.

'Don't say anything. Let's just get out of here,' his saviour said curtly. They turned and went outside. Alice's car was in the visitors' car park; Robbie was happy to sink down in the back seat.

His muscles felt tense, as if he had just tunnelled under the barbed wire of a prison camp and wriggled free. It was not until they had driven into the centre of Bodmin that he felt able to voice his thanks.

'No, no, it was just something we had to do,' replied Alice. 'After all, it was only the inspection for the cycle trail that took you into the tunnel in the first place. But first things first: when did you last eat?'

'Our wonderful forces of law and order didn't give me any food this evening. Lunch seems a long time ago.'

He mused for a moment. 'Now I think about it, I was too busy to have lunch today. Wow! My last meal was breakfast. No wonder I'm hungry.'

'That's OK. I thought you'd be pretty famished. So here's what we're going to do. Geri here lives in Camelford. We'll go back that way and drop her off. She's had a hard time this evening as well; it was her testimony that got you out. Then you and I are going to Delabole for a late supper.'

Alice braked sharply to avoid a hardened drinker as he staggered out of a pub and into the road. Then she ploughed on with her agenda. Robbie noted that she had not sought his approval; she was certainly masterful.

'Geri, could you ring Brian for me, please?' she asked. 'Tell him we're all fine – we're no longer with the police, anyway. Ask him to put some oven chips on, please. I'll make us an omelette to go with them when we get back.'

Alice glanced over her shoulder. 'Brian's a hopeless cook. Ten years of medical training and he can barely cook beans on toast. But he should be able to heat up chips. You're not allergic to eggs?'

They drove past the outskirts of Bodmin and Robbie started to relax. He looked behind him: no, there was no police car behind. He really had escaped.

Leaning forward he tapped Geri on the shoulder.

'I'm very grateful for your testimony. Is there any chance you could tell me what you said, please?'

Geri turned and gave him a shy smile. 'It all started when Rowena came in at the end of the campaign meeting. She told us that you'd both been through the tunnel and then been detained by the police. You were still being interviewed.'

She gave a gulp. 'It brought back something I saw in that tunnel twenty years ago. I've been trying to forget it ever since. I confessed it to Alice after the meeting. She told me I had to

159

come and tell the police in Bodmin.'

Geri drew breath. 'I wasn't keen. I knew I'd be in trouble. Maybe what I'd seen was nothing to do with you. I'd asked Rowena, you see, and she said she hadn't seen anything. But still my conscience wouldn't shut up. It was likely to be connected somehow. I was scared but Alice insisted on coming with me – not just to the station, but right into the interview.'

Her words dried up. Robbie thought she was probably no more used to police stations than he was. Alice took up the tale.

'What Geri told me was a huge shock. But you could have seen the same thing. I had no idea why you were in trouble - I couldn't see why on earth the police should blame you in any way. But if they wanted to make a fuss they needed all the facts to begin with.'

Alice manoeuvred round the roundabout at the edge of Bodmin before continuing. 'For a start I told them you were a top journalist with a major newspaper. That seemed to shake them.'

Robbie felt he was still missing a key element of the story.

Then it clicked. He turned to Geri. 'You mean, you saw the skeleton twenty years ago? On the far side of the cave? The alcove with a hidden entrance, halfway through the tunnel?'

Geri nodded but still didn't seem able to speak. For a moment there was silence. Alice reached the fork at the top of the hill, where the B-road led off for Camelford, turned and followed it.

As he took in her admission more questions occurred. 'What on earth were you doing in the tunnel? Was there anyone with you? And what did it look like? The body, I mean, not the tunnel. Was it wearing any clothes? Was it a skeleton at that point in time?'

'Go easy, Robbie,' admonished Alice. 'If you're not used to dead bodies it must be a pretty unpleasant memory. Geri's managed to suppress her fears for twenty years: she hoped she would never need to talk about it again. If it wasn't for the attention from this cycle trail it might never have reappeared.

'She's been very brave to talk about it. At least give her a bit of space until she's brought it back into focus.'

Her words gave Robbie a better perspective.

'You're quite right, Alice. I'm sorry, Geri. Please don't say any more until you're ready. At least your story convinced the police that I hadn't somehow put the skeleton in there myself. For that alone I'm very grateful.'

There was silence for the rest of the journey. Robbie was feeling worn out, he wasn't used to being held at police stations. He had lots of comments and even more questions, but at this moment all three travellers were too tired to tackle them.

Half an hour later they reached Camelford. As they drew up outside Geri's house she let slip that she'd been asked to go back to the Police Station on Monday afternoon. 'But my friends, the ones with me that night, will be there too, so I'll be alright. And don't worry, I'll let you know how we get on.'

As Geri got out Robbie took the chance to move into the front seat. The silence had made him feel rather better. His mind was buzzing with questions, ideas and schemes for moving the case forward. He looked across to Alice, but she shook her head.

'I know you want to talk, Robbie, but Brian needs to be in the discussion too. We'll be home in five minutes. Just enjoy the sunset over Port Isaac Bay.'

Whatever his partner's misgivings, Brian had done fine work in the kitchen as far as Robbie was concerned. Alice quickly cooked a six-egg omelette and the three sat down to eat. Robbie realised, as he tucked in to what was by far the largest portion, how hungry he had been.

It was now half past ten. 'What I suggest,' said Alice, 'is that you tell Brian and me your story. Take as long as you like. But if you don't mind, we'll park all the follow-up questions until tomorrow. Our minds will be much fresher then.'

So Robbie recounted the events of his afternoon. Brian and Alice listened in silence, apart from the occasional clarifying question.

When Robbie came to a halt there was a pause. Then Brian asked, 'So your car is still parked on some back road near to St Kew?'

Robbie hadn't considered that before. He admitted it was.

'Well, you and I were planning to meet tomorrow anyway. So why don't we begin by letting me take you to fetch back your car? I'll come round for you at, say, ten o'clock? When we're back we can have lunch together.'

'Hey, would you let me take you for lunch?' asked Robbie. 'That would be a way for me to say thank you for all your efforts.'

'I'm sure Alice and I can suggest somewhere,' replied Brian. 'That would give us a chance to start the discussion we've held back from this evening.'

CHAPTER 24

Saturday morning saw Brian arriving on time at the Bettle but there was no sign of his companion, either waiting outside or sitting in the lounge bar.

Eventually, after waiting patiently for a few minutes, the doctor stole past the empty bar and crept upstairs. There he found Robbie tearing about his room, swearing under his breath and almost pulling his hair out in frustration.

'It's the bloody police,' he shouted, when he saw Brian. 'Stealing my property. They should all be arrested.'

It took a few minutes for Brian to calm him down enough to explain what had happened.

'I was up early. Too much adrenalin or something. Anyway, while I was waiting, I was starting to go through the pictures on my camera. When I'm on a field trip I like to delete duplicates as I go along, otherwise I get too many. But I've found they've deleted all the ones I took in the tunnel.'

Robbie was still fuming as they got into Brian's car and set off for St Kew.

As far as Brian was concerned it was another fine day, with plenty to be positive about. He tried to cheer his friend up.

'Look on the bright side. They're not lost forever. Copies of all the pictures you took on Tuesday are on my desktop – remember, you wanted my opinion of the skeleton. We can reload them to your camera when we get home.

'In fact I copied them on yesterday to a friend who's into

forensics. I'll tell you what he said later. So even if the police break into my office they can't delete them entirely.'

Robbie was partially consoled. It was the effrontery that his photos had been deleted that bothered him, rather than the value of the pictures lost.

'It could be the police meant to tell me what they'd done but forgot. We left in rather a hurry. Your Alice was very bossy. No-one wanted to mess with her.'

Brian smiled in agreement. 'So how many pictures did you take yesterday? They're the only ones that you've really lost.'

Robbie thought for a moment. 'There was one of Rowena in the tunnel entrance. Don't misunderstand me: she was in full walking gear. It was her idea. Maybe she just wanted a picture of the tunnel entrance for the campaign brochure?'

'I think you should be very grateful that one's gone missing. I know Rowena. She's very good at throwing herself at men round here – and not just ones of her own age, either. You'd be a youngster compared with some she's taken an interest in. She didn't persuade you to take any inside the tunnel, I hope?'

Then Robbie remembered the 'dark on dark' pictures he had taken in the entrance to the cavern.

'I took a few. The sides of the aperture had been covered with some sort of cloth. It was pretty obscure - doubt it'll help the police, anyway.'

There seemed to be nothing more to be said. Brian drove the rest of the way in silence but his mind was assessing options. Ten miles later they drove through Trelill. There were no signs of a police presence.

A mile further on, turning off down a single-track by-lane, they reached Robbie's car, which looked to have come to no harm.

'The real back-of-beyond. Your car wouldn't have been noticed for a month.'

'Huh. I bet that given time, the police would have found it and done me for obstructive parking.' Robbie was still at odds with the local constabulary.

He started to feel in his trouser pocket for his car keys.

'Wait a minute,' said his friend. 'Now we're here I just want to understand exactly what happened. Have you any observations on the security camera that caught you?'

Robbie thought for a moment. 'Well, as I walked through the police station, there was some sort of Operations Room off the main corridor. The door was open and I glanced in. The far wall was covered with an array of television monitors. I guess it was one of those that betrayed us.'

'Great. Now, can you remember any more? I mean, was there just one monitor covering round here or were there half a dozen?'

The journalist screwed up his eyes in concentration. 'Well most of the monitors – the top two rows - were traffic related. I guess they need to keep an eye on weekend traffic on the A30. Below were a bunch of shopping centre cameras for Tesco and Morrison.'

Robbie pondered further. 'You know, there weren't more than a couple of television pictures that looked like the tunnel. I reckon they'd just got one camera on each entrance. Why are we having this conversation?'

'We wouldn't be if the police had had the sense to treat you as an ally rather than as a potential criminal. For example, if they'd had an intelligent conversation with you about this cloth.

'But given all that's happened,' Brian continued, 'I wondered if you and I ought to make sure the tunnel was properly

165

searched. At least we could take a few more pictures of the mysterious cloth.'

'You mean restorative justice, or something?'

'That might be the phrase. I was conducting a thought experiment. I wanted to see if we could get in and out again without being spotted.'

It was an intriguing question. If he hadn't had his critical picture removed by the police, Robbie would have dismissed the idea as fanciful. But . . . there came to his mind a snippet of a conversation from a week ago.

'I've just remembered something. Someone I talked to mentioned Lambourn was a golf fanatic – played every Saturday. Chances are he's on the course this morning. So if we're looking for a time when he's off duty it'll be right now.'

Almost by default the decision had been made.

Now they moved swiftly. Brian opened the boot of his car to reveal a collection of torches, helmets, high-visibility jackets and pliers. Robbie decided not to ask the doctor if he normally carried this sort of thing around with him. Maybe his patients regularly needed rescuing from darkened cliff-faces?

But if they were going to be a small forensics team, they should dress the part. 'Have you got any gloves?' asked Robbie.

The doctor leaned into the back of his car, reached inside his medical bag, and emerged with two pairs of plastic gloves. 'These'll do, I think.'

The two men put on the rest of the equipment, locked the car and set out for the embankment.

'It's unlikely there are cameras on the railway track up to the tunnel. If there were they'd have stopped us earlier. Rowena and I certainly didn't see any. But we'll keep a good eye out. If it looks like we've been spotted we can just turn back. We can't be in trouble for walking in the countryside.'

'And once we get to the tunnel we mustn't do anything which risks us being spotted. If we can't get inside then we'll just have to accept that – '

'- and collect the information some other way.'

Brian wasn't sure what Robbie had in mind. He assumed – hoped - he was speaking rhetorically.

Fifteen minutes later they were approaching the tunnel entrance. They walked very slowly, looking for a camera round about.

'It'll be well-hidden,' murmured Robbie. 'After all, they don't want it stolen. But I reckon it's got to cover that break in the fencing just over there – that's the way we got in.'

Then they spotted the camera. It had been lashed to a sturdy branch of a pine tree which grew to one side of the old railway track.

'It's not very high up, Robbie. I reckon they didn't use ladders. One just held it onto the branch and then someone else put the rope around it.'

'But if they could reach it so could we. You could sit on my shoulders. Do you think, very gently, we could point it at another part of the tunnel?'

The two men were speaking in whispers. The camera probably didn't capture sound but they weren't taking any chances. They slipped on the medical gloves.

Brian had one more look around for any unwanted police presence but there was nothing. The police must be relying completely on the camera. He was impressed there was any security at all. After all, they could hardly mount a permanent guard days after the skeleton had been removed.

Ten minutes later the two men were inside the tunnel. Acting together it had been easy to shift the camera's focus to the right hand end of the tunnel entrance. Then they crept quickly in at the left.

'I'm pretty sure there was no camera inside the tunnel,' observed Robbie.

'If there was, it would be where the skeleton was found.'

Holding torches they strode quickly on. This time Robbie did not want to inspect the tunnel but simply to reach the skeleton cavern. He relied on counting paces to know where the hidden entrance would be.

Five minutes later they had reached the location. A quick scan of the nearby tunnel confirmed there was no camera observing them. Then Robbie reached inside the opening and felt the cloth on the brick edge.

'See Brian, it's here. What on earth might it be?'

'Well, I reckon the only way to tell would be to take a sample out into daylight. That's why I brought the pliers.'

'Wouldn't that be interfering with a crime scene?'

'Well, the police have taken away the skeleton and are no longer here, so presumably they've done all the forensics they believe are necessary.'

The doctor felt up and down the entrance. 'Look, it goes right the way down. We'll just take a bit – there's plenty more for the police if they ever need it.'

Both sensed they needed to tear off the cloth while the adrenalin was still flowing, before professional caution struck them down. Robbie took the pliers and heaved. 'It's well stuck on,' he muttered. He pulled a few more times. Finally a piece of cloth came away.

'I've bought a freezer bag with me,' said the doctor. 'I came across it as I was preparing to cook last night's chips. Look, put it in here.'

Robbie deposited the sample into the bag. Brian sealed it and slipped it into his pocket. 'Is there anything else while we're here?'

'It looks like the same cloth on all sides of the opening. What about the top?'

'We'll need to get inside the cavern for that. The forensics lads will probably have looked already.'

But a few minutes later, when both men had squeezed themselves inside the cavern, it was obvious the forensics team had not been that observant.

'It's well over eye height,' observed the doctor. 'You'd need to be looking really hard to notice that – or to have some reason to think it might be important.'

'You mean, like finding cloth on the side entrance?'

But now there was someone looking hard. The two men shone their torches on the brick ledge over the narrow opening. And saw something of a glint.

'Brian, how many freezer bags did you bring with you?'

'A couple. There's one left. I don't think we'll need it for anything else. Shall we take them all?'

And a few minutes later a collection of metal discs had been scraped carefully off the high ledge and into the second freezer bag.

CHAPTER 25

The best restaurant around Delabole, the Mill House, towards Trebarwith Strand, was not easy to access. One way in meant a sharp U-turn, the other a steep descent down a narrow road.

Brian, though, knew how to get round this. 'Drive right down to Trebarwith Strand, turn around and come back up. From that direction it's easy.'

Robbie had no compunction about claiming the meal on expenses. He desperately needed to bounce ideas around with others on what was happening. What on earth should he report? Even if his friends could help him to decide no more than that it would be a well-justified expense claim.

The men had agreed, on the walk back to their cars, not to highlight their trip inside the tunnel until they were well into the meal.

'I'm sure Alice will understand eventually,' predicted Brian the optimist. 'But she's had to make one special journey to Bodmin to get you out of the Police Station. She might be annoyed that we risked her making another a day later.'

The journey back in separate cars prevented them discussing their finds in the tunnel any further. By the time they were both back in Delabole it was past noon. Alice was pleased with the proposed meal venue but suggested they needed to be there early as they hadn't booked in advance.

'I'd like us to make a list of topics we need to talk about,' said the forceful head as they settled at their table. 'Otherwise we'll jump all over the place but might miss something important.'

'Yes, miss.' But Robbie's answer wasn't spoken out loud. He might not like being told but could see it was a sensible suggestion.

'One point,' said Alice, 'is how will the discovery of the skeleton affect the cycle trail along a route through the tunnel? That's something I need answering as chair. As soon as the news gets out everyone will want to know what we plan to do. So what do you two think?'

Robbie's first thought was relief that he didn't yet need to confess their further visit to the tunnel. Then he buckled down to giving Alice an answer.

'If a skeleton had been found somewhere along the trail twenty years ago then it wouldn't affect things at all – except maybe to add interest in doing it. But as I understand it from Geri, the skeleton was first discovered then, just not reported. But maybe that blurs the problem?'

'There's a further complication,' added Brian. 'While the police are investigating they won't want the tunnel to be traversed at all.'

'OK Brian, but surely that won't last for long? I mean, once the death is explained there'll be no need to close it any longer.'

'But doesn't it depend on what the explanation is?' asked Alice. 'I know - that's one of the topics we'll come to later. But it can only be natural causes, suicide or murder. What's the impact on my cycle bid in each of those cases?'

There was a moment's silence.

Her husband answered first. 'Death by natural causes is no barrier - even if the bloke's identity is never known. It's just part of life: sad but true.'

'Suicide would be much the same,' added Robbie. 'It'd take a while to sort out. But it'll take ages to move from the cycle trail winning the Green Tourist Award, if it does, to engineering a working trail. It's not a showstopper.'

'So let's go on to murder.' Brian had started to raise his voice in his enthusiasm. A couple at the next table started to give them close attention.

'Best keep your voice down, I think,' advised his wife.

'I think you need to split that case further,' said Brian in a subdued voice. 'I mean, one possibility is a murder that's over - been solved, with someone tried and found guilty –'

'And the other is a murder that's become one of life's great unsolved mysteries,' completed the journalist.

'I'd say that a solved murder would be no long-term obstacle to the cycle trail either,' added Brian. 'It would add historical interest, no doubt, but I doubt if the victim's relatives could stop it happening. They wouldn't want the hassle. They'd be happy to stay well away.'

'But the bigger challenge, Brian, would be if the case was well-publicised but unsolved - and the police were left embarrassed. In that case the Council might want to help them by keeping the public as far away as possible.'

'And it's the Council who'll decide the Award winner. That might make it harder for the cycle trail to win – remember, it'll be judged next month.'

'Mind you, I can think of one bid that would love the case to be an unsolved murder,' said Robbie with a grin. 'That's the bid being put together by Owen Harris. He's desperate for an unsolved murder. That's why Lambourn was so suspicious of the skeleton being found by me just when I did.'

'So are we saying, gentlemen, that the result of this competition might just depend on whether or not this case can be solved?'

'Not just solved, dear, but solved before the competition is judged. Now that's a challenge – especially for the hyde-bound plods over in Bodmin.'

Their meals arrived at that point and brought a natural end to topic one.

'So the second part in our assessment of the case is, "What does the evidence suggest might have happened – and when?" '

Alice was enjoying her wild sea bass but she could see her companions were keen to restart the discussion.

Brian took the lead. 'I had a chat yesterday with my friend in Truro who's into forensics. He was looking at Robbie's pictures of the burial cavern.'

He took a mouthful of steak then continued.

'His view is that the skeleton is of a small man, slim, with no evidence of broken bones. Maybe five foot three inches tall and not much over twenty five years old. And he reckons the body's been there for around fifty years.'

'So he confirms your diagnosis, but makes it more authoritative. And tells us the man was small and thin. Fine work, Brian.'

'Alice told me the gist of Geri's story over breakfast. If the skeleton was fully decomposed in 1990, as she claims, that also supports the notion that he was in there before the railway closed down.'

'But on the other hand, I've interviewed the lineman's daughter. She tells me that the gang were walking through that tunnel every week or so during the working life of the railway. And the way she describes it, they were pretty diligent. Maintenance mattered: it wasn't just a cursory glance.

'I studied that opening carefully,' Robbie continued. 'You might walk past once without noticing. But to do that repeatedly, never once noticing the gap in the bricks, or stopping to have a look inside seems to me unlikely.'

'So that might suggest the late 1960s, just after the line's been closed. OK, let's leave that for now.

'Moving on,' continued Brian, 'what do we know about cause of death? Natural death seems pretty unlikely for a twenty-five year old.'

'And can we eliminate suicide? I mean, can we think of any reason why a twenty-five year old should want to go into an obscure tunnel miles from anywhere to commit suicide?'

There was a silence whilst both men pondered. Alice had finished her sea bass by now; she responded first.

'Well, for a start, they'd need to know the tunnel was there. That's limits it: it's hardly a national monument. And more than that, they'd also need to know there was a cave within the tunnel. That limits the victim much further.'

Alice shook her head. 'I can't imagine anyone would go in there to die unless they lived close beside it.'

Robbie had an alternative. 'What if the railway had some sort of association for them? For example, what if they'd lost their job on the railway when the line closed? That might make them angry enough to finish their life inside the tunnel. But they'd need to be pretty crazy.'

Brian added, 'Robbie's photos show the body was lined up neatly against the wall of the cavern. Someone who committed suicide by taking a huge number of sleeping pills and then lay down to die might lie like that. But if it was a deranged suicide, would the man be arranged that neatly?'

'OK,' said Alice, 'this isn't a court of law. We're just looking at likelihoods. So if we rule out natural death or suicide that leaves us with murder. Do you macho men have any comments on that?'

'A tunnel's an odd place to kill someone,' observed Brian. 'I mean, why on earth would you be there in the first place?'

'The victim might not be there of their own accord, Brian. But isn't it rather a good place to dump a body of someone you'd killed somewhere else? After all, it's taken half a century before it's been discovered.'

'Even so, the arguments we were putting earlier still apply. The murderer must have been someone local to think of the tunnel - and also to know about the void behind the alcove opening.'

'Local at the time of the murder,' retorted Alice, 'say half a century ago. By now they could be anywhere in the world – or they could be dead. I can see why the police might not welcome the case with enthusiasm. It might not do their clear-up rate much good.'

At this point the question of desserts was posed. Delicious-sounding choices were made and a few minutes later were brought to the table. Robbie decided this would be the least bad time to tell Alice about his latest tunnel visit.

'While we were fetching my car this morning we realised we could probably get into the tunnel again without worrying the police.'

He had timed the statement perfectly. It coincided with the head teacher starting to eat her first profiterole. Alice drew in her breath sharply, coughed severely and started to choke. It was fortunate that her husband was on hand to provide medical care in the form of a sharp slap on the back.

A few minutes elapsed for the statement to sink in.

'I don't believe I heard that. After all that trouble yesterday, you want to do what?' Alice folded her arms and looked mutinous.

'Oh, it's alright. We've done it. We went in this morning whilst Lambourn was on his golf course. Would you like to know what we found?'

Alice was caught in a dilemma. She had severe reservations about the men's judgement - but it seemed they'd got away with it.

She sighed deeply and said through clenched teeth, 'Please, please don't go in again. OK, what did you find?'

The two freezer bags were produced. The couple on the next table turned to look as well.

Brian produced and passed round first the bag of cloth which they had prised from the side bricks of the cavern entrance. He was tempted to pass it to the couple on the next table too, since they seemed so interested.

Alice had no more idea than the men as to what it might mean. 'Could you send it to your forensics friend over in Truro?' she suggested.

Once discussion on the cloth had died down, Brian produced the bag of metal discs. 'We found these on the ledge over the cavern entrance. It looks as if they're made of copper.'

'They're quite big: look like old pennies,' muttered the man on the next table to his partner.

'Do you know, I think you're right,' said Brian, turning towards him. 'When was decimalisation?'

'1971,' said the man's partner. 'I'm too young to remember, of course, but it was the year I was born. I suppose that's why they called me Penny. My parents told me it was one event I'd always be able to date accurately.'

'Maybe they thought of you as their own new penny,' suggested her partner.

'I can't begin to imagine why a set of old pennies should be found in the tunnel,' said Robbie. 'But it's put a later time-limit on what happened.'

CHAPTER 26

There was an odd mixture of joyful reunion and fear on Monday afternoon when the four nightwalkers, the first discoverers of the skeleton, met in the room assigned to them at Bodmin Police Station. They'd been invited in from two, with the formal interview, which Geri had been assured would be all together, taking place at three.

Somehow, without it being a conscious decision, the four had moved into different circles after their macabre discovery. It wasn't a guilty conscience exactly, more the burden of keeping a secret so deeply hidden that they couldn't even talk about it with one another.

They still lived in North Cornwall, but hadn't met as a group for years.

Geri was at the Police Station first, waiting nervously as one by one the rest of the group arrived.

'Hi, Gus,' she said as her former boyfriend appeared. There was the hesitation which always arises when meeting a former intimate with whom one is intimate no longer. They gave one another a gentle hug.

'Hi, Trudy. Nice to see you. It's been a while.'

'And you, Gus. I call myself Geri these days.'

'But you're Trudy – hold on, I like the name Trudy.'

'My parents christened me Gertrude. Trudy was fine when I was young. But when that Spice Girl – Geri Halliwell – became famous I realised I could be a Geri too. It's more grown-up. So

178

that's what I am now, please.'

Jack and Nigel arrived together a few minutes later – they'd met in the visitors' car park.

'I'd like to say you haven't changed a bit, Gus,' said Jack, 'but I don't like telling lies until I have to.'

Then he gave Nigel a poke in the ribs. 'Not too much walking along the cliffs for you these days, I'd guess. It's been a long time - how are we all doing?'

For half an hour there was a gentle thaw in various relationships that had long been in the deep freeze.

They knew why they were there. As their interview drew close Geri realised that it would be better to explain beforehand why she'd made the confession that had brought them all here.

The men were silent as she explained how the cycle trail bid had originated and how a journalist, checking the tunnel, had found the skeleton and was now in trouble. 'I had to tell the police that nothing could be blamed on him – it had been there for a long, long time.'

She'd feared their reactions but they were surprisingly sympathetic.

'I always wished we'd said something at the time,' admitted Nigel. 'It's been on my conscience for years. Well done. It'll be good to put things straight.'

After all his troubles with Glendenning, Lambourn decided this interview didn't need to be that formal.

'Technically,' he began, 'you broke the law by not reporting what you found. But I've talked to my boss. He agrees it's not in the public interest to charge you twenty years later. After all, the skeleton's been re-discovered, so we're where we might have been - albeit late in the day.

'That's not a universal amnesty, mind,' he continued. 'If you go speeding along on your motorbike and someone gets hurt' – he looked at Jack, who clearly had some sort of blemish in this direction – 'we'll be after you. But not for failing to report a dead body.'

He glanced round and looked each of them in the eye. 'What I want to do now is to make sure there's nothing else that you spotted that could help us with our inquiries.'

There was a collective sigh of relief.

Nigel was the first to speak. 'It was 1990. I guess we'd all heard of DNA but not yet the internet. Most research was done through libraries.'

He went on, 'We were in the Red Lion and very young. I proposed a night hike to celebrate the full moon.'

'For the record sir, what date was that?'

Nigel had been checking. 'May 1990. Saturday May 17th to be precise. The evening of the Cup Final between Man United and Crystal Palace that ended three all. None of us followed football, we didn't want to watch Match of the Day.'

He described how he'd led them along the old railway track to the mouth of the tunnel.

'Had you been there before?'

'I'd been that far earlier, to check the track was clear. But I'd not been inside the tunnel.'

Gus took over and described their journey through the tunnel. 'We got some way in then we heard a rushing, whistling noise. It sounded like an oncoming train.'

The Inspector frowned. This was the first mention of sound effects. He hoped they weren't going to talk about ghosts.

'Was this . . . all the way through the tunnel?'

'I don't think so. Anyway, we only noticed it near the middle.'

Lambourn looked around. 'Hm. Did you all hear this?'

Four heads nodded.

'So it can't have been just your imagination. Did you have any idea what it was?'

Nigel had the most cogent explanation. 'It was windy. The trees were shaking. It could have been bursts of wind hammering down the tunnel.'

Lambourn was far from convinced but it was clear the others had nothing to add. 'OK, carry on.'

Geri took over. She described how she had been desperate for the toilet and seen a narrow gap in the back of the alcove. She'd grabbed the torch, found herself in a cavern and relieved herself.

'When I stood up I shone the torch round to see where I'd come. There was a collection of odd-shaped rocks like sheep bones, piled beneath a hole, high up on the wall. That was unnerving. But as I looked around further I saw a full-sized skeleton, lying against the far wall.

'I screamed – I was terrified. Couldn't get out quick enough. I dropped the torch in panic and squeezed through the gap back to the lads.'

Jack completed their story. 'So now we were in utter darkness. Gus gave Geri a cuddle. I felt my way over to the opening and scrambled in, used my cigarette lighter to find the torch. I knew it must be near the entrance.'

He paused in recollection. 'Fortunately it was a metal torch. I could see it glinting faintly. I picked it up but it was dead. I could faintly see bones of something across the cavern, but I kept well away. I squeezed back out, then we all got out of the tunnel and back to Nigel's car as fast as we could.'

Nigel took over the narrative. 'We couldn't report it straight away, while we were all together: there were no mobile phones in those days. It was well after midnight by the time we'd emerged from the tunnel, walked back to the car and then dropped Geri back home. She was in a bit of a state. By the next morning reporting it didn't seem so straightforward – and I knew it had to be a collective decision.'

Nigel concluded, 'We met as soon as we could but it was a week later. We went round and round, finally agreed to keep the whole thing secret.'

'Did you ever regret that?' asked the Inspector.

'I realised almost at once that it was a big mistake. But the longer we left it, the harder it was to say anything. We're very sorry. I don't know if there's anything else we can tell you. It's a long time ago now.'

Lambourn had been listening hard and took a moment to work out his next questions.

'Now this is important. Did any of you take anything out of the cavern where the skeleton was found – any mementos or souvenirs, for example?'

There was a pause.

'I saw something on the floor while I was searching for the torch.' This was Jack. The others looked surprised: this was new information.

'What was that, sir?'

Jack felt in his pocket and drew out a plain envelope. He handed it over. 'I put it in here when I first got back to my lodgings, stuck it in a drawer and forgot all about it. It was on the floor beside the torch. I'd no idea what it was.'

The Inspector opened the envelope and held it over his desk. A dull, metal disk about an inch in diameter fell out.

There was a small hole punched close to one edge. It was inscribed but they couldn't see what the words said.

Silently the policeman reached in his desk for a magnifying glass. Then he peered at it closely for half a minute.

The four watched him, waiting for enlightenment. Finally he spoke.

'Looks to me like an identity disk. I should think it's from a British soldier in the Second World War. It's hard to read but the name but it looks like "A. McTavish". Does that mean anything to any of you?'

There was a pause then all of them shook their heads.

'Thank you. It's probably nothing to do with the skeleton. Did you take anything from the tunnel on your way out?' Again four heads shook.

'And you've not been back since?' Four heads shook once more, this time vehemently. On this memories were crystal clear.

'After this meeting in the Red Lion a week later did any of you say anything to anyone?'

'No. It was our dark secret and we didn't tell anyone,' said Nigel. One by one the others agreed.

Lambourn had intended to show the group some pictures of skeletons he had obtained from the Forensic Science Laboratory, taken after different lengths of time decaying. Could this shed any further light on how long the skeleton had been in place?

But on their collective testimony, Geri was the only one that had really seen the skeleton; and that was only for a few seconds.

Showing the woman more pictures of skeletons, he decided, might do more harm than good.

CHAPTER 27

One of the subtle pleasures of the Bettle and Chisel was the generous breakfast which the guests could enjoy, up to ten o'clock in the morning. Robbie had come across this a fortnight ago and had made the most of it ever since. It was a strong reason for not moving on.

But on Tuesday morning this haven was rudely interrupted by a call from his editor.

'I've not broken into one of your interviews, Robbie, I hope? I can phone back later if necessary.'

Robbie hastily cleared his throat and put down a large slice of toast. By now he was the last one in the dining room. 'No, that's fine. I use the first part of the day to write up my notes, deal with email traffic and plan out my day.'

'You've been there for a fortnight. I recall the initial assignment was for just two weeks. So how's it going? Have you something that will grip our readers or is it all rustic and droll? Is it time to move on?'

It was a shock. Robbie wasn't keen to move on at all.

'They're serious about how they're getting a bid together for the cycle trail on the old railway; they've had two business-like meetings so far. I've seen all I need to see from the newspaper's perspective. But there's a second bid that might have wider interest. That's a group wanting to re-energise a local old crime scene. The bid calls itself Arresting Crime.'

'Do they have a scene in mind?'

'Well, they hadn't when I got here. They were floundering. But I came across a skeleton in the old railway tunnel while I was checking the trail for the cyclists. It's far from clear that it was a natural death. That's embargoed by the police for the moment by the way, which is why I can't report it.'

'"Came across a skeleton", eh. Not "a natural death". So your reporter's instincts have been of some local use?'

'I guess it made a change from finding a skeleton in a cupboard, like the politics department.'

'Yes. You say the tunnel was on the old North Cornwall Line? So it might feature in both bids for the Award - who's got the better "tunnel vision"?'

'Well, it might be the police that decide the winner.'

'How do you mean?'

'If it's a natural death, or a crime that's being solved, that might help the cyclists. Whereas if it's an unsolved crime the stigma could scupper the cycle trail for good - but give the other lot something to work up into a major attraction.'

'Hm. Sounds intriguing. I hope you are keeping up to speed with the police investigation?'

'Oh I'm well aware of what the police are doing. I've been over to Bodmin Police Station twice so far.'

His editor did not detect the faint trace of irony. 'Fine. Well, you'd better stay for another week to see what happens. Put more effort into Arresting Crime, perhaps. You've given them hope – now you need to find out what they're doing with it. Just make sure there's an article at the end. It could be a Saturday Supplement piece, I suppose.'

Robbie thought his editor had finished. He was about to put down his phone and retrieve his toast when the man produced a postscript.

'Just one more thing, Robbie. I bumped into Sir Edmund Gibson at the theatre last night. We got chatting in the bar while our wives were powdering their noses. He mentioned that his daughter Rowena hadn't seen much of you last week. He said she sounded forlorn.

'It's none of our business - you're certainly no agony aunt - but he's a strong supporter of our newspaper and I'd like to keep it that way. So please try to keep her in the loop where you can.'

Robbie wasn't in the habit of falling in with every suggestion from his boss. Some of his ideas were odd. And he recalled Brian's words about Rowena. He had no desire to be her latest conquest, if that was what she was hankering after – whatever his boss was hinting.

But it would be good to interview Owen Harris and see how his bid was progressing. Apart from any value to his newspaper, he was sure Alice Southgate would be glad of intelligence on how the rival bid was going.

He'd got Owen's number when Rowena had introduced them in St Teath. Ten minutes later he had a date to meet the chairman of the crime scene bid for lunch, in the White Hart on the following day.

That afternoon he'd drop in on Betsy Chalkpit, the old lineman's daughter. She'd invited him back anytime. Thank goodness not everyone in Delabole needed a formal arrangement before he could see them.

When Robbie got to Mrs Chalkpit's, soon after lunch, he found her grappling with a big pile of ironing. She was pleased to have an excuse to stop.

186

'You've a lot of washing to finish off there,' he observed.

'Oh, it's not all mine. I do it for everyone in the Close. In return my lawn's mown once a fortnight and my hedge is trimmed every month. I guess it's a version of that Big Society that plum-voiced fellow keeps talking about. Except that we've been doing it for years, before the politicians ever thought of it.'

'Well, I won't keep you from your chores for long. It's just I had one or two extra questions about life on the old railway.'

'Eh bless you, I don't mind stopping. The ironing's not that urgent – it's not needed till Friday. Would you like a cup of tea?'

'And a chocolate biscuit,' Robbie added – but only to himself.

'So what else do you want to know?' she asked, once they were both sitting comfortably with mugs of tea in their hands.

'Well, you told me about the tunnel being used to store munitions during the war. That led me to find an article about it in my Archive. Had you any idea what the inhabitants of Trelill made of it? I think, if it had been me living there, I wouldn't have much liked it.'

'Well, I was born in 1941 so I was an infant during the war. I can't give you a firsthand account. But my Mum and Dad knew all the folk in Trelill and how they felt. And the short answer is: no, they weren't happy at all.

'There were huge, locked iron gates at either end of the tunnel to reduce the risk of vandalism – and some sort of fire screens inside them. In general the villagers opted for silence. My Dad said that they thought the less fuss they made, the less risk there was of the wrong person getting to hear about it and deciding to make mischief.'

'Thank you, that's really interesting. So it wouldn't be that well known. The less glamorous history of the railway.'

Robbie put his mug down and Betsy gave him a refill. He recalled the phone call from Geri the evening before and the new information, from her police interview, about the noise in the tunnel.

'There's one other thing that's come up but it might not make any sense.'

'But if you don't ask you'll never know.'

'True. OK, it's a question about noise inside the tunnel. Did your Dad ever speak of a rushing sound inside the tunnel?'

'You mean something that sounded like an oncoming train?'

'Yes, that's right. Maybe on very gusty days?'

Betsy looked at him closely. 'I don't know where you've heard that. It was one of the best-kept secrets of the tunnel. Railwaymen didn't speak about it in case it scared away the passengers. Of course, if you were inside a train with the windows shut, you wouldn't hear it anyway. But there was only a single track. Even the thought of meeting an oncoming train inside the tunnel was pretty frightening.

'My Dad came across the sound occasionally, over many years as a lineman. He reckoned it only happened when there was a strong, gusty wind – and it had to be blowing from the north.'

'Did you ever hear anything?'

'I heard it just once, a windy day during the first summer I worked there. It was scary, I can tell you. I knew it couldn't be but for a horrible second I thought it was a train. It didn't happen very often, mind.

'In fact, my Dad reckoned the roar stopped happening as the line drew towards its close. He used to say it was the final breaths of a slowly-dying line. In later years it was one of the things he attributed to the ghost.'

CHAPTER 28

Owen Harris was already in the bar when Robbie reached the White Hart on Wednesday lunchtime. As the weather was fine the older man suggested that they adjourn to the garden for their lunch. 'It'll be quieter out there.'

It was hardly busy inside.

They ordered ploughmen's lunches, seized their pints of cider and strolled outside. Robbie had drunk too much last time, he resolved he would fetch the refills today.

'Thank you for agreeing to see me. I wanted to find out how your campaign for "Arresting Crime" was going.'

'Not as well as I'd hoped, Robbie, is the honest answer. Well, you were here for that talk by Inspector Lambourn. I didn't know if he was being deliberately cagey about any unsolved crime to make his force look efficient; or if he simply didn't know of any – which might mean they were horribly inefficient.'

Owen paused and sipped his drink. 'My colleagues and I have been asking everyone we can think of that's lived here long enough – say half a century - but we've not come across any peculiar corpses. I don't know if that means nothing exciting ever happens here or just that the old folk have gone senile.

'No, Lambourn was not as helpful as I'd hoped,' agreed Robbie. 'Not the world's most charismatic speaker. It was rather disappointing.'

The pair started to attack their lunches.

189

'I was thinking about your bid,' mused Robbie. 'Do you have to start with a physical body? Have you thought of making up a crime in the abstract, then looking for anyone who's gone away that it might apply to?'

Owen paused between mouthfuls. 'Hm. Sounds a bit different. Go on.'

'Well, for example, why not start with motive? What motives can you think of for someone being killed?'

'To be honest, there are a few people I know that I'd like to do away with. There's a wrecking crew that play on my golf course, for example, if "play" is the word. Was it Mark Twain that declared golf was the best way of spoiling a good walk? Well this lot prove the opposite. Once you're behind them it's like following a troupe of arthritic snails on a go-slow.'

'You mean, they don't just stand aside and let you through?'

'Never. But they do it to all of us. If anything happened the trouble wouldn't be finding a suspect. The list would be a yard long.'

'How many of them are there?'

'Most times there's four.'

'Well, what if all four were to disappear from the area at exactly the same time?'

'We'd all be extremely grateful. We'd suspect they'd gone to plague another golf course for a month or two – maybe gone for a joint holiday in Spain.'

This was harder work than Robbie had expected. He stabbed his pickled onion and tried again.

'OK, let's leave motive. How about method? Remember, you're after something tourists will find intriguing. They'll hardly be gob-smacked if it's a straightforward shooting. Come on, what interesting ways can you think of to dispose of your

190

wrecking crew?'

Owen thought for a moment. 'Maybe they could each be hit on the head with a golf club and then be buried in a series of bunkers around the course?'

'That might arouse some interest. Especially if they weren't all found at once, but over a period of months. Trouble is, the golf course might not like it. Can you think of something more subtle?'

'Well, they all drink green tea regularly in the clubhouse. Foul stuff. But it tastes so horrible you could easily put something in it.'

'Right, let's take that a bit further. Let's assume, for a minute, that you could get hold of some deadly poison. Say one of the murderers was married to a doctor. What would be needed to get that poison into their tea?'

'The barman at the clubhouse hates them as much as the rest of us. They sit for hours at a window table – they're as slow drinking their tea as they are playing golf. While they're there they rubbish the real golfers as they plug away outside. When the players see the crew most of 'em won't come in. The wrecking crew halve the bar takings when they're around. So the barman could just put poison in their teapot when he takes them the tea.' His eyes started to gleam.

Owen was taking the example rather seriously. Robbie hoped the man didn't know any doctors with access to poisons. This was only meant to be a theoretical exercise.

'OK, you're starting to get the idea. But the trouble is that it's all happening in the present. You couldn't use it for half a century. The police, the victims' families, even the killer – if caught – would all refuse permission: "intellectual property rights" or something. What we've got to think about now is the

191

same thing, set further in the past – say fifty years ago.'

The pair continued to make inroads on their lunches. Robbie spotted Owen had finished his cider and was quickly on his feet. 'Let me get you another. Same again?' He returned a few minutes later with a pint for Owen and half for himself. 'I'd have a pint but I've got to drive back to Delabole.'

Owen had been thinking. 'Do you really think it would work to start the thought process for Arresting Crime with someone who'd just disappeared?'

'Could do.' At least the man was trying.

Owen sipped his cider and reflected.

'You know, I did have a friend . . . he worked in St Kew. Adam, he was called, he went away very suddenly. One Friday he and I were drinking in the Red Lion in St Kew, as we did on a regular basis. The next week he wasn't there. And I never saw him again. Do you think he could be the basis of our Arresting Crime?'

'He might. Let's try. You must have thought about it at the time: why did you think he'd gone away?'

'It was mid-December. I assumed he'd gone away for Christmas with his family. But he never came back.'

'Had he ever talked about his family?'

'Not to me. But everyone's got some sort of family, haven't they?'

'Most do. Did no-one else notice that he'd gone?'

'I don't think he had many friends, to be honest. He had a flat in the Children's Home – the Laurels. He was on call most of the time, he said, so he couldn't really cope with visitors.'

'This sounds promising. Now imagine what might have happened to him – and where they'd have put the body.'

There was a pause. The two men drank more cider. 'This

isn't so easy, you know,' protested Owen. 'He could have gone anywhere.'

'Well was there anyone else you know who dropped out like that?'

'There was my brother: he was called Neville. He went off to the United States in 1963. But I can tell you exactly what happened to him. He was killed in a car crash a year later.'

'Gosh, I'm so sorry.'

Owen shrugged. 'It was a long time ago. Neville went away to start his own business. He was fed up with life here – thought we'd been farmers forever and needed a change. We didn't hear from him for a long time. My Dad fretted away so in the end I flew over to check he was alright. Got there in time to find Neville had been killed in a head-on car smash.'

Owen paused, obviously saddened by the memory.

'Mind, I'm not sure Neville would be much use for our crime puzzle. We all knew where he'd gone. Apart from anything else, he's buried here in St Teath.'

There was another pause. Both men sipped their drinks.

'The idea of starting with questions around someone who'd just gone away is a good one.' Owen looked enthused. 'It might help stir the public's imagination. All we'd need then would be motive and method.'

'And you'd have to invent clues. For example, when did the incident happen? For most crimes on television, the pathologist gives a time of death from the dead body. But with no body you'd need something else.'

'You mean, like a copy of the victim's latest bank statement – so you could see when their account was last used?'

'Or a ticket showing their last journey. You might even need to review the history of the old North Cornwall Line: when did trains last run?'

Robbie hadn't intended to talk about the railway – the embargo was still in place - but it was hard to resist. 'Even if you had a skeleton it would be hard to analyse. No flesh, so unless there's a bullet hole in the skull you couldn't say for sure whether there was foul play. Forensics would tell the police how long it had been there. But it'd be a wide range.'

Owen was brainstorming as well now. 'These days the police can do a lot with DNA. I mean, if they can take a DNA sample from a mammoth fossil from Outer Mongolia they must be able to do something with human bones a century old.'

'Yes. Mind, you'd have to find someone to match the sample with, preferably a close relative. With current budget cuts I doubt they'd want to take DNA samples from everyone in North Cornwall.'

Owen finished his drink, seized his glass and stood up. 'Can I get you another – and maybe the dessert menu?'

Absentmindedly Robbie handed over his glass. He felt frustrated when he saw Owen bring them back both pints of cider. But the desserts on the menu he'd got hold of looked very tempting.

He chose an Eton Mess while Owen settled for a treacle sponge. Robbie returned to the bar to place their orders.

'Someone lent me an Archive about the railway,' he said, once they had settled down with their desserts. 'It started when the line reached Delabole.'

'1893. My grandfather had influence in those days.'

'I don't recall mention of a Harris. Maybe he was in one of the parts I haven't got to. Was he significant?'

'You must have seen a mention of Sir Anthony Aristotle? That was my grandfather. His son got so fed up with being teased at school that he shortened the name to Harris. Much less pretentious, so I've stuck with it.'

'The Archive suggested some rivalry between Aristotle and Trevelyan.'

'Yes, there was a real feud. They were like chalk and cheese. My grandfather ran the Slate Quarry – centuries old – while John Trevelyan was an upstart businessman from Padstow. They never really got on.'

'You know we were talking about motives. Well, a feud's got possibilities. It gets whole families involved in trying to do one another down.'

'Mm, I see what you mean. Maybe I'll ask my committee to look for old feuds. That might give us some new ideas. We badly need a fresh start. There's only a fortnight before entries need to be in.'

Robbie's head felt befuddled when he left the White Hart - again. Two and a half pints of the local cider had left their mark. He decided on a long walk round St Teath before taking charge of his car.

At the far side of the village he came across the local church. That reminded him of Owen's sad tale about his brother.

Robbie let himself into the churchyard and started to look for the young man's gravestone. There were hundreds, it was as well he wasn't in any hurry.

Finally, he found it: the final resting place of Neville Harris. A simple gravestone marked a short but eventful life. Neville had been born on August 12th 1934 and had died on July 10th 1964. So he was nearly thirty when he died. Killed in a head-on car crash, Owen had said.

It occurred to Robbie that Neville was roughly the same age

as his skeleton. He could foresee Owen taking it quite hard when the police embargo was lifted.

It was all very frustrating, a jigsaw with not enough pieces. Robbie shook himself, strode back through the churchyard and decided that he was now fit enough to drive slowly back to Delabole.

CHAPTER 29

Thursday morning: well over a week since Robbie had found the skeleton. So what did he think now?

One possibility was that the victim had been Adam. The name had come up twice now in his interviews. Trevor had been confused – or deliberately ignorant - about where the man had ended up. It still wasn't completely clear, from the story he'd told, why the tunnel still caused him so much fear. But was it his place, on the story he'd been told, to drop Trevor Hucknall into the mire?

Their conversation at the Riverside had been in confidence and newspapermen did not disclose their sources. Before he could say anything to the police he would need a completely different source for the idea – maybe from his research group? And it would do no harm to check for alternatives.

This caused him to wonder who might have noticed a small, lean twenty-five year old disappearing unexpectedly from the scene fifty or more years ago. Eventually that led him to ring Miss Trevelyan. It was a long shot, but she was the right sort of age. Miss Trevelyan said she'd be pleased to see him later that morning – say for coffee at eleven?

As he walked through Delabole, Robbie mused on the phone call he'd received from Inspector Lambourn the previous evening.

'Good evening, sir. Could I have a few words? I've got more

information you might be able to comment on.'

Robbie thought he sounded conciliatory. He must now accept that the journalist had nothing to do with planting the skeleton – and might have more to offer as an independent witness.

'I met the first skeleton finders a couple of days ago. Two new points. First, they mentioned they'd heard a sort of noise inside the tunnel. They said it "sounded like an oncoming train". It may be irrelevant but I'd like to know what it was. Did you hear anything like that?'

Robbie rejoiced to be treated as a resource and not a demon. He struggled to make sense of the phenomenon.

'I didn't hear anything. But it wasn't windy when I was there. Did they say anything about the wind in 1990?'

'They said it was gusty. I've got a call out to the Met Office asking for more details.'

'There was what looked like a ventilation shaft vent where we found the skeleton. Could that have anything to do with it? Could what they heard be a burst of wind howling down the shaft?'

'That's an interesting idea, sir. Thank you. My second question might also be irrelevant, but I'm trying to make sure we cover all angles.'

'Good policy. Fire away.'

'Well, one of Geri's group found a piece of metal in the cave, which he handed over. It was an old army tag. It bore the name "A. McTavish". I'm chasing it up with Army Records but does the name ring any bells for you?'

Robbie paused. He had heard the name somewhere . . . Then he remembered.

'Do you know, Inspector, I have come across that name –

and only recently. I've been reading the local Archive of the railway. There was an Alastair McTavish stationed near here during the war. He was based at Davidstow Airfield. He used Trelill tunnel to store his depth charges.'

'Ah, that's very useful. So it must have been left there during the war. Nothing to do with the skeleton at all. That's one mystery solved at any rate.'

There was a pause and then the Inspector concluded, 'A shoal of red herring. You can see why a simple policeman might think the whole thing had been set up by someone wanting to create a murder mystery, can't you? Anyway, thank you for your help. I may be in contact again.'

When Robbie reached Miss Trevelyan's bungalow she greeted him effusively.

News of the skeleton was starting to seep round the village. The police hadn't made any announcement but enough people now knew that it couldn't be hidden completely. As the finder of the bones, Robbie was a local celebrity. His companion, Mick Hucknall, was not around so the journalist didn't even have to share the limelight.

Robbie had planned to start the conversation by returning the boxes of Railway Archives and asking some questions about the material he had read, but the skeleton was the topic of the moment. He found himself being asked far more questions than he'd expected. But he could see no reason to hold back any of the facts which he had already told the police.

'Does anyone know who the poor man was?' the old head teacher asked, once the raw facts of the discovery had been laid out.

'Well, I was wondering if you might be able to help there.'

'An old woman like me? The police must be desperate – or very short staffed. I don't know, these government cuts are going too far. I'd want to be at least a sergeant. Will they be able to give me a uniform?'

Robbie couldn't help smiling at her sparky humour. 'But it's because you are, if you don't mind me saying, moderately old that I thought of you. You see, the age of the bones means this all happened roughly half a century ago. Probably before 1970; maybe soon after the line closed in 1966. And it almost certainly involved someone who lived round here. So you'd have been around at the time.'

'Goodness, I see what you mean. I've lived in this village since 1956. So I could have been the murderer!'

'Miss Trevelyan, I promise you, that thought had never crossed my mind. We don't even know if it was murder. No, the thought that had occurred to me was this: given your wide network of acquaintances, you might have known the skeleton while he was still alive - before he disappeared. So is there anyone that you can think of that might have turned into that skeleton?'

'Goodness me, that's a big question. Do you know, there was a detective I used to read stories about when I was a child called Sherlock Holmes. He'd be too clever for modern television. He used to refer to the need for sustained thought as a "three pipe problem". Well, you and I don't smoke, but this seems at least like a "fresh pot of coffee" problem. I'll muse as I make it.'

Miss Trevelyan returned a few minutes later with a determined, thinking look on her face. She set down the coffee tray as Robbie opened his laptop. 'In case we think of anything,' he explained. He was pleased to see that fresh coffee also meant more biscuits.

'It's far from easy,' Miss Trevelyan began. 'So many people have left the area over the years. But we are a community so most of them pop back sooner or later to see relatives and so on. What we want is someone who went away without any warning – and with no relatives making any fuss.'

'Well, they might have made a fuss. At least if they had nothing to do with his disappearance. Look, can we call the skeleton X for a moment? X must have had friends who missed him as well. Surely there would have been a big commotion. Can you remember anything like that? Say in the late 1960s?'

There was silence while Miss Trevelyan pondered. Robbie took the chance to eat another biscuit.

'Do you know anything more about X that might help me?' she asked at last. 'For example, how old was he? Do we know anything about his size?'

Robbie had been holding back this information so he could cross-check any ideas from the head teacher and narrow down the options. If she had produced half a dozen candidates this might have worked. Now he could see he was being over optimistic. The journalist was wary of asking a leading question. But it surely couldn't mess up the legality of the investigation to give her a few more facts. He would need to blur which facts came from where, though.

'I talked to the police yesterday. The Forensic report is still awaited. But I have some idea from what I observed. For the purposes of this discussion, let's say that X was not very tall – say, only about five foot three inches; quite slim; and probably in his mid twenties. Does that help?'

A dreamy look came over her face. 'I can think of one

handsome young man, short and thin, who went away from here in the early nineteen sixties. He went off to America, or so his family said.'

'Can you tell me his name, please, so I can look into it? I promise I won't tell anyone the idea came from you.'

'Well, it was someone called Neville Harris. His brother still lives around her – a farmer by the name of Owen.'

This must be the other side of the story he'd heard from Owen the day before. 'I'm sorry. I don't think it could be him. Remember, the railway was still running in the early 1960s. And I've talked to the daughter of a lineman – Betsy Chalkpit. She told me the tunnel was checked at least once a week, right until the railway closed, for any loose fittings on the rails. If Mick and I could see the gap in the recess as we walked through last week then the line gang must have done so too – one time or another. But they never reported anything.'

Miss Trevelyan obviously watched television crime assiduously. 'What if the gap had been covered over from the inside, so the cavern couldn't be seen?'

Robbie shook his head. 'That would need some sort of wooden framework. There was no sign of anything like that when I was there.'

There was a pause while both mused on the problem.

Then Robbie remembered the ledge over the opening. Did that offer other possibilities? 'It might not have needed a big wooden framework, I suppose. If the covering could be arranged, somehow, so that it hung down close to the opening.'

Miss Trevelyan was persistent. 'Well, what if the cover had just been a black curtain, hung to fit over the hole? That'd make the gap hard to see, wouldn't it?'

Robbie gave the idea some thought. It wasn't that foolish.

He didn't want to divulge the information to the old lady, but could this make sense of the traces of cloth in the entrance?

'My, that's a Sherlock Holmes calibre suggestion.'

The old lady seemed to bask in the praise. Maybe she could be a detective after all.

Musing, the journalist unpacked the idea further. 'What sort of cloth? Black velvet, perhaps? I suppose if it was put there in the 1960s it might well have decayed away over the next fifty years. But how would you make it hang?'

'Well, fashions for curtains have come a long way during my lifetime. Look – you see I've got curtain rods. Those used to be items you'd only find in stately homes. In my younger days, people used to improvise – for example, they would put lots of coins along the hem of a curtain to make it hang properly.'

'Coins?'

She stopped for a moment to think. 'I suppose if such a curtain was turned the other way up, and looped over a ledge, it might be kept in place from all the coins in the hem which were now at the top.'

Miss Trevelyan looked at him for further approval. 'Is that an idea worthy of Sherlock Holmes too?'

CHAPTER 30

Robbie's late morning walk back from Miss Trevelyan through Delabole took him past the Southgates'. He was buzzing with excitement.

On the off-chance, he knocked to see if anyone was at home. It was term-time, so he knew Alice would be at work, running her school with an iron fist; but maybe the doctor came home for lunch?

To his delight, Brian came to the door. His surgery closed for lunch and he was due back later in the afternoon; he had a couple of hours free in the meantime.

'Come in and share my beggar's portion. Alice doesn't like me over-eating, so there isn't much, I'm afraid.'

'Any chance of a drink?'

'You're right, that is more under my control. But I'd better not have more than a glass; I'm being a doctor again later this afternoon.'

The pair made their way through to the kitchen and Brian got out some cheese and a couple of rolls. Then he took a half-drunk bottle of Chardonnay from the fridge and poured them each a glass.

'Cheers. I'd have rung to talk to you this evening anyway, so it's good you're here. I've heard back from my forensic friend. Given the urgency, I sent him our sample of cloth by courier on Saturday evening. I asked him to give it top priority. He rang me back with some results just before lunch.'

'That was quick.'

'They're not overworked at the moment. The criminal classes are slacking. He managed to slip it into a gap in their schedule.'

'So what's the result?' As he spoke, Robbie took a swig of his wine and started to grapple with the task of squashing cheese into his roll.

'Well, they reckon the cloth is some form of velvet. Not modern material, though, just some form of cotton. Probably the sort that was on sale everywhere before the Second World War.'

'Old-fashioned - so the sort of material that would disintegrate if left in a cave or a tunnel for a few decades?'

'Precisely. But the most unexpected thing he told me was that he could also analyse the glue that was holding the cloth onto the bricks. It was some sort of araldite.'

'He couldn't tell you where it was sold, I suppose?'

'Oh yes. There's just one outlet, he said, on the High Street in Bodmin; and there's been a CCTV camera outside it since 1960.'

Robbie was about to punch the air then stopped and grinned as he realised his friend was joking. Life was never going to be that simple.

'No, they've no idea. But they applied all sorts of techniques to find out its precise chemical makeup. It matched exactly to araldite. And he tells me this type of glue was not invented until 1945.'

'So assuming it's something to do with the skeleton that gives us the earliest date at which the deed could have been done. That's pretty useful.'

There was a pause while both men tucked into their rolls

and drank their wine. Robbie poured himself a second glass, which emptied the bottle. 'Outside dustbin, I suppose?'

'I came round here for two reasons,' he continued, when the bottle had been disposed of. 'Well, three, if you include this wine, which is delicious. Firstly, to bring you up to date on the police investigations. Lambourn rang me last night. I don't know what your Alice told him last week but whatever it was it's done the trick – he's treating me with real respect now.'

Robbie went on to recount the gist of his phone call with the Inspector. 'It's not obvious how it helps but he's made me feel we're on the same side.'

'Great. And what was your other reason for coming?'

'Well, I went to see Miss Trevelyan this morning. I'm on my way back now, as a matter of fact. What a terrific old lady. We had a very good discussion.'

He could see Brian was itching to know what had made him so excited.

He deliberately took another sip of his wine to make him wait. It was good to have something that was so badly wanted.

'Miss Trevelyan, on her own initiative, came up with the suggestion on what the cloth might once have been used for.'

'Go on.'

'She asked if the gap might not have been covered over by dark velvet curtains.'

It did not take the doctor long to latch on. 'Hey, that's an idea. That would explain why the gap was never noticed by the maintenance gang.'

'She also told me something else about how curtains were arranged in her youth. That is, you would weigh down the hem, to make sure the curtain hung properly, using weights or coins.'

'Hey, that's great,' said Brian, then stopped. 'But that doesn't

206

work, does it? If the killer had hung up curtains with all the coins in the hem, and the curtains disintegrated, they'd be left on the floor of the cave.'

'But what if the coins were already in the hem of the curtain, from when it had been hung in someone's house? The killer brings it along, then realised that the coins could be used to help keep the curtain from sliding down until the glue's hardened, so arranges it with the hem at the top – maybe with a few stones to add to the weight.'

'Or – here's another idea - maybe he doesn't want them hanging at the bottom because, in a wind gusting down the tunnel – or out of the ventilation shaft - the coins might clink together and draw attention to the drape.'

There was silence as the two scenarios were evaluated. Either could make sense. The men couldn't think of anything else that worked any better.

'I'd better make sure there's another half-drunk bottle of Chardonnay in the fridge for when Alice gets home,' muttered Brian.

He went into the larder, came back with a fresh bottle of white wine and applied the bottle-opener. 'You can drink more than me. But we must leave some to put back in the fridge.'

'Thanks. You know, Brian, this whole idea makes it far more likely that the skeleton arrived while the trains were still running. There'd be little point in messing about with curtains after the lineman no longer came.'

'And I've got another observation,' he added. 'In either of our scenarios the killer never comes anywhere near to handling those coins. In either case they're fastened away inside the hem, last touched by the killer's wife or mother.'

'OK. I agree. So?'

207

'Well, last Saturday we were immensely careful not to touch the coins in case they had the killer's fingerprints on. We wore medical gloves all the time until the coins were safely inside the bag. But now there's no need to be careful. They can't possibly have any useful prints. So why don't we have a look and find out the dates on them all? That must help narrow the date range on when it all happened.'

Brian was not hard to convince. It had been frustrating to have a bag of coins and not be able to examine them one by one.

He unlocked the plastic bag from his study safe. 'Alice saw me put them away on Saturday,' he explained. 'I did that in case I needed to prove to a court that the evidence hadn't been tampered with. Where's the best place to lay them out?'

Robbie spotted a whiteboard standing on its side in the corner of the dining room. 'How about this?'

'It's Alice's, but I'm sure she won't mind.'

Quickly they arranged the whiteboard on the kitchen table and unpacked the bag of coins. There were about fifty old-denomination pennies. A couple were so old and faded that it would take a Forensic Laboratory to deduce their year of issue. The rest, though, were legible.

Robbie noted down the years on a piece of paper as they carefully moved them, one by one, across the board. He laughed, 'Looks like a special form of shove-halfpenny.'

The last few coins were too dirty to read. Brian fetched some vinegar, poured it onto a J-cloth and doused the coins. Now the years were legible. Robbie added their numbers to his list as they too were moved across the board.

Soon would come the moment of truth. Robbie took a second sheet of paper and carefully rearranged the years he had noted into ascending order. He counted the number of years in his second list to make sure he hadn't lost or double counted any. Then the pair examined the rearranged list together.

'Normally distributed,' said Brian.

Robbie didn't know exactly what he meant but it sounded like a term of approval. Most of the dates fell in the middle of the range, anyway. The earliest was 1934 and the latest 1950.

'So the events in the tunnel could have taken place in any year after 1934,' pronounced Robbie.

'No, no, it's the other way round. What these coins show is that it could not have taken place before 1950 – otherwise how would a coin that late have been included in the hem of the curtain? Well done, Robbie. We've narrowed the range of death even further.'

CHAPTER 31

By Thursday evening Robbie Glendenning was after intelligent company.

He'd phoned Brian, hoping for a chance to push their theories further, but the doctor was out on call. Alice, who'd answered the phone, was also busy: she had some plans for school she needed to check over.

He'd eaten alone, not wanting to display his lack of skill at darts. Afterwards he'd gone to his room, hoping to have a phone conversation with George.

But for some reason she was not answering. Odd: wasn't she supposed to be housebound? He hoped she hadn't been rushed off to hospital with her daughter. Then he noticed a text message on his phone. But it was not from George, it was from Rowena.

'do u fncy mnlght swm? cm to trligga at mdnght. ro x'

His first thought was that she had texted him by mistake – maybe she knew another Robbie? Or was it a general invitation to friends and acquaintances around Delabole? He would be more interested if it was just for him.

Then Robbie recalled his editor's entreaty to "keep Rowena in the loop". He'd been inclined to ignore it. Maybe this was a way he could do so? He wasn't sure what temperature the sea would be at midnight, but a pretty girl might distract him from the cold. At least he could tell his editor that he had tried.

He'd started updating his notes when his phone rang. His heart raced – was this George returning his call? It turned out to be Inspector Lambourn. Even so he felt mildly encouraged – it was good to be consulted.

'Good evening, sir. It's the Trelill tunnel case again. There's something more I'd like your comments on.'

'Go ahead, Inspector.'

'We've made progress on the identity medal found in the cave. You remember – it was owned by A. McTavish. The Army got back to me earlier today.'

'And was he a Scotsman with war-time service in Davidstow?'

'That was the peculiar thing, sir. The Army had an Alistair McTavish whose record was exactly as you said. He came from Glasgow. But they tell me he died thirty years ago. So the skeleton couldn't be him.'

Robbie grimaced. 'That's one line of enquiry closed off, I suppose.'

'Yes. The odd thing, though, was that though the name matched, the identify number on the disk was not his.'

Robbie paused to consider. 'How bizarre. You mean there's more than one military McTavish in Cornwall?'

'That's what the Army tells me.'

'But if it was a soldier's identity disk, as you say, could the Army tell you more about this one?'

'Well sir, the identity number corresponded to another McTavish, a much younger man. One who joined the Army to do his National Service in 1955.'

'I see . . . So what's your question?'

'Well, the strange thing was that this fellow turned out to be

211

his son. He was called Adam, so he had the same initials. Have you any comments on this one?'

Robbie felt a surge of excitement. Was this the Adam he'd heard about?

'And this son – the one who matched the cave ID – is he still alive?' He did his best to adopt a neutral tone of voice but this was the crucial question.

'We haven't managed to establish that yet. But at least now we've got an Army link and a family connection to start the chasing.'

'Thank you for letting me know, Inspector. I'll give it some thought.'

After such an unexpected phone call, Robbie filled out the rest of the evening getting his notes up to date. At a quarter to twelve he discarded his valuables, seized his towel and swimming trunks, slipped on his fleece and strode around the pub to his Stag.

A few minutes later he was out on the road and then down the lonely side road to Treligga. There was no traffic, no clouds and a full moon. The trees were rustling in the breeze but otherwise there was silence. Now his eyes had got used to it the moonlight was amazing. At midnight in Treligga not much was happening.

He walked down the road to the gate, then up the path of Rowena Gibson's cottage. There was no light on inside. Perhaps it was all a joke or a ghastly mistake and she was fast asleep?

It was too late to wake her up. He walked slowly back down the path. Then, glancing back as he reached the road, he saw a notice on the gate. It was written in large handwriting, making it readable by moonlight. He didn't know how he'd missed it.

'Robbie, I've gone on down to Tregardock beach. Please join me. There won't be anyone else. Love Rowena'

Why hadn't she bothered to wait? He was only a few minutes late. Maybe, though she hadn't told him so, others were coming too? Perhaps she was planning a bigger party and had gone on ahead to prepare?

Robbie wasn't interested in a crowded beach party at midnight. He was tempted to turn round and go back to Delabole. But it was clear from the note that Rowena was looking forward to his company.

Robbie wasn't averse to being on an empty beach by moonlight in the sole company of a pretty girl. Especially one intending to go for a swim. It would be one more chance to appreciate her curves. He shrugged his shoulders and turned towards the path at the end of the village that he knew led down to the beach.

He hadn't brought his torch but by now his eyes were used to the moonlight and the track across the fields was clear. In the distance he could just make out the paler shade of the sea, stretching across Port Isaac Bay.

Now he was away from the village and his senses were on high alert it was slightly creepy. There were subtle sounds that he couldn't quite identify, from night insects or small animals rustling in the long grass. There were also the rustic smells of the countryside. For night hikes to be much fun, he decided, he needed company.

After ten minutes his track joined the way down from the other farmhouse and the path became narrower. He needed to be more careful here, the thorny gorse bushes could easily snag his fleece.

213

The journalist continued on until he came to the kissing gate which marked the start of the cliffs.

He paused. Ought he to be able to see the beach from here? He couldn't remember the exact configuration. Should he be able to see Rowena in the moonlight? Not if she was sitting still, of course, but she would surely be moving about to stay warm.

The clear sky made for good night vision and a distinctive chill. He shivered; he was glad he had brought his fleece. He would keep it on as long as he could: let Rowena be the first to get undressed. He remembered she seemed to be indifferent to the cold. It was certainly going to be cold in that sea.

So engrossed was Robbie in his own thoughts that he did not notice the figure arising from the bushes behind him. Did not see him at all, until the figure raised a heavy stick and brought it down sharply on his unprotected head.

After that he noticed nothing whatsoever.

CHAPTER 32

George Gilbert had started to drive to Cornwall at teatime, hoping to give Robbie a surprise. Polly's doctor now knew the cause of her illness and, joy of joys, it was treatable. The ambulance had come to take her to the London Hospital for Tropical Diseases and George's nursing duties were at an end.

'She's got to be kept in strict isolation. And you need a break,' the doctor had told her. George hadn't resisted too hard. She was fed up with hearing of Robbie's research over the phone. Her analysis of train schedules and weather data was complete and ready to share.

Her phone had rung on the drive down and she saw the call was from Robbie when she stopped at Taunton Dean Services. She decided not to reply to make her news a complete surprise.

But the call reminded her she needed to sort accommodation. Usually when coming to Cornwall she had her cottage but this time it had been let. After a pause she looked up the notes from her first chat with Robbie. Yes - there it was: the number of the Bettle and Chisel.

She rang and someone answered; plenty of noise in the background. They had just one room left. Great. Later she wondered if that what they told every enquiry.

'What time are you expecting to arrive, madam?'

'I'm on my way from London. It might be a couple of hours.'

'That's all right, we cater for late arrivals - we're open till midnight. Pick up you key at the reception desk. That's behind the main bar.'

If the internal geography of the Bettle and Chisel had been less random, George might have met Robbie as he left for his midnight swim. Subsequent events would then have been very different.

As it was, she was at the rear collecting her keys as the man she had come so far to see hustled out the front door.

George slipped upstairs to check her room. All was fine so reassured, she went down to fetch her suitcase.

There was no-one else about. There were a few more guest rooms nearby but all their doors were shut and any one could have been Robbie's.

She'd had a long drive, no wonder she felt exhausted. George decided it would be enough of a surprise for Robbie to meet her over breakfast.

It was nearly nine o'clock before she awoke, realised the time and hurried down to breakfast. But she'd had still beaten Robbie to the dining room.

She checked with the Polish waitress as she was offered a choice of grilled kippers or full English breakfast. 'No, Mr Robbie he not here yet. It is early for him. By nine thirty he should be here.'

Nine thirty came and went. Even though she made her meal last, George had long finished kippers and coffee and was starting to feel irritated.

At ten o'clock the breakfast room closed and Robbie still had not appeared.

George went to the reception desk and rang the bell. The

same waitress appeared, now in a new role.

'You are after Mr Robbie? We should see if he is in his room asleep. He drinks robustly. Sometimes he has a – what you call it? – an overhang.'

George followed the waitress upstairs and noted Robbie's door. The waitress knocked gently and then much louder, but to no avail.

'Do you have a key? He might be ill or something.'

The waitress had anticipated this possibility. She fumbled with a ring of keys, picked one and opened the door.

The two women stepped quietly into the room. It was clear that Robbie Glendenning had not been there for some time. His bed had not been slept in.

The waitress shrugged her shoulder. 'Maybe he sleep last night with a friend?'

George didn't know how to take this. Was this how Robbie behaved on fieldwork? The waitress was Polish: did she realise what she was implying?

Or maybe she did? George's surprise visit might teach her more than she'd expected.

Then she spotted Robbie's phone. 'Something odd must have happened for him to leave this behind. He's a journalist – takes it everywhere. Could we see if it tells us where he's gone?'

The waitress wasn't in any mood to say no. This was as exciting an incident as she'd seen for some time. She sensed the possibility of a massive row.

George looked at the most recent calls. And there, top of the list, she saw the text message dated yesterday, inviting Robbie to a midnight swim.

Disturbed, she showed it to the waitress. 'Maybe this is where he's gone.'

217

The waitress read the message. 'It's from "Ro". That likely be Rowena. She been showing him round this last week.'

'Has she? Could you be really helpful and tell me where I might find this Rowena please? Maybe I can go and catch Robbie there.'

The waitress missed the nuance in the word "catch". But she wanted to be helpful – after all, George was a guest here too. 'I never been there but I think she lives in cottage in Treligga. That's – '

'I know where Treligga is, thank you,' interrupted George brusquely. 'A few enquiries will find me the house. In fact, I think I'll go and have a word with this Rowena right now.'

George was not normally a reactionary. Her mind liked to remain open to all possibilities for as long as that was possible.

But her mind was a whirl as she drove to Treligga. She had assured herself that Robbie was only a friend. So if he had formed an attachment with someone local, on what basis could she possibly be envious? Was she in fact jealous, and if so what did that say about her emotions? Three years after the death of her husband, during which the ability to love anyone else had seemed lost forever, was she at last feeling a stirring of emotion? Was Robbie far more to her than just a crime-solving colleague? And if he was, would her response be too late?

She managed to maintain an icy calm as she drove to Treligga, asked at one house, then knocked at the cottage of Rowena Gibson.

'Hello,' she began, as a cheerful-looking Rowena came to the door, a large dog trailing behind her. 'I'm a friend of Robbie Glendenning.'

'So am I,' replied Rowena. She looked her visitor up and

down. She saw an attractive woman with curly hair, but her green eyes seemed almost in pain and her body-language shouted stress. 'You must be Robbie's friend from London. George? Robbie told me about you. I'm very pleased to meet you. Come in. Would you like a coffee?'

She was either an outstanding actress or else completely innocent. No way could she have anticipated George's visit. She must be innocent. It was as well, thought George, as she followed her in, that she had not started off making damning accusations.

As the two women sat down together with their coffees, George explained as unemotionally as she could exactly what had brought her to Rowena's.

The younger woman was indignant. 'I wouldn't dream of sending such a message – not to anyone. Robbie's been good company over the last couple of weeks but once he'd mentioned your name I made sure nothing at all happened between us.'

She reached in her handbag. 'Look, here's my phone: there's my number. That won't be where the message came from.'

'In any case I'd be crazy,' she went on, 'to ask a man to go anywhere with me at midnight – least of all a deserted beach. You'd need a wetsuit to go in the sea at midnight. I tried it once: it turns bloody cold once the sun goes down. No way, not even with someone as special - I mean as sweet - as Robbie.'

George had written down the details of the call from Robbie's phone. She consulted her notebook. 'No, you're quite right. It's not the same number at all. Well, there's a puzzle.'

Rowena mused for a moment.

'I admit I took Robbie for a swim down at Tregardock, two weeks ago – I was just being friendly to a fresh face. Well, a fresh male face, to be honest. He'd told me that he'd never been down there and I wanted to show him how remote it was. That was before I knew anything about you.

'But George, if someone else knew about that – and it wasn't any great secret - I suppose they might think it was a way of luring him to a remote spot.'

George was feeling less stressed now, able to think more clearly. 'Except that the message itself would only get him as far as Treligga.'

Rowena was still feeling edgy. 'I didn't see him at all last night, if that's what you're suggesting. I was worn out from taking my dog for a walk. I turned out the lights and went to bed at half past ten. There's not much to do in Treligga.'

George pondered for a moment.

'But would it have been possible for someone to leave a message on your doorway, to send him on to Tregardock? He'd got what he thought was your text message. He'd come to the cottage and see no lights on. Then see the message and think you'd invited him on to Tregardock.'

Rowena could see it was a possibility. She stood up and opened the front door. 'If any message was left here, it would have to be pinned on. There's quite a breeze.'

She started to study the doorway, beam by beam. George joined her. At least it was a well-maintained cottage; there'd not much hope with old paintwork.

'How about the gate?' asked George. 'He'd be bound to see that. And putting it there would make him less likely to come and rouse the house.'

She wandered down to the gate and examined it closely. There was something unusual. 'Is this hole new, do you reckon?'

Rowena joined her. 'That's exactly the sort of hole you'd get from a drawing pin in the gate. I don't remember seeing it before. You might be right.'

'The only message that he'd believe would be one urging him to Tregardock beach. I mean, he thinks he's going down for a swim. That's the nearest spot. Could you show me exactly where you went last week?'

'Sure. But if you don't mind I'll bring Rex. Do you like dogs? He's a Labrador retriever.'

'Aren't they the breed that can follow scents? I don't suppose you've got any item of Robbie's that we could use to set Rex onto the chase?'

'Hang on a minute.' Rowena slipped back inside the house.

'Would this do? It's his walking hat. I was so rude about it when he came here the first time that he refused to wear it again. He must have left it behind.'

A few minutes later an excited Rex had been given a good sniff of the hat – which George agreed was hideous – and was sniffing about in a determined manner. He came out of the gate then set off up the road.

'That's no good. The beach is the other way,' said Rowena in disgust.

'Hold on a minute – how did Robbie get here last night? If he came in his old Stag wouldn't he park it somewhere over there?'

Rex was circling a spot now and woofing loudly. He had found one end of the trail.

Rowena seized the dog's collar and pulled him back to her gate, then urged him in the opposite direction.

For a moment the dog seemed uncertain. Then his tail started to wag and he picked up another scent, this time heading for the path across the fields.

The two women followed him, horribly uncertain of where he would lead them.

CHAPTER 33

Two hours later George Gilbert was sitting in the kitchen, explaining the whole sorry sequence to Dr Brian Southgate, as he got out rolls and cheese for a snack lunch. George had known Brian for many years – he'd been a good friend of her late husband. Brian had been surprised to see her at his door but would still enjoy her company. Coffee, rather than wine, seemed more appropriate.

'This huge dog set off on the track across the fields towards the coast. Then, as Rowena and I got to the kissing gate on the path which overlooks the beach, the dog went into a frenzy. He'd obviously picked up a strong scent again. There was something beside the hedge that he'd latched onto.'

'It wasn't Robbie?' The doctor's professional voice was unnaturally calm.

'That's what we feared, of course. We both looked very carefully. The grass was chewed up all right but there was nothing else that we could see.'

'So you carried on?'

'We tried to. But Rex wouldn't go any further towards the beach. Instead, after a bit, he started going the other way, back towards the road that leads to that other farmhouse.'

Brian could see that though George was outwardly calm she was having difficulty in keeping her emotions under control.

After a moment she went on, 'But the trail didn't lead as far as the farmhouse. It stopped again, this time by the roadside. I

223

could imagine that that, too, would be a good place to park a car.'

'So do you think there was a gang? One to remove his Stag from Treligga, say, another to drive down and kidnap him from beside the kissing gate?'

'But there wouldn't need to be two of them, would there? I mean, what if someone was waiting near the kissing gate, did something – something horrible – to Robbie' – her voice faltered but she swallowed hard and managed to keep going – 'then fished Robbie's car keys out of his pocket, walked back to Treligga, fetched the Stag round and down this other side road, and finally shoved poor Robbie into the boot and drove off.'

'Mm.' Brian mused for a moment. 'All that backward and forward movements would take him at least an hour. But I suppose he had the whole night to do what he wanted. Have you alerted the police?'

'Give me a chance, Brian, I've only just got back to De-labole. The whole thing seemed so bizarre I thought I must be dreaming. I mean, Robbie's just a friendly journalist. He wouldn't knowingly cause offence to anyone. It's not as though he's reporting on drugs or crime. I wondered if it was all a grotesque misunderstanding – some sort of joke that had gone wrong.

'I knew from what he told me on the phone that he'd been talking to you and Alice. So I thought that before I started to involve the police I'd come round and get your take on the whole thing. I was glad to find you at home. By the way, what are you doing here? Shouldn't you be at work?'

Brian explained how he usually came home from lunch. 'The surgery is very close. But given what's happened, I'll take the afternoon off. Fewer people claim to be ill on Fridays anyway, they don't want to muck up their weekends. My colleague will cover. Now, before we get all tangled up with the police, let's just give this whole matter some serious thought.'

It was as well, thought George, that Brian was so calm and disinclined to panic. No doubt it was his professional training – years of coping with emergencies in hospital wards. He'd insisted that she ate some lunch while they considered the whole episode carefully.

'The first point that strikes me,' said the doctor 'is that this was a well thought out plan: subtle but slick. It was a plausible scheme – very likely to work - and it did.'

'It was certainly aimed precisely at Robbie.' George had been thinking about the text message. 'This was no random mugging.'

'We haven't any evidence it was a mugging at all, George. But whatever it was it must have been planned by someone local, who knew all about Tregardock beach. I mean, not many visitors ever go to that stretch of coast.'

'They would need to know Robbie had recently been there, so he'd be willing to go tramping around in the dark again. And also,' she added, 'that Rowena was the girl he'd been with.'

'But given time one could entice Robbie much further away from the area. So doesn't the way it was done suggest that this character was in a considerable hurry?'

'Maybe he feared Robbie would spill the beans about something he'd just discovered? By the way, do you know what interviews he's conducted recently?'

'No idea. But if this character's working against the clock then we've got one detail in our favour,' the doctor pointed out. 'Your surprise presence down in the Bettle has made you - and

225

hence me - aware that something's gone wrong far sooner than he might have expected.'

'How do you mean?'

'Well, Robbie and I had several chats over the last couple of weeks and I saw how he worked. He was acting on his own terms. No-one told him who to interview. There was no place where he had to turn up and would be missed if he didn't. If you hadn't found that phone message it could have been days before anyone had any inkling that he'd disappeared and raised the alarm.'

The thought was disturbing.

George was quick to move onto a consequence.

'If that's our main advantage, we need to keep it that way as long as we can. I'll phone Rowena - ask her not to tell anybody else what we found.'

A further thought came to her. 'I'd also better make sure the Bettle doesn't let anyone into his room. Robbie didn't take his laptop to Treligga. It'll have all his notes. We don't want that to disappear.'

The doctor nodded and then stood up to bring them both an orange from the fruit bowl in the living room.

George seized the chance to ring Rowena.

'Hi. It's me — George.' She could tell from the answering voice that Rowena was very upset too.

'No, I haven't heard anything either,' the analyst responded. 'But I've been thinking. It's really important that you and I don't tell anyone what we suspect and what we've found. Just at present that's our only advantage.'

She explained in more detail. Rowena agreed and the call ended.

As he returned Brian was still thinking furiously.

'Robbie has been putting a lot of effort into identifying the tunnel skeleton. He's been to see lots of families with links to the old railway line. Maybe he learned something important from one of them. So your assertion that he's a "harmless journalist" might not be how he's seen by someone round here.'

'But any crime to do with the skeleton must have happened decades ago.'

'Yes. But if it wasn't just an accident – if there was a killer involved – then that person might not have gone away. He or she might still be around. And they might fear that Robbie was on the way to exposing them.'

George considered. 'In fact, when you put it like that, it's odds on that Robbie's disappearance is directly connected with the skeleton. So where does that take us?'

'Well, let's try to see into this villain's mind. I'm sorry George, but let's fear the worse - just for a moment. We can be sure he doesn't just want to do away with Robbie and have him found quickly. If he did, he'd have left him in the bushes at the cliff top. But if he had done that, from how you described it, Rowena's dog would have found him.'

'It's obvious, Brian, such a blatantly violent act would alert the police. They'd be here in droves, searching everywhere. No telling what they'd find. Our villain couldn't be sure that wouldn't lead to him or her being arrested.'

'Alright. So he needs somewhere to hide Robbie that he can reach in the limited hours of the night.'

'On the same logic, Brian, it would need to be somewhere where Robbie's not going to be found very quickly.'

'Maybe the assailant's got an escape plan to leave the area, that with a bit of time he can then put into practice?'

'Brian, this chap must be quite old, mustn't he? I don't know how quickly the tunnel skeleton decayed, but even if it's only thirty years ago then he must be well over fifty. Well, how many body-sized hiding places can a fifty year old find at short notice?'

'Unless he lived in the back of beyond and had a secret cellar it wouldn't make much sense for him to use his own house.'

There was silence for a few minutes.

It was Brian who came up with the suggestion. 'I can think of one place to hide a body that's not far from here, which might not be looked at for quite a while. And it's also somewhere this particular villain would know intimately – so he might not mind going there in the middle of the night.'

He paused, smiling, to give her chance to catch up. But George looked merely puzzled.

A few clues might help. 'Can you follow my train of thought? Am I on the right track?'

'Oh,' George put her hands to her face. 'You're not thinking of the Trelill tunnel? He surely wouldn't dare?'

'It would take some nerve. But remember, the skeleton that was found had lain undiscovered for several decades. Unless the cycle trail wins the Green Tourist Award and the tunnel becomes a regular thoroughfare it could be left for many more. The villain might just gamble that the cyclists don't win – the stigma of the skeleton is a bit of an obstacle, after all. He might well be right. As for the police, well, they've examined it carefully – why should they go back?'

George pondered for a while. 'OK, it's a long shot, but I can't think of anything else. So you think we should ring the police and ask them to look?'

'Gracious no, it would take ages to jump through all the hoops which the police would raise before they could take decisive action like that. No, I was thinking of a much more direct approach.'

'I don't know what you mean.'

'What I had in mind was this. Robbie and I found a path in there last Saturday so I know the way – at least in daylight. And most of the bits and pieces we would need are still in my car.'

'OK. I'm game to try anything that might help find Robbie. But if this doesn't succeed then we must alert the police.'

'Fair enough. But time is not on our side. Have you finished your lunch? It would be good if we went right away.'

As the two drove over to the point where he and Robbie had parked to enter the tunnel a week before, Brian described the process he and Robbie had gone through to by-pass the security camera and enter the tunnel.

George tried to listen but did not say much. In truth she was not really taking much in. A fear was gnawing in her stomach as to what they were going to find.

Brian was in a hurry now. He parked the car, hastily equipped them both with jackets and helmets and put his emergency medical bag inside his rucksack. Then he led George onto the old railway embankment. Neither of them felt like talking as they followed the old track through the wood and up to the mouth of the tunnel.

Brian quickly looked for the police camera. It was still in place, the police must still be treating the tunnel as a potential crime scene. A week ago he and Robbie had tilted it back after they got out, so it recorded the entrance fencing once more. This time he'd brought a folding stool. Using this it took him only a minute to reach up and tilt it, slowly and harmlessly, till it pointed away to the right hand side.

Then he and George scrambled through the gap in the fencing on the left and into the tunnel.

'I need to pace it from here. Robbie reckoned it was two hundred and thirty yards.' Brian strode carefully forwards.

George followed him, seeing the tunnel in her torch light but not really caring, wondering what they would find.

All too soon they reached the alcove with the narrow opening at the rear.

'I'd better go in first,' said Brian. George was about to protest and then realised he was trying to protect her. He must have encountered death often enough during his medical career.

'I'll wait outside, in the main tunnel, till you give me a call.'

For a long, long minute there was an agonising silence.

Then came a shout from the inner cavern. 'Robbie's in here, George. And he's still alive. Not in the best of health but still alive. And just about conscious. Come on, squeeze in. I'm sure he'd appreciate a hug.'

CHAPTER 34

The attack on Robbie Glendenning certainly seemed to have galvanised the local police into action, thought Brian, as he drove back from Bodmin Police Station later that day.

A fifty-year old skeleton in a long-abandoned tunnel might be suspicious, but without ancillary clues on who he was and how he had died it was never going to command much police time. A violent assault on a senior journalist, while he was innocently overlooking Cornish cliffs, was something else altogether.

Brian had stayed to give Robbie what medical treatment he could inside the tunnel. Meanwhile George, after seeing her friend briefly, had hastened back to the mouth of the tunnel and called up the emergency services.

It had taken an ambulance half an hour to reach Trelill from Bodmin and a further half hour before the stretcher was ma-noeuvred down the hillside and then along to the patient within the tunnel. An hour later the badly injured journalist was in Intensive Care in the Royal Cornwall Hospital in Truro. George had accompanied him on the alarm-blaring, high-speed journey.

Robbie had now slumped back into unconsciousness but the medical staff told her to relax: her friend was in the best place possible.

The journalist had a severe head injury and was also dehy-drated – he'd probably drunk nothing since the previous eve-ning. Nonetheless, the medical team were confident that sooner or later he was going to regain consciousness.

George didn't share their certainty and wondered if this was a professional front for her benefit. A local policeman from Truro had also been assigned to the case and was sitting beside her. He, too, expected to wait for some time.

Brian had been interrogated at length by Inspector Lambourn. He had told the policeman what George Gilbert had told him over lunch of the known events of the previous twenty four hours and her preliminary search down to Treligga and Tregardock. Lambourn had immediately sent a Scene of Crime team down to the cliff top but they hadn't found anything useful.

The policeman asked him for George's details. 'It's an odd name for a woman,' he muttered as he wrote them down.

'Her parents were Beatles' fans. Their names were John and Paula,' explained Brian by way of explanation.

'The poor kid's lucky she wasn't called Ringo,' the policeman muttered. He noted that he already had a record of Rowena's address from his interview with her the week before.

Brian had gone on to explain the line of reasoning which had led him and George to explore the railway tunnel in search of Robbie.

'We knew it was a long shot. But it seemed to us that the assault must be linked somehow or another to the interviews Robbie had been doing and to the skeleton in the tunnel. That was the one place we could think of where the assailant might put a second body, given he didn't have much time.'

'But if it hadn't been for this George' - his face wrinkled with the nominal oddity - 'coming down unexpectedly late last night, Robbie might not have been missed for a week. How do you mean, "didn't have much time"?'

'We thought about it like this. From the timing of the phone message the assault couldn't have happened before half past twelve. Assuming he was working alone, the villain then had to fetch Robbie's car round from Treligga to the cliff-top, ready to take him away. By now it would be at least two am. This time of year it's light by five. That would only leave his attacker two or three hours of darkness. I knew where the tunnel was. It was suitably close, less than ten miles away and it could be reached in time. So George and I decided it was worth having a look.'

The policeman looked unconvinced. Robbie might have told his friend where it was but how did he know the way into the tunnel? And why had his entrance not shown up on the security camera? Lambourn's doubts about the authenticity of the body-in-the-tunnel story seemed about to re-surface.

'But you must agree that the two cases are connected?' Brian urged him, sensing his doubts.

Lambourn did not like witnesses doing his thinking for him and made no comment.

Instead, he asked for details of Robbie's car, which had disappeared from the scene.

'I don't know its number. But it was a Triumph Stag. Fairly old, the colour was dark green.'

Brian also gave the policeman Robbie's Bristol address. George had passed this on while the stretcher was being loaded.

'Will that be enough for the DVLA database to give his car number?'

It was a reasonable question but the policeman was unwilling to give anything away.

Eventually the interview drew to a close and Brian was free to return to Delabole.

As far as the doctor could see, until Robbie was able to talk, finding his car was the one action the police could pursue. Of course, no-one knew what Robbie might be able to tell them once he'd recovered consciousness. He might even have seen his assailant. When he got home he would ring George to find out if there was any change in his condition. He could only hope the journalist had remembered some vital detail of his attack.

There was one other avenue open to the police and Inspector Lambourn had spotted it. To pursue it he needed the number of the caller who had left the crucial text message on Robbie's phone the evening before.

After a moment's thought, he rang the Police Station in Truro and was put through to the policeman stationed by Robbie's bedside.

'Any change in his condition?'

'I'm afraid not, sir. He's still unconscious. Could be hours or maybe days. I'm famished, sir. Do we need a continuous guard all that time?'

'At least for the moment. Think of it as a diet. We'll take stock tomorrow morning. But there's one thing that might help resolve things. Is there a woman there with him?'

'George Gilbert? Yes – do you want a word with her?' He handed over his phone.

'Mrs Gilbert? Your friend Dr Brian Southgate has told me most of what happened earlier on today. He's gone back to Delabole now. But there's one question I forgot to ask him which you might be able to answer.'

'Fire away. I'll do anything I can to help catch whoever did this.'

'Well, do you know what happened to Mr Glendenning's

phone? In particular, I'm after the number of the caller that left the explosive text message – the one that led him down to the coast.'

'As far as I know his phone is still in his locked room at the Bettle. I told the management to make sure they kept it locked. But I did make a note of the number – hang on a minute.' She reached for her handbag, flipped through her notebook and read it out.

'Thank you very much. That's very efficient. I'll need to interview you too, but that doesn't have to be this evening.'

Early that evening, Mary Tavistock's doorbell rang. She was surprised to find two young-looking police officers standing outside her cottage in St Teath. She'd not seen either of them before.

'Mrs Tavistock? Good evening. Is your husband in, please?'

'I'm afraid he's out. He's gone for a drink at the White Hart. It's the weekly darts contest. Can I help?'

But her help was not what the policeman was after. Instead he turned, had a brief word with his female colleague and then strode the few dozen yards down the road to the White Hart Inn.

He had been told to make a quiet detention but it looked as if that might not be possible.

The darts competition had just begun. The policeman sought guidance from the barman. Mr Tavistock was pointed out to him. He was an older man with curly grey hair and a short beard, looking fit and healthy. He was sitting at a table with several men of a similar age.

'Excuse me, sir. Are you Mr Archie Tavistock?'

'Yes that's right, Officer. Is something the matter? Has my

235

dog got loose again? Or have you come about my Council Tax arrears?'

A more serious thought occurred to him. 'Surely Mary hasn't been taken ill – she was alright when I left her half an hour ago.'

'It would be better if we had a word outside, sir.'

A few minutes later those watching through the windows of the Inn, including several of the darts team, were somewhat surprised to see Archie Tavistock being encouraged into the back of the police car, which then drove swiftly away.

CHAPTER 35

It was some time since Inspector Lambourn had personally conducted a serious crime interview. There was more than one piece of evidence pointing towards Archie Tavistock, but there were also plenty of gaps – and the Inspector knew he must handle it all very carefully.

Tavistock had been left to fester in one of the interview rooms for half an hour when he arrived with just an unsweetened cup of machine coffee for company. Lambourn had noticed that he walked in with a slight limp.

The policeman had deliberately left him to smoulder; it might help make him lose some self-control.

'Good evening, sir. Thank you for coming in.'

'I didn't have much bloody choice, did I? Your plods managed to barge in on the darts competition with St Tudy's. It's a key match, but they wouldn't even let me take my turn before they brought me along here. I argued, but they said all this community-friendly policing was no longer cost-effective and they'd been told to cut it out. They'd better be ready to take me back again when we've finished.'

He'd been brought from the pub early in the evening but he must have drunk a pint before he came. Good, thought the policeman, that might help loosen his tongue.

'Can I ask, sir, how you spent yesterday evening?'

'The way I usually spend my evenings, I should think. At my age the days all seem very similar – they blur together. I was either at home with my wife or in the White Hart, pondering the injustices in the world. Who will we shoot first come the revolution? I suppose this visit will at least give me more material.'

Inspector Lambourn could guess who might be top of his new list.

'Well, one of my officers talked to your wife as you were being brought here. She said that on Thursday you were at home all evening.'

'Well, there you are then. I told you I was at home or in the pub.'

'OK, let's leave that for a moment. Can you tell me your car make and number?'

'It's a dark red Vauxhall Astra. AGH 756E. It's a bit battered though – like me, it's seen better days. Hey, is this about some sort of road accident?'

'I'll ask the questions if you don't mind, sir. And where is that car at the moment?'

'As far as I know it's parked next to my cottage in St Teath. Is this about car insurance? You see -'

'I haven't invited you here, sir, to talk about car insurance.'

There was a pause whilst the Inspector glanced down at his notes and decided on his next question.

'Have ever met a journalist that's been working around the Delabole area recently – Mr Robbie Glendenning?'

'A rather tubby man that looks like he never combs his hair?'

'I'm not sure he would like that description, but – yes – it sounds like you've at least seen him.'

'I've met him for an interview. That's him interviewing me, you understand, not the other way around.' Tavistock started to laugh and then realised the policeman wasn't taking it as a joke.

'And when was that, sir?'

'A few days ago. Tuesday afternoon, it would be. He wanted to talk about this Arresting Crime bid we're trying to get together.'

'And was the interview amicable?'

'Very friendly. The main point of contention was when he started asking about how our scheme could contribute to a lower carbon economy.'

'And how did you answer that?'

'I told him we'd already been talking to the local Wind Farm. They've got plenty of land and a spare building but they don't get many visitors. The idea we've been working on is that we'd build some sort of crime scene inside their annexe. It would be an extra reason for tourists to come along - a bit like the Courtroom Experience in Bodmin. All we really need is a good, juicy crime. I don't suppose you've got any, have you?'

'I'll ask the questions, sir. That'll make it more efficient. It's already quite late.' He checked his notes.

'So Glendenning didn't talk to you about the old railway tunnel?'

'No, that's the competing bid you're thinking of, creating a new cycle trail. He and I just talked about crime – as it were.'

'Do you have any first-hand memories of the old railway line?'

'What is this – This Is Your Life, Archie Tavistock? I've lived around here all my life. Of course I remember the old railway – but I wasn't sorry when it was shut down. Too much smoke and noise, I'd say.'

The policeman glanced down at his notes again.

'Going back to your car, sir, I wonder if you could explain to me why it should have been seen last night, parked beside the main road that runs from Delabole to Polzeath, just past the

239

turn off to Treligga?'

Tavistock looked rather uncomfortable. There was silence in the room.

'Well?'

'It's like this, Officer. My wife told you I was at home all evening. Well, that's the truth as far as she knows. See, I promised I'd stay in all evening. I was supposed to be waiting in for a phone call from our family in Bournemouth. They're expecting their first baby any day now. Mary had insisted they told us soon as there was any news. But then she had to go over to stay with her aunt in Plymouth because she'd suffered a fall. So I said I'd stay in all evening and wait for the call.'

'Yes?'

'But after she'd gone I remembered. I'd agreed with my friend that if it was fine it'd be a good night to go sea fishing. It was practically full moon.'

'So why did that lead to your car being left on the main road along from Delabole?'

'Well, we'd decided to go to the small cove on the coast down past Dannonchapel. That's about a mile on from Tregardock Beach. You can get to it across the fields. It's a couple of miles from the road but it's remote and peaceful once you reach it. Under a full moon it's almost magical.'

'So you went fishing with your friend? Could you tell me his name, please?'

'It's Tom – Tom Wellbeloved from Treknow. I'm afraid that he didn't turn up. He rang me on my landline about eleven to say that he was still at the Port William in Trebarwith Strand but he'd had too much to drink and didn't fancy coming out on the cliffs afterwards. So I went fishing on my own.'

Again there was a pause whilst the policeman pondered his

next line of questions.

'Do you have a mobile phone, sir?'

'Of course. I'm not daft you know. My wife insists I take it with me for safety whenever I go anywhere near the edge of the cliffs.'

'Could I see it please?'

Tavistock felt in one jacket pocket and then the other. He stood up and reached round to the back pocket of his trousers. Then he looked irritated. 'That's odd, it must have slipped out. I'm afraid I seem to have lost it.'

'Lost it, eh? That is a pity. I'd like you to try really hard with this next one, sir. When did you last use it?'

There was a longer pause. 'I certainly had it on Tuesday lunchtime. I remember using it while I was in the pub to book myself a doctor's appointment. Since then - let me see. I was expecting my wife to contact me on Thursday evening from Plymouth. But she didn't – or at least, I didn't take any such call. But if I'd lost my phone I suppose that would explain why she tried but couldn't get through. We had a bit of an argument about that earlier today.'

Tavistock concluded, 'The best answer I can give to your question is sometime between Tuesday afternoon and Thursday evening.'

Lambourn wasn't sure where to go next. These were more convincing answers than he'd been expecting. Was this because Tavistock was innocent – or because he knew these questions would be coming and had rehearsed a very clever line of answers?

'Another question, sir. Do you ever use a walking stick to help you cope with your limp?'

'Sometimes. But I don't take it with me when I go fishing, if that's what you're wondering. It would get in the way – tangled up with my rod and so on.' Tavistock started to look really fed up. 'Are there any more deformities you want to question me on?'

'I also notice that you've got a plaster on your left hand. What's the reason for that?'

'I fell against the rocks while I was fishing last night. I badly scratched my hand. The plaster's just there to protect it for a day or two.'

The policeman continued to ask variants of these questions without learning anything more. In truth it was only the phone number that was remotely decisive. He started to wonder if there was any chance that Mrs Gilbert had copied the phone number down wrongly from Glendenning's phone. For a fleeting moment he wondered about driving over to Delabole to seize the journalist's phone from the Bettle and Chisel. But it was very late. It could wait until tomorrow.

On balance Lambourn decided he needed more evidence before he could arrest Tavistock. Maybe that would be forth-coming once Glendenning had recovered consciousness.

In the meantime he warned the man that he might want to talk to him again. On no account should he go away. He then offered him the office phone to call for a lift home. After all, he no longer had his mobile – apparently.

CHAPTER 36

Down in the Royal Cornwall Hospital in Truro the injured journalist remained unconscious throughout Friday night. Without telling an outright lie, George Gilbert implied she was some sort of relative. She was allowed to get what rest she could while sitting in an easy chair in the visitors' lounge.

In truth, given the traumas of the day, she might not have slept well even in her own bed.

On Saturday morning the ward sister declared there was no change. George scurried away and found a cafe offering a cooked breakfast. She'd not eaten since the previous lunchtime. A large helping of bacon and eggs started to revive her.

When she got back two senior medics were assessing Robbie behind the movable curtain. The analyst waited anxiously for their verdict.

'At least he's no worse,' said the consultant as he emerged from the curtain. 'He's taken a severe blow to the head but the X-rays show that, mercifully, the skull isn't fractured.'

'How long will he be unconscious?' asked George.

'You should be thankful he's got a hard head. Chances are he'll come out of the coma in the next forty eight hours.' The consultant also explained there were also effects on his body from his ordeal, scratching and so on, but these were not long-term injuries.

It was fortunate, thought George, that her friend had not been left in the tunnel without fluid for another day. The drip on his arm meant that he was being gradually re-hydrated. From now on it was an exercise in patience.

As soon as she could George phoned Brian and Alice Southgate to give them the latest prognosis and to find out their news.

Brian asserted that he and Alice intended to drive over to Truro that afternoon. If Robbie had recovered consciousness they could greet him – even if only briefly. If he had not then he urged her to come back with them to Delabole. 'You'll be more use later on,' he said, 'if you've had some proper rest yourself.'

Brian put two further points. 'Once you're back in Delabole you'll have your own car again. Leave your phone number with the ward. You can be back in Truro within an hour of Robbie recovering consciousness. The other thing, Alice wondered, is: would you like to give up on the Bettle and come and stay with us? We've got plenty of room and we'd love to have you.'

Sadly there had been no change in Robbie's condition when the pair arrived. George was dozing, making the most of the chair in the visitors' room. The Truro policeman, who had seized another chair, looked bored out of his mind.

Brian introduced himself to the medical staff – it was useful being a doctor. He made sure they had his number so they could report any change to him as well as to George. There seemed nothing else the trio could do so they headed back to Delabole.

Alice was driving. Brian enlivened the journey by bringing George up to date on their discussions with Robbie over the past fortnight. He recounted their discovery of the metal discs in the cavern, the realisation that they were old coins, the insight that they had probably been used to weight down a curtain and the conjecture that the curtain had been used to cover the entrance to the cavern from the tunnel.

'All this must be on Robbie's laptop,' George reflected wistfully. 'It's a pity we haven't got access. That would tell us who else he interviewed this last week and his latest thinking. After all, it was because someone in Delabole feared he knew too much that he's where he is now.'

'By now the police will have seized it,' asserted Alice. 'It's twenty four hours since Robbie was found and the police were alerted. Cyber-crime experts will be working out the password so they can get into it.'

'But they won't find it in his room,' replied George. 'I rang the landlord yesterday morning - as soon as Rowena and I realised there was something wrong. I asked him to put Robbie's valuables into a safe and to say nothing to anyone. I was amazed to learn they had a safe at the pub, to be honest.'

'Delabole's a working village,' explained Brian. 'Tradesmen often stay in the Bettle but we've no bank. So they might turn up with cash they've just been paid with. They'd want to keep it somewhere more secure than their own room.'

Brian paused. 'So his laptop will still be in the safe. The landlord might hand it back to you, me and Alice if we all turn up together. We're a respectable bunch of local citizens and he knows us all. We mustn't give any hint that Robbie's been found, but we might imply that it could help us find him.

'But we don't know Robbie's password either,' objected Alice.

'I deal with computers all the time,' replied George. 'I gave Robbie a few tips when we met in Looe on how to make a password more secure. I don't know how much he's changed it but I can make an informed guess.'

That evening George sat at Brian's desk trying to work out the missing password on Robbie's computer while Alice cooked lasagne for their supper. Brian had been sent to the Spar to buy an extra bottle of wine.

The conversation at the Bettle had gone much as Brian had predicted. No difficulty had been raised on handing over Robbie's laptop to the three of them. It helped that Brian had paid the rent on Robbie's room for a further week.

But he'd asked the landlord to install an extra padlock on his door. 'You're open many hours a day. Your staff can't be everywhere. You wouldn't want to risk someone forcing the door and rifling his belongings.'

Brian also knew, though he had not told the landlord, that the key to his room was no longer in Robbie's possession. If his assailant had it, the doctor thought it unlikely he would risk coming to search the room. Nonetheless he wanted to eliminate the risk altogether.

George had handed in her key. She hadn't said where she was going but the pub was used to short-term stays. A low-profile exit would ruffle no feathers.

Now she scowled at her friend's laptop. When they'd talked a year ago she had encouraged him to combine letters and numbers – for example george2009. He must have updated it since. But to her amazement she found that he hadn't. Whatever he'd intended, his laptop was now open for business.

She was just about to see how Robbie had organised his notes when Alice called her to supper.

Over the meal, Alice told George about the bid to turn the

North Cornwall Railway into a cycle trail up from Wadebridge.

'That would interest visitors staying in my cottage in Tre-know,' George observed. 'Especially if a cycle hire shop started up in Delabole. They'd be able to cycle all the way down to Wadebridge.'

'Coming back would be a strain,' commented Brian. 'Uphill all the way. I'm not sure I'd fancy that.'

'Maybe you'd need a special deal, whereby a minibus and trailer would be provided in Wadebridge to bring them and the bikes back again?'

'You mean: come to Delabole, the tourist centre of North Cornwall? It would need to expand to make that true. There's not one teashop in the village.'

'But that's a matter of supply and demand. A steady stream of tourists and one or two teashops would soon spring up. It only takes a large front room in a cottage on the main street. After all, they've several like that in Port Isaac.'

The mention of Port Isaac aroused opinions on parking. It was a relief to talk about something other than crime.

Once the meal was over George showed them the documents folders on Robbie's laptop. 'His recent notes will be kept here – "green_tourist_award"'. She flipped it open. 'Look, here are his interview notes. Each one is entitled "notes_" followed by the name of the person interviewed.

'He's done a lot of interviews,' commented Alice. 'We encouraged him to meet people who knew something about the old railway. He's done well to find that many. We hoped it might help turn the trail into living history.'

George scanned down the list. 'None of these names means anything to me. Can either of you help?'

'I know that one,' said Alice, pointing at the screen. 'Miss

Trevelyan is a former head teacher. She ran the village school in the 1960s and 70s. Look, she's been interviewed twice – once earlier this week. Has he been to see anyone else more than once? I wonder what made her so popular?'

George spent the rest of Saturday evening reading through the notes. Even without any complication from the skeleton, there seemed to be the basis for some interesting articles.

Another document was entitled "ideas". This contained thoughts about the skeleton – notably on its dates. It was good to have the arguments about dates, based on the coins and the use of araldite, set down clearly.

Ideas on dates reminded her of something she'd brought down to show Robbie. 'There was one piece of research Robbie asked me to do about trains and weather.'

'Let's hear it,' said Brian. He was sitting at the far end of the settee, reading a dull looking medical journal.

'Well, somehow or other Robbie unearthed a weather archive for the last century in Padstow. He asked me to see if there were any periods when the weather was so bad that the trains didn't run at all.'

'The weather here is not too severe,' said Alice. She knew all about this: the subject was on the primary school syllabus. 'If it snows in Scotland it doesn't rate a mention, but a light flurry in London is the main news of the day. Snow there can disrupt travel for days.'

'But I've been working through this archive. It showed there were one or two periods when it did snow here,' commented George. 'For example, in the cold winter of 1947, there was plenty of snow – and more recently in 1963.'

'You can't expect us to remember that far back – they're

both before any of us were born,' responded Alice.

'Yes, but I was only looking during the time the railway was operating: it closed down in 1967. Robbie suggested I began with the period after the war.'

'It seems clear from the coins that the skeleton can't have been put there before 1950,' said Brian.

'OK, we'll leave out 1947 as well. Now I've got the daily weather in this part of the world. The 1963 bad weather actually began in late 1962. It snowed on Christmas Eve and didn't clear away until March.'

'The railways wouldn't be closed for that long,' challenged Brian. 'The snowplough isn't a modern invention.'

'No. But it's interesting to put the weather data alongside the log kept at St Kew during the 50s and 60s. Harold noted the time every train arrived and left his station. It turns out that trains stopped running between Christmas Eve 1962 and New Year's Day 1963. And if the trains weren't running the track maintenance wouldn't operate either.'

'If you were going to be without trains round here, I guess the Christmas holidays would be the best time for it to happen,' observed Alice.

'I'd say that would be the worst: all those poor folk on holiday, not able to get home,' responded Brian.

George didn't want to precipitate a row. 'Anyway, that's when they stopped. I was going to ask Robbie if that was a period during which the skeleton could have been dumped and the curtain installed.'

'Those dates would fit the dating on the skeleton,' enthused Brian. 'My expert reckoned fifty years old. 1962 would be a better fit than the 1970s.'

'One late interview suggests Robbie's ideas were moving in

that direction. Look.' George fiddled with the computer so it displayed the interview notes.

'With Betsy Chalkpit last Tuesday - the lineman's daughter. It's a comment she makes about the weird roar that was heard occasionally in the tunnel. She heard it in 1960, said it sounded like an oncoming train.'

Neither Brian nor Alice had heard this detail. George was encouraged to continue.

'Betsy also said that her father – the lineman here in the 1960s – asserted that the roar died down as the line reached its closing days.

'That might just have been his imagination. But just suppose that the roar was linked not to the wind through the tunnel, but rather to it gusting down the ventilation shaft and out through the cavern entrance?'

'In that case,' said Brian, 'the curtain glued across the entrance would stifle the roar - so it wouldn't happen after Christmas 1962.'

Alice voiced a doubt. 'But we know the roar was heard again in 1990. It was heard by Geri and her friends, the night when they first found the skeleton. She told me so herself.'

'That's alright. By 1990 the curtain must have disintegrated or Geri wouldn't even have seen the cavern. Once the curtain had gone the roar would happen again – probably from some time in the 1980s. It's all starting to fit.'

250

CHAPTER 37

There was still no news from Truro about Robbie by Sunday morning. Brian phoned the Intensive Care ward but learned there was no change. 'They said we just needed to be patient,' he told the others over breakfast.

Robbie's lack of progress made George even keener to "do something". Brian was anxious to dampen her zeal.

'It's only two days ago that whoever is behind this – and remember, we think that it's someone local - lured and then attacked Robbie. Almost killed him outright then left him to die in a remote tunnel. If they think that we know as much as he did they'll probably come for us too.'

'But Robbie didn't realise he was in danger,' replied George. 'He put himself at risk by wandering about on his own on the cliffs at midnight. Surely, in broad daylight in the middle of Delabole, we'll all be perfectly safe?'

'Hm. What do you want to do, anyway?'

'I was thinking of re-visiting the people Robbie saw last week. It must be something one of them said that put him in danger. Maybe if I can replay the interview the same insight will come up.'

'It might be what Robbie said to the person that did the damage. Made them aware of his thinking. Either way they're key people. I'm surprised the police haven't been round to check what they were doing on Thursday evening.'

'But until we hand over Robbie's laptop or he recovers

consciousness the police don't know who he went to see.'

'And once they start tramping about the village his attacker will be given a clue that Robbie's been found and is still alive,' added Alice. 'Right now the brute will be thinking they've got away with it.'

'Hm. Who did you plan to go and see, George?'

'One of the last people Robbie saw was Owen Harris over in St Teath. He's the chair of the Arresting Crime bid.'

'George, you're not seeing him on your own. He's probably completely innocent, but he's a strong man.'

'OK, what about Miss Trevelyan? Robbie went to see her twice. I gather from his notes that she's ancient: she must be harmless. I've hardly been seen around the village so the attacker won't know who I am. And for your peace of mind I'll drive there so I can't be nobbled on the way. If Alice rings up to make the appointment beforehand, Miss Trevelyan will know that you both know that I'm there. Surely that's safe enough?'

Eventually, after a long argument, George won. Alice rang Miss Trevelyan, who invited George round for coffee later that morning.

In the meantime George immersed herself in Robbie's notes of the previous meetings and tried to work out her best line of questioning.

Miss Trevelyan was as pleased to see George Gilbert as she had been to see Robbie on his earlier visits.

'You're George. Alice tells me you're a friend of Robbie's. She said he wasn't very well – I hope he's soon better. Do come in, my dear. It looks like rain. Now, at this time of day would you prefer tea or coffee?'

George sat in the lounge whilst her host bustled about

making coffee. She had not brought her computer but made sure her notebook was to hand.

'Thank you for seeing me so quickly,' she began, when Miss Trevelyan returned with a coffee tray and placed it on the table between them.

'Normally Sunday morning would be a bad time to catch me. I attend the Anglican Church in St Teath. But right now there's an interregnum.'

George looked puzzled. The former head was quick to see that she needed less technical language.

'I mean, the church is between vicars. The last one left in December and they're still busy choosing her successor. It often takes a year. In the meantime the services are led by the vicar from St Endellion, but he only comes every fortnight. Today's the week when there are no services.'

George didn't care much about ecclesiastical niceties. She glanced at her notebook to check the first topic she wished to cover.

'I'm here to try and add to Robbie Glendenning's inquiries about the North Cornwall Line. I'm afraid he's not around at the moment.'

'That's right, Mr Glendenning was trying to learn more of its history to help with the bid. Wouldn't it be good if the line was restored as a cycle trail?'

'Well, it might help me let my holiday cottage down in Treknow.'

'Oh, you've got a cottage here – so you're local too,' the old lady smiled.

'I let it occasionally but mostly I use it to get away from London.'

'And what do you do there?'

253

George explained something of her work and then moved on to her agenda for the day. 'One of the things Robbie and I are interested in is the times when the line was closed – for example, due to severe weather.'

'It wasn't often bad enough to stop the trains in Cornwall. They were too vital to life here – livestock as well as people. Trains were often delayed but rarely cancelled. The odd train might not run, but it would be rare for there to be no traffic at all.'

'How about the severe winter of 1963?'

'Ah, now that might be the exception. Everyone struggled then. It was cold all over the country, of course.'

She mused for a moment. 'In 1963 my school had to close for two weeks at the start of January: half the pupils couldn't get in – the roads were too icy. They didn't bother to grit round here. But the rest of us battled through – it was exhilarating. Many of the children arrived on sledges.'

'I think Robbie borrowed some of your Railway Archives. Could you lend me the one for 1962-3?'

'Of course, my dear. As long as you sign it out. I'll get it when we've finished talking. But before I fetch it, tell me a bit more about yourself. For example, how close are you to Robbie Glendenning? He was very discreet – didn't tell me much about you. Is he your fiancé or anything?'

George was rather taken aback. She hadn't expected a discussion this personal. But Miss Trevelyan was an old lady who lived on her own and was probably quite lonely; she had certainly been very supportive to Robbie.

'We met a couple of years ago in Looe,' she began. 'Trouble is, we're both so busy that we don't have much time to spend together. And recently my daughter Polly's been very ill so I've had to stay home looking after her.'

Miss Trevelyan pondered. 'Does the existence of a daughter mean you've had a partner before?'

An intimate question asked in a gentle way. George felt no embarrassment.

'I married Mark when I left University – I was twenty two. Polly came along shortly after. We loved her to bits but we never had any more children. We were both so busy. Mark was on business abroad when he was killed in a plane crash in 2008. I still miss him a lot.' She covered her face to hide her sorrow.

The older lady could see that she was upset. 'I'm sorry, my dear. It was very rude of me to probe into your private life before I knew you. I'd never imagined there would be so much sadness. It's just that I'd met Robbie, and he and you seemed so well-matched to one another . . .'

'That's alright. You're probably right about Robbie. We just need some encouragement – maybe from someone older who knows us both.'

George paused for a moment. Was this the opportunity she had hoped for to learn more about Miss Trevelyan?

'Could I ask a personal question in return? I understand you've lived around here all your life. Was there ever anybody you had a special relationship with?'

'Goodness me. I've not been asked questions like that for half a century.' Her face softened as she gave a subdued smile. 'You've been honest with me though so it's only fair that I'm honest with you. There once was a young man whom I hoped to spend the rest of my life with. We did spend time together – it started in the summer of 1961. He was a little younger than me but that didn't matter. But he had big rows inside his family. In the end he couldn't stand it anymore and set off for the

255

United States. I never saw him again.'

'He never returned? Oh, how tragic. Miss Trevelyan, I'm so sorry. Now we've both accidentally barged into one another's innermost secrets.'

The older lady was still replaying the events of the 1960s. 'It was even worse than that. If he'd stayed there and met someone else I could perhaps eventually have understood. But it wasn't as easy as that. He was killed in a car crash and came home in a coffin. He left as a handsome young man and returned in a box – he's buried in St Teath's churchyard. I was well over thirty by then. It put me off seeking any more relationships.'

'Miss Trevelyan, "well over thirty" is no age to settle for being single. I'm forty myself, and, as you've discerned, Robbie and I have hopes of making a go of it – if we can ever manage to coordinate our work patterns.'

'If one could live life again, George, there are lots of things we might change. At the time the grief overwhelmed me. But I couldn't talk it over with anyone. His family didn't even invite me to the funeral.

'Still, being head teacher at Delabole was more than a full-time job. It gave me a great deal of pleasure, of a rather different sort. So take note, my dear, we should always be positive about the hand that life deals us.'

George Gilbert returned to the Southgate's for lunch aware there was still a mystery to solve but feeling that she was making progress. A few more pieces of the jigsaw had been exposed, even if it was not yet obvious where they fitted.

'After lunch, I'd like to go down to that churchyard in St Teath's. Miss Trevelyan wouldn't tell me the name of her young man, but there can't be that many gravestones for young men buried in the mid 1960s.'

Brian was unsympathetic. 'You're not wandering about a deserted graveyard on your own – even if it's just a couple of miles away. Robbie's attacker is around somewhere. I'm sorry but you'll have to put up with one of us coming with you.'

This time George did not argue too strongly. The brooding presence of an evil force was starting to grip her imagination.

Over lunch George told her hosts about her conversation with Miss Trevelyan. The story of her unconsummated romance was not one that they had heard before, despite both living in the village for many years.

'You've done well to winkle that out of her,' said Alice. 'She must really like you. Re-directed love perhaps helps to explain why she was such a dedicated head teacher for so many years. I'm pretty committed to the school, but I still manage to make sure I've something left over for Brian.'

Her husband gave a smile of appreciation.

After lunch, while Alice settled down to consider some more school reports, Brian drove George down to St Teath. The dark clouds heading towards them suggested a downpour was imminent. Neither had been in the churchyard before. They were dismayed how far it stretched.

'A lot of people have died here,' observed Brian.

'They've had many centuries to do so.'

A mid-1960s gravestone would appear strikingly more modern than ones from earlier times. They split up, so they could walk slowly past different groups of graves, while staying within sight of one another.

The threatened rain had just started to fall when they found an isolated grave on the far edge of the graveyard. There were no flowers nearby or any other indication that it had been recently visited. It looked almost abandoned.

'"Neville Harris, 1934-1964" read George. 'This must be the one. It's the only one we've found for 1964. Poor chap: he was only twenty nine. I wonder if he was any relation of the Owen Harris I read about?'

As she spoke a streak of lightning flashed down beside the graveyard, followed almost at once by a deafening roar of thunder. Simultaneously the rain started to pelt down.

'Quick, into the porch,' urged Brian. The pair raced across the graveyard and into the porch entrance.

Still catching their breath, they sat side by side on the stone bench which ran along the porch as the lightning flashed and the rain crashed down outside.

'We're going to be here for some time,' observed George. She had only been wearing a summer dress and was shivering. Even the few seconds' exposure as they'd ran for the porch had been enough to leave her soaked to the skin.

Brian had come better prepared and was still dry under his cagoule. He saw that his friend was very cold and wondered how he could distract her. His eyes scanned the wall facing them. At the end nearest to the church door there was a list of vicars of St Teath, along with the dates of their ministries.

'Are there any trends in the length of times vicars were here?'

A mathematical puzzle was always a good way of capturing George's attention. She twisted her head and gazed at it carefully. 'Typically,' she observed, 'vicars stayed here for around ten years but one or two stayed much longer.'

At the bottom of the list the current interregnum was being played out. The last vicar had left at the end of the previous year but his successor might not be in post for another few months.

For a few minutes she pondered on whether the lengths of stay were reducing over time. There were fewer vicars in the eighteenth century than the nineteenth – although some tenures overlapped the centuries.

Then a thought struck her. 'Hey, look at 1964 – the year when Neville was buried. That was in the middle of a fifteen month interregnum. No wonder we didn't find many gravestones for that year.'

'It wasn't that we didn't find many,' responded Brian. 'We didn't see any more at all. It's very odd that there should be just the one.

It was two hours before they were back in Delabole. Brian had rung ahead to warn Alice and a deep hot bath had been run. George could exult in a long, bubbly soak as she warmed up from her sustained drenching.

But she could not completely relax. Something was not consistent. There had been two such different accounts of the life and death of Neville Harris.

Miss Trevelyan – Grace, she had been asked to call her – had been ignored by the family and not even invited to Neville's funeral. That did not make sense. Surely no-one in Neville's family could deny her the consolation of a last farewell? Was there any other reason why she might have been excluded?

And why should there be just one gravestone laid in 1964? It would make more sense if there was none at all during an interregnum. But one? Was it just a coincidence that the grave was right on the edge of the cemetery, well away from all other gravestones?

Then the lines of concern came together. Grace was a well-educated woman. Might she have been excluded because of fears that she would notice if a funeral was not authentic?

And if so, was there something suspicious about the grave itself? George pondered the dates involved and whether they had deeper significance.

CHAPTER 38

It was very early on the Tuesday morning that any alert villagers in St Teath, glancing out of their bedroom windows, would have noticed a police presence in the church cemetery. No-one knew what it was about and the police certainly weren't going to tell them.

One stolid policeman stood on duty at the entrance to the graveyard. His attendance was scarcely needed. There were no mourners wanting to adorn the graves of their relatives in St Teath at seven o'clock in the morning.

His colleagues proceeded to the far side of the graveyard, where they erected a white forensic frame tent over one of the graves. Gradually other pieces of equipment were brought into the tent from the police van.

At half past ten another police car drove through the village and out on to the farmhouse on the road beyond, owned and occupied by Owen Harris. He was asked, courteously but firmly, to accompany the policemen to Bodmin Police Station. The police car drove back slowly through the village and Harris had a distant sight of the activity in the graveyard. He said nothing but gave a sigh – it wasn't clear whether it was of sadness, anger or despair.

Arriving at Bodmin Police Station Harris was given chance to "enjoy" a solitary cup of coffee from the Kenco coffee machine in a poorly-furnished interview room. There was a table and chairs and a sound recorder, but not much else. After quarter of an hour he was joined by a solemn-looking Inspector Lambourn.

'Thank you for coming in sir. I'm sorry you had to wait, we're rather busy today.'

'I didn't have much choice, Inspector. Your colleagues said I could come of my own free will or else I could come here under arrest. I preferred the former. Can I ask, what is all this about?'

'Various matters, sir, you'll see as we go along. First of all, I'd like to take you back to last Tuesday – that's exactly a week ago.'

'Yes, yes, I agree it is Tuesday. I don't travel very far these days. As far as I recall last week was a normal Tuesday in St Teath. What's the question?'

'Did you go into the White Hart Inn at any point?'

'Inspector, I go into the White Hart on most days. I'm a single man in my declining years. I'm retired. I've never been one to sit at home watching daytime television and I don't paint landscapes. The White Hart is a fine pub. I get on well with the landlord – and most of the clientele.'

'Can you tell me who you had lunch with last Tuesday?'

'As I've just told you, I have lunch there most days. Quite a few of us do. It's hard to remember exactly who I saw when.'

'Try sir. We can bring in other witnesses to your lunch if necessary but it would be simpler if you just told us.'

There was silence whilst Harris seemed to rack his brains. The policeman was in no hurry: time was on his side. He was content to let Harris ponder.

'I'm not certain but it could have been Archie Tavistock – among others. Normally there are three or four of us around the table. Archie's often there on a Tuesday, it's the day his wife goes shopping to Wadebridge. It suits them both for him to be somewhere else. He's not much of a shopper – prefers catching fish to buying it, as you might say.'

'Good. That confirms what Mr Tavistock told us. Now, here's a further question. Do you remember Mr Tavistock using his phone at any time during your meal?'

'Inspector, if Archie had gone to the corner of the bar, stood on his head and sang us a carol I might have remembered. But using a phone? He could have done. Well, not to make a call, of course. He doesn't have that many friends and most of them were with him in the bar. But sometimes his wife would ring him from Tesco's, to alert him to some mega-bargain she'd spotted – cheaper engine oil, for example. I honestly can't remember. But why can't you ask him?'

'We have sir, but he's not certain either. So you can't be sure whether you picked up Mr Tavistock's phone over lunch - or was it on some other occasion?'

Harris seemed to quiver – it wasn't clear if with indignation or with shock. 'I haven't picked it up at all. Really, Inspector, if you've brought me all this way about a missing mobile . . .'

'Let's leave that for a moment. Now, sir, you know Mr Robbie Glendenning the journalist?'

'I've met him a couple of times – in the White Hart, as it happens. I told you, I spend a lot of time there.'

There was a knock at the door and a constable entered. He placed a note in front of the Inspector, muttered 'It's as we expected' and then left. The Inspector glanced at the note then continued the interview.

'When is the last time you saw Mr Glendenning?'

'Let me see. Yes, we had lunch together last Wednesday. He's a journalist, you know – his main task is interviewing people. He wanted to know about our bid for the Green Tourist Award – that's the one you came to talk to us about a few weeks ago.'

'And you've not seen him since?'

'Nope.'

'So if he alleges that last Thursday night you enticed him onto the cliffs over Tregardock Beach, hit him on the head, dragged him away and left him to die in Trelill Railway Tunnel, he's mistaken?'

It was a gamble to give so much carefully-garnered conjecture to a witness but Lambourn wanted to see what impact it would have.

Harris seemed to choke. 'I don't know what you're talking about.'

'Maybe he was confusing you with someone else?'

'Inspector, this is fantasy. I've no idea what you're on about. I thought police work was about collecting hard evidence, not blind guesswork. Why on earth should I want to do anything like that to poor old Glendenning?'

'Exactly, sir. Why indeed? Now I'd like to move on to something else. I gather your brother Neville Harris is buried in the graveyard at St Teath?'

'He is. I buried him there myself in 1964. Brought his body back from the United States, where he'd been killed in a road accident. It was a very sad time for the family.'

'Was it, indeed?' Lambourn paused, to make sure he pitched his next statement as he intended.

'Mr Harris, for reasons which I won't go in to, my team have been looking very hard at that grave. In fact, this morning we put in a team to have it exhumed. That note which was just brought in gives me some preliminary findings. And do you know what: the most amazing thing was, they could find no body in there at all. Have you anything to say on that?'

It was half an hour later. Harris, looking as if he might faint, had asked for an adjournment to take in the news. Lambourn had decided to allow him a short time on his own.

It suited the Inspector to have a little time to work out his next line of questioning.

'So, sir, we'd got as far as the empty tomb in St Teath. What can you tell me about that? Is your brother taking after Lazarus?'

Harris took a deep breath. 'OK, you're right – there never was a body in there. I hoped that the truth would never come out, but I suppose it had to eventually.'

'Can you elaborate on that, sir?'

Harris drew another deep breath. 'It was all a very long time ago. The truth if you must know is that I arranged it all for my Dad. He was only in his sixties but he'd had many hard knocks and was failing rapidly. I knew he would never travel to the United States to see where my brother was buried. After the fatal road accident my Dad pined so much for him. In the end I told him I would arrange to have Neville's body brought home to be buried in St Teath. There was the interregnum in the church at that time, you see, which gave me the idea and also made it possible to arrange.'

'I don't suppose that you can tell us the place to go in the United States where we could find Neville's remains?'

'We're talking about something half a century ago, Inspector. I'm not a man who spends much time dwelling on the past. There was a long controversy about the accident. My brother was, shall we say, an enthusiastic driver. He never took speed limits very seriously. He regarded them as a challenge rather than an edict. In the end he wasn't buried – he was cremated.

'I hung on to the relevant documents for many years but eventually – twenty years ago - I decided they wouldn't be needed. They went the way of a lot of other papers in my de-cluttering. So I can't give you any more details, I'm afraid.'

'If what you've just admitted is true I imagine it offends some church law or other if nothing else – even if it was half a century ago. But I can think of a less innocent way of putting it.'

Inspector Lambourn paused once again for effect.

'What you're saying is that your brother disappeared from the scene at almost the same time as a skeleton came to be in laid down in the nearby tunnel in Trelill.'

'That's not a pleasant way of presenting what happened. We don't know when the skeleton appeared. Coincidences do sometimes happen, you know.'

The Inspector looked at him coldly. 'It wasn't very pleasant for the skeleton, sir – whoever he was. But there is one way we can advance our understanding from here. Can I ask you to give us a DNA sample?

'Once we've processed it that'll give us something we can compare with the DNA sample we've already had from the skeleton.'

CHAPTER 39

Even when classified as urgent a DNA sample takes forty eight hours to be processed by the Forensic Service. So it was Thursday afternoon before Owen Harris was collected once more from his home near St Teath and brought by police car to Bodmin Police Station.

This time there was no delay. Inspector Lambourn was waiting for him, eager it seemed to continue their confrontation. A keen-looking sergeant, whom he introduced as Sergeant Springer, was also present. Lambourn turned on the recording device and announced the date and time and the names of those present. Then he turned to Owen Harris.

'Good afternoon, sir. Thank you for coming in again. Can I remind you that we're still dealing with the case of the skeleton in Trelill tunnel. I got the result of the DNA analysis an hour ago and I thought we should discuss it as soon as possible.'

Harris nodded. Lambourn wondered if he knew what was coming.

'I don't know how much you know about matching of DNA samples, sir?'

'Not a lot. Only the snippets I've picked up from Midsomer Murders. It doesn't come up much in traditional farming.'

'Well, it's a complicated piece of science and it's advancing all the time. When DNA was first unravelled in the 1980s it was like an advanced fingerprint, but one that related to the whole body. As the science advanced, it was found that blood relatives, had a similar DNA to one another. You might not be able to say exactly what that relationship was – they might not be able to distinguish a father-son link from a grandfather-son connection, for example - but it considerably narrowed the options. In many old cases that had been insoluble vital new facts emerged. Amazing, eh?'

'I suppose so,' conceded Harris.

'In particular, when a long-dead skeleton was found to have a DNA code similar to the code of a living person, that would be a big clue as to their identity.'

'Go on.'

'I just wanted to make sure we weren't blinding you with science, sir. Well, the striking thing about the DNA sample you gave us on Tuesday is that it shows you are a very close relative indeed to the skeleton that was found in Trelill tunnel – in fact you were his brother.'

The Inspector stopped talking and looked hard at Harris. Harris didn't look too surprised but the news didn't seem to have floored him either.

'I feared that was where you were heading, Inspector. In fact I've feared it all along, ever since rumours started to circulate that a skeleton had been found in that blasted tunnel.'

'So do you accept, sir, that the skeleton is in fact your brother Neville – the one whom you were telling me only two days ago that you had buried in the St Teath churchyard – and then later, in version two, that had been cremated in the United States?'

'Good heavens, no, Inspector. Whatever made you think that I only had one brother?'

The Inspector's eyes bulged. The man must think he was an idiot.

'If that's the line you're going to take, sir, maybe you could run through your immediate family for me – that is, all the brothers that you might be going to mention as this interview goes on.'

'I only had one other brother, Inspector and that was poor Edwin. And no sisters, in case you've got other skeletons stashed away in the morgue that you want to try and fit me up with.'

'Do tell me about Edwin, sir. Every detail you can possibly remember. Every single known fact about his existence. Any documents that might have survived your de-cluttering, what was it, twenty years ago. Any family photographs or school reports. Any witnesses to his life who are still sane and breathing. A birth certificate, maybe? In fact, anything that might possibly help to provide me with hard evidence that this man really existed at all.'

An hour later, Inspector Lambourn and Sergeant Springer decided to stop for a break and a chance to take stock.

Owen Harris was left alone in the interview room with a cup of canteen tea and a plate of plain digestive biscuits. Lambourn and Springer proceeded to the canteen where they ordered two mugs of strong, sweet coffee and two large slices of Victoria sponge. Both felt in need of refreshment.

'The trouble is, guv, he's had two days at home to work on this latest story,' said Springer. 'It's harder than you might think for us to prove that someone never existed when there's a witness saying they once did.'

'All the more so when it's so long ago. I mean, goodness knows how tight they were with conventions on registering births and the rest back in the 1930s. That's before the welfare state.'

'It's probably worse for a child on an isolated farm,' added Springer. 'And not just any child, but one whom Harris described as "simple". In those days his mother might have prevented him from being seen – tried to airbrush him from history. And it's just about possible that someone could destroy all the documents that might have backed up their story. It's all a very long time ago.'

'But there must be older people in that community who could back up or else counter his story in a convincing way. For instance, did he go to school and if so which one? It's just that it'll take us a day or two to find them.'

'It's a good job we've got enough evidence to arrest him. We certainly don't want him roaming his village this evening, setting up additional witnesses to support his claims.'

When the interview resumed, Inspector Lambourn started by going back to one of Harris's earlier comments, which he hadn't picked up at the time.

'You said, sir, something about "fearing this is where the inquiry might be going once that skeleton was found". What did you mean by that?'

'Well, I meant I thought the skeleton might be Edwin. We all played in that tunnel sometimes in our teenage years – it wasn't hard to get inside it, you know. Not many trains in the years right after the war.'

'By "all" do you mean yourself, Edwin and Neville?'

'That's right. Edwin was the oldest and Neville was next: I'm the youngest. Neville was something of a bully. He always wanted to tease poor Edwin but the lad didn't know how to stand up for himself. Neville would give him a dare and he would meekly try and fulfil it. He'd been hidden away from society all through his childhood, you see, and he had no self confidence at all. He daren't refuse.'

'When did you last see Edwin, sir?'

'Let me think . . . He disappeared off the farm one day early in 1955. Even before that happened it was a dreadful time. The house was icy cold and we couldn't afford the fuel needed to heat it. My mother was dying of tuberculosis and my Dad was cracking up under the strain. Basically the farm's business was going bust. Neville and I kept out of the way as much as we could.'

He paused, his eyes clouding over. 'That was the context. Then I remember coming home one winter's day and finding that Edwin wasn't there any more.'

'So surely your father would call the police?'

'Well, Dad wasn't thinking straight. Edwin was twenty five by then, physically if not emotionally. My Dad said if he wanted to run away that was fine by him. He didn't do much on the farm and it meant one less mouth to feed. All my Dad's energies were going into making my Mum's final days as peaceful as possible.'

'So this brother of yours just wandered off and you never saw him again?'

'It wasn't for want of trying. Neville and I searched the farm and the surrounding area for days but we never found anything. I wanted to go to the police at that point but I was afraid I would get my Dad into trouble for not going earlier. To say nothing of it being the last straw for my Mum if she saw the police wandering about. Neville insisted that it was best for us to keep quiet.'

There was a pause in the questioning. His story sounded

271

almost believable.

'So now, sir, what do you think happened to Edwin?'

'I was always suspicious of Neville's insistence that we kept it all secret. I wondered if he knew more about Edwin's disappearance than he had let on. For example, had he challenged him with a dare which had gone horribly wrong?'

'Did you ever talk about wild dares, sir? Ones that Edwin might have taken seriously?'

'The most devilish one that Neville came up with was for someone to be tied up and laid down between the rails in the darkness of the tunnel while a train passed over them. That could cause anyone to faint or have a seizure.'

'So what happened after that, sir?'

'Neville and I had been close, we were only two years apart in age. But we were never close after Edwin disappeared. Gradually we drifted apart. Neville just didn't want to stay around these parts. It was almost as if he wanted to get as far away as possible - as if he had a deeply troubled conscience about something very bad that had happened.'

'Are you saying that was really why he went to America?'

'I'm saying he had a strong desire to get as far away as possible, at all costs. America was the culmination of that desire. He left the UK in early 1963 and never came back.'

'And the rest of your family?'

'My Mum had died from tuberculosis in 1956. My Dad survived that and also survived Neville leaving us. But it all took its toll. He died from a heart attack in 1966.

'I was left alone with the remnant of the farm. It took me all my working life to turn it round, it's been a long slog. All you've discovered in these last few days confirms my worst fears.'

CHAPTER 40

Robbie Glendenning remained unconscious in the Intensive Care Ward of the hospital in Truro for almost a week. After her Sunday back in Delabole George Gilbert drove over every afternoon to see him, hoping against hope that he might sense her presence - or even hear her voice - and respond in some way. But until Thursday nothing happened.

The medical team on the ward were unfailingly positive, urging her day after day to be patient. They said his body was well on the way to recovery from all its knocks and deprivations. He had suffered an extremely severe blow on the head but there was no reason for him not to make a full recovery.

On Wednesday there had been some good news from the police. They had found Robbie's dark green Triumph Stag in an out-of-the-way spot at the far end of the car park of Bodmin Parkway. A railway official had spotted that it hadn't moved for several days and had reported the fact to the police.

George reflected that if Robbie had not been found in Trelill tunnel it was a well judged place for the car to have been left. For with no proof he'd been assaulted it could easily be taken that Robbie had driven to Bodmin Parkway Station and then caught a train to another part of the country. As a senior journalist he could have been alerted to another story and gone to chase it.

So without her intervention last Friday police interest – if it existed at all - would soon have died down.

The Stag was apparently undamaged and had been taken to the Regional Forensic Science Laboratory in Exeter. Unfortunately the roof had been left open when it was abandoned and the thunderstorm on Sunday afternoon had left the interior soaked. That would be bad news for the owner when he came to drive it again. More to the point, the scientists doubted they'd find any useful traces in the soggy interior of the DNA of Robbie's assailant.

In her time spent travelling and watching an unconscious Robbie, George tried to reconstruct the journeys that must have been taken by his assailant, assuming he was acting alone and hence relying on buses to assist his journeys.

The man had to start off late on Thursday evening waiting on the coast near Treligga. Then he had taken Robbie's car – plus Robbie – to Trelill, maybe using a wheelbarrow to carry him from the roadside to inside the tunnel.

George noted a supplementary set of questions. Where had the wheelbarrow come from? Where had it been abandoned? Might it have DNA traces? It could have been thrown into the hedge anywhere on the journey to Bodmin. Thinking about it though, she feared it would probably also have suffered the Sunday thunderstorm. She concluded that finding it was not a priority.

But how had the assailant got home from Bodmin Parkway? Of course, he might have gone off somewhere by train - but all their deductions had suggested he was a local.

George checked on the internet. There was a regular, hourly bus from Bodmin Parkway to Wadebridge, starting at seven in the morning. If the Stag had been abandoned late in the night the assailant was probably on the first bus of the day. He wouldn't want to be found anywhere near the journalist's car.

She must ask Inspector Lambourn whether the bus driver for that first journey last Friday had been questioned about his passengers. On an early morning bus there might only be one or two at the start. The driver wouldn't know who they were but he might remember something about them.

From Wadebridge, George knew there were two bus routes to the Delabole area. One trundled around the coast before ending up in Camelford. The other went straight up the A39. From there the assailant would be on home ground. He could potter about in Camelford and catch a later bus back to Delabole.

As George forced herself to think through exactly what had happened, she realised the man would have had no sleep on Thursday night during a strenuous sequence of tasks. Robbie was no lightweight. By Friday morning, the assailant would not want to hang about in Camelford. He would be desperate to drop out of sight and catch up on his sleep.

How could he do that? George let her imagination roll. The simplest way would be to drive to Camelford the evening before, leave his car there and then take the last bus back down the coastal route, getting out near Treligga. It would be worth asking that bus driver if anyone had got out there.

It was on Thursday afternoon that the longed-for recovery occurred. George had just arrived and taken her regular seat by Robbie's bedside. She greeted his inert body cheerfully, as she'd done every day that week.

This time though, there was some sort of response. Robbie seemed to grunt. Then, slowly, his eyes opened. They shut again almost at once, but a few seconds later they reopened, this time for longer. And this time with more focus. He blinked: a mirage? It looked like George, sitting at his bedside.

'Hello Robbie,' she greeted him. 'You've been asleep for a very long time. You're in a hospital. Let me tell the nurses that you've woken up.'

There was a flurry of activity as the hospital staff hustled to check their newly-conscious patient. As Intensive Care they had a huge battery of tests they could apply. George waited in the visitors' lounge until the various procedures were deemed complete. Waiting was not so hard now she had seen for herself that Robbie was starting to recover. She also took the chance to ring Brian and tell him the good news.

Half an hour later, one of the nurses called her back in. 'You can have just a few minutes. He'll go back to sleep very soon. We've given him some very strong pain-killers. One of their side-effects is that they'll make him feel dozy. But he's on the way to recovery. We told you to be patient.'

By some magic of serendipity, none of the relay team of policemen who'd been around for most of the week was present. George didn't care, she wanted Robbie all to herself. She reached forward and gently held his hand; poor chap, he looked so fragile.

'Robbie, how are you? Can you speak? Do you remember anything? Or do you want me to do the talking?'

Then she remembered tip one from an interview course she'd once attended: "Don't ask too many questions at once. Let them answer the first before you move on to the rest." Shut up woman, she thought, irritated with her lack of self control. Let him speak.

'The last thing I can remember,' he said, speaking in a low

voice that matched the quiet mood of the ward, 'is standing on the cliffs overlooking Tregardock Beach. It was in the moonlight. I was looking to see if my new friend Rowena was down there. I'd had an odd text from her, you see. Then I got an almighty crack on the head – it still hurts, you know.'

He paused and reached to feel the bandage that still encircled his head. Then he looked straight at her. 'But George – what on earth are you doing here? Are we still in Cornwall? Bless you; how did you know I was in trouble?' He shook his head gently. It was all too much to take in.

'Robbie, you look very sleepy. We're in Intensive Care in Truro. It's a long story as to how each of us got here. I don't think you can take it all in right now. It's enough today to know you're on the mend. We've communicated. I'll come back tomorrow and we can talk properly.'

CHAPTER 41

Miss Trevelyan was rather excited to receive a call from the Bodmin Police early on Friday morning. 'A case we are currently investigating means that we need to check on events sixty or seventy years ago,' she was told. 'You've been identified as a reliable witness who's lived in the relevant area for a long time. Could we come and see you this morning?'

Despite her role as head teacher, the old lady had not had that much to do with the police in her professional life. It was only a small primary school and her pupils were not normally in trouble. However, she'd watched crime series on television and had some idea of what might happen. She must answer the question asked, not babble on about unrelated matters. Accordingly she dressed smartly so she was ready, if required, to travel to Bodmin Police Station. She hoped, though, that she would not have to spend the night in a cell.

Sergeant Tom Springer and WPC Sharon Highsmith drove up at ten. Miss Trevelyan welcomed them in and offered them a cup of coffee, which they accepted. It was evidently going to be more Midsomer Murders than Lewis.

'How long have you been living around here?' Springer was going to ask the questions and Highsmith to write down her answers.

'I was born in Camelford in 1929. My parents both died when I was young and I was brought up by my grandfather, John Trevelyan and by my aunt. He had a house on the edge of

St Kew.

'I was always interested in teaching and knowledge. I went away to Teacher Training College – let me see, that must have been 1948. I qualified as a primary school teacher in 1951. I taught for a few years near Plymouth then the opportunity came to teach in Delabole Primary. I was so pleased to be coming back close to home.

'There were only two teachers at the school. When the head left in 1965 I applied to take over and was successful. I remained there for the rest of my teaching career. Once I retired in 1989 I could see no good reason to move away. I had lots of friends here and still felt part of the community.'

'Thank you. That sets the stage nicely. Now the case we're working on involves the Harris family. We've been talking to Mr Owen Harris, who currently resides on the far side of St Teath. Have you had anything to do with the family over the years?'

The name was a shock. Miss Trevelyan took some time to gather her thoughts. Promises of silence made decades ago would have to be set aside. Sharon Highsmith prepared to write down her answer.

'I want to answer the question as fully as I can. To declare my interest, as it were, I want first to make sure you understand there was a feud between the Harris and Trevelyan families. It dated back to the start of the railway. I only heard about the feud from my grandfather so I only knew one side of the dispute. I always told my pupils they needed to hear both sides of a story before they made any decision about who was right. But as I understood it, it all started with an argument about the Trelill tunnel. My grandfather was for it and Owen Harris's grandfather was against it. He wanted a viaduct instead.

'Anyway, whatever the rights and wrongs of that, the upshot was that my grandfather forbade the Trevelyan family to have anything at all to do with the Harris's. It was an edict that lasted until my grandfather died in 1946.

'So there were reasons why I had no personal dealings with the Harris family until I returned to the area in 1955. And even then the family feud had a dampening effect. I was busy with my new job. The Harris family had a series of misfortunes. Mrs Harris died of tuberculosis, I think, in 1956. The farm was going to rack and ruin. Mr Harris was going down with it. The lads – that's Neville and Owen – kept out of the way as much as they could.'

Sergeant Springer was itching to intervene. This was the nub of his inquiry. Then he realised that the old lady hadn't finished – not by a long way.

'I suppose it was because they kept away from their home that they spent more time round about the area. And that was when I started to get to know them – or rather, Neville. We were both in our twenties. He was slightly younger but it didn't seem significant – not to me, anyway. We were both hungry to make up for all the years this ridiculous quarrel had kept us apart. Looking back, I suppose that the fact the relationship had been forbidden made it all the more attractive.'

She paused. Springer and Highsmith felt no urge to intervene. They sensed that somehow or other this was a crucial piece of testimony.

'Of course, we had to be careful. As a teacher I was in a position of trust in the community. I had to lead by example. Attitudes were different to what they are now. This was before the pill had revolutionised common attitudes towards sex in relationships. So it was a very low-profile relationship between us; it took a long time to mature.

'Even Owen knew nothing at all about it. Neville warned me he was still caught up in this wretched, long-standing family quarrel, with its hatred of everything Trevelyan, which Neville and I just laughed about. We had each other and that was far more important.

'But we kept it very quiet. It was autumn 1962 before Owen had any inkling there was anything going on between his brother and me. Neville told me, on one of our secret dates, that when Owen found out he was incandescent. Said he'd kill him if he didn't give up on the relationship. Neville just laughed – told him to get lost.

'But it was clear we couldn't just carry on as we had been. Imagine the publicity for a teacher involved in a bitter public quarrel. So Neville went up to London to try and arrange something more ambitious than being a destitute farmer's son. He said it would involve him spending time in the United States.

'I understand he left for the States just before Christmas 1962. He had intimated, and I'd been hoping, he was coming back to propose to me over the Christmas holidays. But he never did. In fact he never wrote at all.'

The old lady stopped, tears in her eyes. In her self-imposed emotional isolation she had never shared these details before with anyone. Now, even fifty years later, the pain of it all hit her afresh.

Sharon Highsmith spotted a box of paper handkerchiefs on the sideboard, grabbed it and pressed a few into her hands. 'It's all right. Take as long as you want. Why don't I make us all another cup of coffee?'

A quarter of an hour later, after a coffee break orchestrated entirely by her guests, the interview restarted.

'Can I ask you, Miss Trevelyan, how much you've had to do with Owen Harris?'

'Very little – as little as possible, I'd say. It's almost as if Owen still pursues the feud between our two families – which is ludicrous. He never even invited me to the funeral service for Neville, which I understood they held in 1964.

'And how about his older brother, Edwin?'

Miss Trevelyan looked bemused. 'What older brother? There was only ever the two of 'em.'

'I can't explain why, just at the moment, but this is the crucial reason why we've come here. Can you be absolutely sure that there was no older brother?'

'As I explained, because of the feud I had no contact with the Harris family until the late 1950s. So I can't be absolutely sure – I can't say I knew the household and went in and out all the time. In fact I never went in at all. But I never once saw or heard anyone talk about Edwin. But there couldn't be another Harris – surely? Unless, I suppose, he died very young.'

Springer was still not completely satisfied. Maybe he needed to explain more about his underlying problem?

'In the case we're dealing with, Miss Trevelyan, the suspect asserts categorically that there was this other brother. He wasn't just a child, but grew to be an adult. His story depends on it. That's why my Inspector has asked me to do everything I can to try and find some other evidence of him. It would only need one reference - one document in which he is mentioned - for our suspect to claim he was vindicated. And make us look a bunch of idiots.'

'We don't want that. You're certainly not idiots. Would it

help to look through the school Archive about the railway line? It's a long shot but I seem to remember Harris's farm ran alongside the old railway line, so maybe there's a connection. I've got it here; it's all labelled and so on. It's based on material assembled by pupils at the school from 1893 to 1967.'

'I'd be amazed,' said Springer, 'if Edwin had managed to find his way into that. But I suppose it would show my boss that we'd really tried if we gave it a quick search. Could we do so here and now?'

Miss Trevelyan cleared her dining table and fetched out the boxes of Archive from 1930 to 1955. The two police officers were relieved to discover that although each year had a separate container, the boxes were by no means full and the war years were almost empty. 'Can I help with the search?' she asked, 'I can read the material as fast as you two and we'll get through it all faster.'

They set to work, dividing the boxes into three piles. They soon found that by skimming the primary sources (the hand-written material produced by the pupils) and speed-reading the typed summaries from the teachers, they could get though a box in just a few minutes. They had eight or nine boxes each so it would take them an hour. Springer started to become interested in the details of the railway operations mentioned in the summaries until he was taken to task by Highsmith. But in box after box there was no mention of Edwin Harris.

They were almost onto their final boxes when there was a gasp of amazement from Miss Trevelyan. She had reached the box for 1944-5. Her hand shaking, she passed over the summary document which she had been reading to Springer.

And there, on the final page, he saw an account of an incident during the Second World War centred around the

Trelill tunnel. Some lads had tried to break in past the entrance barrier and had been caught by a guard posted by the village.

And on the last page the lads were named: Owen, Neville and Edwin Harris.

The sergeant read the account carefully. It sounded authentic.

'And these archives have been in this house since you retired?'

'I've lent one or two out sometimes, but basically I've had them in my care all the way through. I always told my pupils that an accurate archive would be useful one day.'

'I think I need to phone my boss,' said Springer. 'He's not going to like this, but he did send us to find what evidence we could. What a pity we were so successful.'

CHAPTER 42

While Miss Trevelyan was recounting her life story to the two police officers, Robbie Glendenning was giving an account of his more recent past to George Gilbert as she sat beside him in Intensive Care.

He had already been told that he'd made such good progress in the past twenty four hours that he would be moved to a general ward later that morning; and he could expect to be out altogether within the next few days.

'You'll need to take it easy,' the doctor warned him. 'But there's nothing broken. It might not feel like it, but your skull really isn't fractured so there's not much more we can do. The wounds are all healing nicely. A few gentle cliff walks in the fresh air, looked after by your friend, will do you more good than extra time in here.'

'That's great,' said George, once they were on their own. 'You look so much better than you did yesterday. Isn't the human body's ability to recover from adversity amazing?'

There appeared to be nothing seriously amiss with Robbie's long-term memory. He quickly remembered George had been busy looking after her daughter Polly – that was why she shouldn't be here - and he asked after her.

'I've been ringing the hospital every day, Robbie. They know what the illness is now and they know how to treat it. It's just a matter of time. But it's very infectious, so she's being kept in isolation. I couldn't visit her right now even if I was in London.

But every remote tropical cloud has a warm local lining. It's freed me up to come and visit you instead.'

George was longing to tell Robbie about how she and Brian had managed to find him, and also about her discoveries in St Teath but was aware she must not compromise his testimony.

So she suggested they began by Robbie trying very hard to remember every detail he could of his experience.

'Take your time. We've got till they move you to your new ward. There might be details lodged in your subconscious that will come out if we talk around it all. We want your attacker in jail.'

'George, I've been doing my best to remember everything ever since I woke up this morning feeling so much better. But I've not managed to come up with much. And I don't know if my bits and pieces are already well-known.'

'Go on, tell me and then I'll help you put it into context.'

'It all began when I found a text message on my phone.'

'Yes, I found that. I came to stay in the Bettle as a surprise. It was some surprise. Once you didn't appear for breakfast I got the waitress to check your room and we spotted the phone. That was a vital clue.'

'I'm amazed I left it behind. I hardly ever travel without it. It was just that the message talked about having a swim, so I decided to leave all my valuables back in the pub.'

'If I asked, would you be willing to go for a midnight swim with me one day?' she asked mischievously.

Robbie looked slightly embarrassed. George sought to reassure him.

'Don't worry, I've met Rowena. I accept that she's quite pretty. Maybe it's as well I came down when I did.'

Robbie decided it was best to hasten on. He noted, though,

George's half-formed invitation. He'd remind her of it one day.

'When I got to Rowena's the lights were out. But there was a note on the gatepost inviting me to Tregardock Beach. I'd been there the week before – '

'With Rowena?'

'Yes, with Rowena. You and I weren't in touch at that stage. And it was in the daytime.' He paused but could think of no other redeeming features; best to press on. 'Anyway, I got to the kissing gate near the top of the cliffs and stopped to see if I could see her down below. Then, without any warning, someone came up behind and hit me hard on the head. I went out like a light.'

'I'm sure the police will want to ask you, but can you remember anything else about the attack? Any noise, for example – a grunt or something? Or was there any smell – tobacco, maybe, or alcohol? Was there any animal involved?'

Robbie forced himself to replay the moment of the attack slowly in his mind.

'I certainly didn't hear a dog. But I think, now you press me, that there was a faint smell of cider from behind in the seconds before the blow. That wasn't me: I know I often drink cider, but that Thursday I'd dined alone and had a bottle of red wine at the pub.'

'OK, you were done in by a cider drinker. That's not much, it covers half the local population, but it's something. Now, let's go on. Any memories of the time between the moment of attack and waking up here in hospital?'

Again Robbie didn't answer straight away but forced himself to replay what few memories he'd been left with.

'I think I can remember feeling very hot and squashed. And there was some sort of roaring noise – one that changed pitch from time to time.'

'Go on. You're doing very well.'

'Then, at another point, I was scarcely conscious and it was very bumpy. I was jerked up and down. I think I heard someone cursing under their breath. And I half-remember my head hanging over an edge.'

'And then?'

'After that it was really - intensely - dark for a long time. Then I imagined I saw your lovely, concerned face peering at me. I must have been hallucinating or something.'

'Maybe. Anything else? Any more tastes or smells?'

'I was really thirsty. Absolutely parched. That helped make me lightheaded, I suppose. Then some kind soul poured water down my throat – another dream?'

There was another pause. He continued to dredge his memories.

'I've also some sort of impression of being strapped into a vehicle with lots of lights. Then a slow, alternating pattern of light and darkness. And I could hear what sounded like your voice, talking, very faintly - but only occasionally.'

'That's good, Robbie. Suppose that now I give you a few more clues, from what I know, and see if you can do even better.'

'No. Let me work out a few more things first. Am I right in thinking that the vehicle with lights was an ambulance? Bringing me here from some location – some location where you, miraculously, managed to find me?'

'Exactly. So where do you think you might have been left?'

'Well, when I wasn't thinking about my own story, this morning, I was also wondering about why anyone should want to do me in. Whom had I offended so badly? And the obvious reason, of course, is that I got too close to the truth on the question of the skeleton in the tunnel. Hey – is that where I was taken?'

'That's where Brian and I found you last Friday afternoon – a week ago. No wonder it all looked so dark. It really was pitch black.'

'But if I ended up in there that's much too far to be dragged. I must have gone by car. Wait - was I taken in the boot of my own car? That variable pitch roaring noise – it was someone changing gear – he not only did me in, the bastard stole my car.'

He seemed more indignant about the loss of his beloved Stag than about the blow on the head. Then a new thought came to him.

'But if the police could find my car, they might be able to get my attacker's DNA. From the driver's seat, or the steering wheel, or something. Assuming he didn't wear gloves. And that it's not been driven off the cliffs and into the sea.'

'No, I can tell you he didn't do that. In fact there's some good news on that front. Your car's been found by the police at Bodmin Parkway Station. Unfortunately the roof was down and it got soaked in a massive thunderstorm we had on Sunday. '

'But what about the boot – that's where I was so squashed, of course? My assailant would have to grapple with the boot lid – it's very awkward. You've got to reach right underneath, twist the catch and then give it a hefty pull. Do you think that might collect some DNA? And it's under cover. It might not be washed out by the rain at all.'

'That's a brilliant thought, Robbie. If you don't mind, I'll ring the police with that insight right away. It would be a shame if they were so busy on the driver's seat that they missed the DNA trace inside the boot.'

CHAPTER 43

Friday afternoon. Inspector Lambourn was just concluding a difficult interview with Owen Harris. The old farmer was relishing the boot being on the other foot and wanted to make the most of it.

'So you're saying, Inspector, that now, finally, you accept that I was telling you the truth. I did have a brother called Edwin, so the DNA evidence proves that it's his body that was found in the tunnel.'

'The evidence collected by my officers seems to indicate that, sir. Uncontrovertibly, one might say. As I say, I apologise, on behalf of Bodmin Police, for arresting you a couple of days ago. It was a necessary step, given what we then knew. The wheels of justice sometime take a while to turn; it's just a pity when we get caught in the cogs. Still, you'll be back home in time for the next darts match at the White Hart this evening. Would you like to use the office phone to ring for a taxi?'

'I presume you have some standard arrangement with a local taxi firm for taking wrongful arrests home?'

'Yes – no – oh, I don't know. That's what a lawyer would call a loaded question, sir. Generally regarded as unfair when used by barristers.'

'I thought all questions posed by barristers were unfair? That's why they charge so much for their services. And talking of legal services, can I take it that you will be destroying my DNA sample, now I'm not being charged with any offence?'

'I think it was at your own meeting a couple of weeks ago, sir, that I explained that the police were forced to discard any DNA they'd collected which was not linked to a criminal undertaking. The law requires it. Parliament regards it as one of the bulwarks of liberty. "A man is innocent until proved guilty" and all that. The basis of our system of justice.'

'Cut the waffle. So you're giving me your word as a senior policeman that my DNA sample analysis will be destroyed, taken off your DNA database, straight away?'

'That forms the basis of our procedures, sir. I'll do it as soon as we've concluded this interview. Mustn't threaten our long-established system of justice, must we? Now, if there's nothing else you want to raise, no other points of esoteric law you'd like clarified, I'll get you that taxi number.'

Owen Harris had made it as far as the reception area of the Police Station when the call came through to Lambourn's office from the Forensic Service in Exeter.

A slow smile spread across his face. 'The man's DNA found on the inside boot lid of Glendenning's car? No possibility of error? Excellent.'

Swiftly he rang the front desk.

'Is Owen Harris still there?'

'He is, sir. Waiting patiently for his taxi. It's a terribly slow service, this time of year. For some reason they give priority to tourists.'

'Ask him to wait a few more minutes. Whatever you do don't let him leave the building. I'm coming down there as soon as I can to re-arrest him. He may have wriggled out of one charge, but he'll have some difficulty, I think, in dodging this one.'

CHAPTER 44

It was George's suggestion, once Robbie was discharged from hospital, that the pair should go together to visit Miss Trevelyan.

'She's very fond of you, you know. I had to be very careful, when I went to see her last week, not to let on that you'd been badly injured. But now you've been discharged that's no longer a secret. By now she must have heard the stories going round the village. She'd love to see for herself that you're still in one piece.'

It was Friday afternoon. The old lady was indeed pleased to see them. She invited them in and made sure that they sat side by side on the settee, while she fetched a tray of afternoon tea. It was a while, she thought, since she'd been a matchmaker. The two seemed well-suited to one another.

'You've had some experiences since we last met,' she told Robbie. 'Are you fully recovered?'

'I'm on the mend.' Robbie proceeded to tell her the gist of his story. She was horrified and then thrilled by the tale.

'Your comments on the interregnum at St Teath were very helpful,' George told her, when the topic of Robbie's attack and recovery was exhausted.

'Well, I was a teacher for forty years, but I think that's the oddest commendation I've ever been given. How?'

'Well, I went to have a look for the grave you told me about.' George suddenly remembered that this wasn't just any old grave. It was the one that Miss Trevelyan still thought contained the body of her long-lost lover. She struggled to slide away from the detail.

'And later I realised that the date on it was during an earlier interregnum. That gave me an idea which I passed on to the police.'

'So it was you that put the police on to me?' the old lady asked George.

'I don't think so. Apart from your gun-running in Port Isaac and the arson attacks in Camelford I should think you're fairly innocent.'

George smiled to show she was joking, but Miss Trevelyan had got the joke anyway. George continued, 'I didn't know the police had been to see you. What was that about?'

'They wanted to know about the Harris family. So I told them all about Neville – he was my special friend, you see.'

George smiled back at her.

The old lady continued, 'But it was the other brother - Edwin - they were interested in. I'd never heard of him and I told them so. But in the end we searched through the Archives and found his name. He was mentioned along with Neville and Owen in the account for 1945, would you believe. The police could hardly credit it. I don't think they believed he'd existed either.'

The journalist was equally suspicious. 'You're saying the only hard evidence of his existence is this one mention in your Archive?'

'Yes.'

'But how did they know it hadn't been added later? Didn't they check if you'd lent it to anyone else?' asked Robbie. 'I know you'd have kept a record of anyone borrowing it – you even had my name down.'

'No – I don't think they realised I kept a formal track of each volume of the Archive, like a library. There's an idea. Should we see if that particular year was ever borrowed?'

This task was easier than the searching through twenty five years' worth of Archives for a mention of Edwin. Miss Trevelyan fetched her large loan-recording notebook and put it on the table. Slowly they turned back the pages.

It was George who spotted the entry. 'Look, it was taken out once – back in 1990.' Disappointment crept into her voice. 'But not by anyone I've ever heard of. Jonathan Selvey. Was he a friend of yours?'

'He was one of my former pupils. I never forgot their names – their looks changed, of course, as they grew up. But he wasn't at school while the railway was running – he was far too young. In fact I was surprised he'd take an interest in the Archive at all, so long after the line closed. But he said his landlord had a question he wanted answering. I never knew what it was.'

She pointed at another date, further across the page. 'But he brought it back – and only a week later. I've no idea why he wanted it.'

George and Robbie could hazard a guess but until they knew more it was only a suspicion. But it made the existence of Edwin even more problematic. Were there any other sources that could move the question forward?

'This Archive is authoritative – but it can't be the only document around from that era,' observed Robbie.

'Hey - did any letters from Neville throw any light on Edwin?' asked George. 'Have you still got them hidden away somewhere?'

This was not a question that Miss Trevelyan ever expected to be asked. But she wanted to give George every encouragement.

'Most of the time that Neville and I were lovers we both lived around here so there was no need for us to write. Our notes simply proposed locations and times. Once we met we could pour out our hearts to one another face to face.

'The only time that we needed to write was in the autumn of 1962, when Neville went up to London to find an alternative career. With his ailing father and his hostile brother he could see it would never work for him to stay around here – not if he wanted to marry me, anyway. But I was busy teaching and he was so busy chasing possibilities and contacts that we only wrote to each other once a week. Mind you, I've kept all those letters. They were very special times.'

Miss Trevelyan's eyes seemed to fill with tears. But there was something special, too, about sharing these times with this "young" couple.

'Was it those letters that made you suspect Neville planned to come back and see you one more time before he went to the United States?' asked Robbie.

'It was far more than just a plan, young man. He wrote to me from his lodgings in London. I still remember the date he put on the letter: Dec 15th 1962. "My dearest Grace," it began.

'He told me that he'd just bought a return plane ticket to New York, due to fly out in early January. A plane ticket – nowadays we're all so used to flying but back then it was a novelty. I'd never seen a plane ticket, let alone used one. Neville told me he'd bring it down to show me.'

'What did he plan to do in America?'

'He had met some American businessman. He wanted to hire a British farm manager to run his estate in New Hampshire. Neville had seen his advert, gone for interview and been offered the contract. He was going over to check it out. The plan was that, assuming all was OK, Neville would return, we'd get quietly married and then we'd emigrate to the New World.'

There was a few moments silence as they each contemplated this alternative future which had never happened.

'So he was coming down for Christmas to propose to you? Oh, how romantic. It must have been a wonderful letter,' commented George.

'It was very explicit. He told me the time of the train he was coming down on: late afternoon on Christmas Eve. He asked me to meet him at St Kew. I borrowed a car for the occasion.'

'But surely the most convenient station would have been here in Delabole?'

'St Kew was what he said - and I wasn't going to argue. St Kew wasn't the right station for either of us. It was one stop after Port Isaac Road, two stops beyond Delabole. Neither of those stations was much used by then. But we thought it reduced the chance of him being spotted – or of us being seen together by his family. You see, the plan was he would spend his Christmas in this house here, just with me.'

'But he never turned up?'

'It was even worse than that. I stood waiting at St Kew for hours in the cold – the train was badly delayed. We didn't know it then but the bad winter of 1962/3 was just beginning. We didn't have mobile phone contact in those days.'

'Mobile phones can be a mixed blessing,' murmured Robbie, thinking of how one had been used to nearly entice him to his death. But the old lady wasn't listening. She was still in her world of 1962.

'Then, finally, the train steamed in. It was dark and cold. It wasn't a full-length platform at St Kew. If you happened to be in the wrong end of the train you had to make your way through to reach a carriage that was on the platform, so you could get out.

'For a time I couldn't see anyone. Then, in the cloud of steam near the engine, I thought I saw Neville. It was someone like him, wearing a tweed jacket like he had. I rushed forward and threw myself into his arms.

'But it wasn't Neville at all. And much worse than that, it was his brother - Owen.'

'Owen? I can see that would be a mutual shock. Oh, you poor woman. So what happened next?' said George.

'Did Owen have anything to say? Maybe he knew something about Neville's change of plan?' added the pragmatic Robbie.

'Owen was still nursing the old feud. He first unwrapped himself from my arms. Then he scowled ferociously, turned his back and walked out of the station.

'Of course, I waited around longer, in case there was a telephone message to the station from Neville. Or maybe a later train. But it was the last train from London before Christmas. There was no message. I never heard from him again.'

CHAPTER 45

George and Robbie walked slowly back from Grace Trevelyan's cottage, both deep in thought. They hadn't dared to say more in front of the old lady but they knew that her beloved Neville Harris was not, as she still thought, buried in the St Teath churchyard.

'I wonder how far back airlines keep their passenger flying records?' mused Robbie.

'I bet they'll keep them forever. Air passenger miles don't have a use-by date, do they? As long as the airline survived, anyway.'

'It wouldn't be called British Airways in those days but I bet its records still exist somewhere. No doubt the police could access them if required.'

'The question, Robbie, is not whether someone pretending to be Neville Harris flew out to New York in January 1963. The crucial question is what happened to that return ticket? Did "Neville" fly back again?'

There was a long pause as each of them pulled together all their known facts and deduced what had probably happened on that fateful Christmas journey.

'We know that Neville was in London, sorting out his travel plans,' began George. 'And we've just heard how Owen got off the London train.'

'So our best guess,' mused Robbie, 'is that Owen met

Neville by chance on the last Christmas Eve train down from London. Both men coming back to Cornwall for Christmas. They'd be compartmentalised carriages in those days. It was a long journey. It's easy to imagine that, towards the end, the two men would have had a compartment to themselves.'

'And then something happened to provoke the storm. Perhaps Owen started talking about them spending time with their Dad and Neville let slip that he wasn't coming to see his Dad at all, he was coming down to propose to Grace. We know, from what Grace has told us, how Owen would feel about that.'

'So we conjecture that the two brothers had a massive row about her, came to blows, and somehow or other Neville was killed.'

George continued. 'What was Owen to do? He could have got out at his planned stop at Port Isaac Road and left the body on the train. But it would be found when the train terminated at Padstow and the police would be alerted.'

'Yes. Then as now newspapers are desperate for hard news over the Christmas holidays.' This was a business Robbie knew well. 'Pictures of the body's face would be in all the papers and soon recognised – not least by Grace. One interview with her and the police would quickly be beating a path to the Harris's farm.'

'Then Owen remembered the Trelill tunnel – the only one on the line. Not far from his farm, as it happened. Remember, he'd explored it as a boy and had found an inner cavern halfway along.'

Robbie was into the task now. 'He knew the train would go slowly through the tunnel. Somewhere in the Railway Archive I learned there was a fifteen miles per hour speed limit. It would only take a minute to pass through but if Owen was ready and waiting, with the body at the window, it could just be done.'

'How would he know they were approaching the tunnel?' George wondered. 'He wouldn't be able to see anything out of the window. It was late December, the train was running late due to the bad weather and it was already dark.'

Robbie recalled the tale of Hyacinth Trevelyan. 'But he was local – he knew the long-established tradition. The engine would always blow its whistle once it was close to the tunnel. That would give him the necessary warning.'

Robbie collected his thoughts and then continued. 'So Owen got himself ready. He peeled off Neville's jacket, seized all his documents, including his airline tickets and passport –'

'- then dumped the poor man out of the train window into the darkness of Trelill tunnel.'

'After that he slipped on Neville's jacket, ready to get out five minutes later at the next stop.'

'I bet Owen was as shocked as Grace, Robbie, when he stumbled along the platform and was so lovingly welcomed by her at St Kew. She'd be the last person on earth he wanted to meet.'

So how did it continue? Robbie took up the tale.

'Then Owen had a huge stroke of luck. The cold winter weather, the worst for years, came at exactly the right time. There were a series of days after Christmas when the snow stopped all trains and all the maintenance work. He used one of those days, probably Boxing Day, to go back into the tunnel and drag his brother's body into the inner cavern. And then – a stroke of genius, maybe even a separate visit - to glue in a dark curtain to hide the cavity's entrance.'

It was all possible, indeed horribly likely.

'So on the scenario we're building, Robbie, what would have happened next?'

Robbie tried to imagine a little further. 'Just hiding Neville's body wasn't enough. He might not have come on the train but Grace was still waiting for him in Delabole. Owen needed to simulate a credible disappearance. Once again he was fortunate. On the journey down to Cornwall Neville must have told him of his plans to go to the United States. Everything was ready. So Owen took his brother's place – he had his ticket and passport, after all – and contrived to make it look as if Neville had flown to America as planned.'

'We know Grace mistook Owen for Neville at St Kew. The two men must have looked fairly similar. Passport photos are never that precise.'

George let the emotion of that meeting flow over her for a second and then continued, 'Afterwards Owen crept back to the UK, still pretending to be his brother. Then he made sure everyone back home was left thinking that Neville had started his new life in the United States.'

'But the deception didn't end there. His father kept asking questions about him. Owen needed Neville not just to move away but to be demonstrably dead. So he concocted a story about Neville being killed in a road crash and went over the United States for an imagined cremation. But his Dad still fretted away, wanted to see the tombstone for himself. So later, during the interregnum, he would arrange for the coffin of his brother to be "buried in St Teath".'

'Robbie, we'll need to make sure the police have all the hard information and our conjectures. Do you think they'll be able to nail Owen for it?'

'No doubt he'll wriggle. But if the 1963 flights, not just to the United States but in both directions, are established then Owen will need to prove he was in the UK in the beginning of 1963 if he wants to prove those journeys were not him. Proving anything half a century back is nigh on impossible but on our reconstruction that would certainly be beyond him.'

George was still feeling the sadness of Grace's encounter with the wrong brother. 'I bet he's obliterated any memory of meeting Grace Trevelyan when he got off the train at St Kew late on that Christmas Eve. The encounter would be so horrible that he'll have blanked it out. But her testimony will prove that Owen was in the train – the same one as Neville planned to travel down on. And she's still got her letter showing that was when Neville intended to travel.'

'George, there's another question for the police to ask Owen. It's small but critical. We know, from what Grace said, why Neville was travelling to St Kew. But why ever should Owen travel one or two stops past his own station?'

'Yes, why indeed? Do you think Grace Trevelyan will be willing to testify?'

'George, I'm sure that once Grace understands what really happened to her beloved Neville, nothing on earth will stop her testifying. And I'm sure she'll be a very compelling witness.'

The two continued to walk through the village, musing on what had happened and how easy or hard it would be to prove in a court of law.

'The trouble is, Robbie, to you and me it all hangs together, it's utterly convincing, but there's not a trace of direct evidence that Owen murdered Neville – or even that he was murdered at all. Even if he was on the same train as his brother, that doesn't prove he killed him and then shoved him out the carriage window.'

'And he could assert that no-one knew how bad the weather would be in the days ahead. Trains in Cornwall were almost never stopped for long by bad weather. He would have no idea he'd have a chance to deal with Neville's body in the tunnel over the Christmas holidays.'

George had another difficulty. 'Right from the start I've been bothered about the man's lack of clothing. I still don't see why Owen would choose to strip his brother naked. I mean, he'd have to cart every item away. It's a big risk. If he was spotted carrying his brother's clothes or trying to dispose of them that would destroy the whole illusion. I doubt if anything Neville was wearing was distinctive or worth very much. So why on earth did he bother?'

Their euphoria dampened, the two walked on in silence.

'So how does all this fit in with your earlier theory of Adam McTavish?' asked George. Robbie had given her a summary of Trevor's "confession" in the Riverside and the phone call from the police but the idea had been subsumed by more recent events. 'Didn't both events happen around the same time?'

Robbie was silent as he put together dates. 'Actually, George, they were the same time – Christmas Eve 1962. You don't think they might have overlapped in some way?'

George mused for a moment. 'Suppose that Adam was dumped in the tunnel on almost the same day as Neville. How might it affect Owen's behaviour on Boxing Day, when he came to put Neville into the cave, if he came across a second body in the tunnel, not just the one he'd put there?'

'When I last interviewed Owen, he admitted to me that he knew Adam. They were drinking buddies, about the same age. So he'd recognise him. What we don't know is if Adam was still alive.'

Handling uncertainty was George's forté. 'Let's try the alternatives. First suppose that Adam was dead. Owen would have no idea who had put him there or how long it'd be till he was missed. But he knew Adam worked locally in St Kew so sooner or later someone would come looking for him.'

'That's right. Leaving two bodies in the same cave would make it almost certain that sooner or later they'd both be found. Owen could smooth over Neville's disappearance by a trip to the States but he could nothing to discourage a search for Adam.'

George was quickly onto mitigation. 'The best solution would be to move Adam somewhere else, somewhere more obvious, so when they started looking he'd be quickly found. He mustn't leave the two bodies together.'

Robbie could see a snag. 'But for Owen, acting on his own, that wouldn't be easy. He'd find it much harder to move Adam any distance, working on his own, than he had to drop Neville down from the train. It's two hundred yards to the tunnel entrance in either direction for a start. And he didn't know the trains would be stopped for a week.'

'OK, Robbie. So option one leads to problems. Now let's consider option two: he finds Adam still alive in the tunnel – probably inside the cave. I bet the lads from the Laurels knew about the cave as well. When they brought him into the tunnel they'd put him as far out of sight as they could. What happens then?'

Robbie thought back to his interview with Owen. 'We know from his various efforts that Owen is a calculating creature. If a body is later found where it's locally known that an injured man was once dumped, the assumption will be that it's the same man

– especially if by this stage the body has been reduced to a skeleton. Remember this is 1962. DNA is completely unknown. So it would suit Owen to treat Adam for his injuries and then encourage him to clear off as fast and as far as possible.'

'And that would be one reason why he'd strip every item of clothing off Neville and give them to Adam. And why he'd make sure Adam left his army identity medal behind. You know, Robbie, that's a much more convincing reason for the skeleton being naked than we've had before.'

'But the thing is, George, on this scenario Adam McTavish would be a witness to Owen's appearance in the tunnel and to his connection with Neville. Adam could give strong supporting evidence that Owen had known about his brother – he'd come to deal with him inside the tunnel.'

George concluded, 'So it all depends on whether Adam McTavish is still alive. If he is, and the police know where he is, all that's needed is for them to ask him.'

CHAPTER 46

The police – and in particular the dogged Inspector Lambourn - had had a busy week. Despite long interviews over several days, Harris had not been able to provide any explanation for how his DNA had been deposited on the inside of the boot of Robbie Glendenning's car.

But the time spent on the interviews had given the police chance to assemble additional evidence. The driver of the bus from Bodmin to Wadebridge on the Friday before had been interviewed. He had remembered that there were only a couple of passengers on his first bus: a pretty young lady in a very short skirt and an older man with a stick. He had regarded them as rather an odd couple, which is why they'd stuck in his mind.

Later, the bus driver had been invited to come in to Bodmin Police Station for an identity parade. A bunch of retired country folk had been assembled, but Owen Harris had been picked out without any hesitation. The driver, who had hoped that the parade would be made up of short-skirted young ladies, went away feeling slightly cheated.

This success had led the police to quiz the driver of the last bus taking the coast road from Camelford on the critical Thursday evening. Again there had been very few passengers. And this driver was fairly certain, from the photographs he'd been shown, that one of those passengers was Owen Harris. He would attend another identity parade shortly.

Harris's line of stout denial was starting to look thin against this rising volume of evidence.

Lambourn noticed that there was one line of defence that Harris didn't care to pursue: what possible motive could he have for attacking the journalist? This question needed more work. He doubted, though, whether this would make any difference to the verdict of the jury when he came to trial.

George had gleaned all this from Lambourn, when he phoned her to check that Robbie was recovering well. She was a woman used to finding out information from senior managers and he had been no match for her wiles – especially as she had been the initiator of one of his key strategies.

'There's one more piece of news that your friend might be interested in,' Lambourn concluded. 'Glendenning and I were talking about it on the evening he was assaulted. It's that our colleagues in Scotland have managed to track down Adam McTavish. He's alive and well, now living in the Outer Hebrides.'

In the Bettle and Chisel the final meeting was about to take place of the group campaigning for a cycle trail from Wadebridge to Delabole.

A big roar announced the arrival of Robbie Glendenning, George Gilbert beside him. News of his assault and his recovery had spread round the village "like smoke from a steam train in Trelill tunnel" as one old-timer put it. At eight o'clock Alice Southgate arrived, exactly on time, and the meeting began.

Alice reminded them that this was the critical point in pulling together their bid. 'I've set aside the weekend to draw together the various pieces,' she announced forcefully. 'It'll go to the Council on Monday.'

This plan was received with approval. 'So how far have we reached,' she asked, 'on the questions we asked a month ago?'

Nathan's legal report came first. He had heard from all thirty landowners. Two thirds were happy to discuss permissive footpaths. Only one had written, digging in his heels to make the trail's progress more difficult.

'Who is it?' asked Alice. 'Maybe someone here knows something that will help influence his views?'

'The thing is, it was all private correspondence. Now I've told you what he said, I don't want to name him in public. Though some of you will know him, he drinks mostly at the White Hart. Someone I used to lodge with, actually, in an earlier life.'

Suddenly a link arose in Robbie's mind. What was this fellow's surname? He'd only ever heard it once – they just kept referring to him as Nathan. But had he not seen it written down, earlier that day? It couldn't be, surely?

'Could I butt in for a minute?' he asked.

Alice looked around for any dissent. But no-one was going to refuse the man who had suffered so much in helping put together their bid. 'Carry on.'

'It might not be relevant,' he said, 'but could I ask you, Nathan, when your "earlier life" ended?'

'Twenty years ago – late 1991.'

'And were you called Nathan in those days?'

'I was christened Jonathan. All my friends called me Jack. Even Geri here – I knew her as Trudy then – called me Jack. I only chose to be called Nathan when I started to become a solicitor.'

'Thank you. We'll talk more when this meeting's over. I may have a way of removing this obstacle to the cycle trail – or rather, I think you have.'

The meeting had finished by nine o'clock. Chairman Alice was brilliant at making contributors stick to the point and at cutting out red herrings. Whether the cycle trail would ever happen would be down to the Award judges at the Cornwall Council, but they had all done the most they possibly could.

After the meeting, Robbie and George sat either side of Nathan at one of the far tables. Robbie did the questioning though George knew exactly what he was going to ask.

'We're speaking privately now, Nathan, off the record. Was your landlord Owen Harris?'

'I've no idea how you two knew that, but yes, he was.'

'And were you with Geri – or should I say Trudy - in Trelill tunnel, the first time the skeleton was found?'

'I was. But I was too worried to be the one to alert the police. I feared for my career as a solicitor, you see.'

'And did you mention the find to your landlord?'

'He could see I was upset. I wasn't home until two on that Saturday night. I was badly shaken, the whole story just slipped out. He promised he would keep it secret – and, as far as I knew, he did.'

'And soon after that did Owen ask you to go and borrow a particular Railway Archive from Miss Trevelyan?'

Nathan pondered for a moment. In the trauma of the hidden skeleton he'd forgotten the event entirely. But now it came back to him.

'How on earth did you know that? He did. But I've no idea why.'

'I believe we do. You must tell this to the police. First thing tomorrow morning. A really serious case hangs on it. And the correct identification of that skeleton. Please can you do that?'

Later that evening Robbie and George walked slowly back, hand in hand, to the Southgate's.

'Well, everything we've learnt today – this afternoon and this evening - must help nail Owen Harris for the murder of the skeleton in the tunnel. Especially once the police interview Adam McTavish.' George sounded relieved.

'If Nathan doesn't tell the police I'll tell them myself. Once they learn it was Owen who inserted the only mention of Edwin in the record, he'll find it hard to make that defence stick.'

'He might claim that what happened in the train was some sort of dreadful accident, after which he was acting in panic. Nobody could be sure how Neville died, fifty years after the event.'

'But Grace is a redoubtable lady. Her testimony, Neville's final letter and Adam's testimony will make it hard for him to escape justice.'

'Don't you think it's implausible,' asked George, 'that two bodies should arrive in the same place at the same time from two different sources?'

'Well, the cave inside the tunnel was special. No-one knew of it except a few locals so it's not surprising that it was the hiding place both lots chose to use. The coincidence is on the timing. But both events were triggered by Christmas. So maybe it's not as bizarre as you'd think.'

'There's one other thing that doesn't make much sense to me,' ventured George. 'Why on earth did Owen bring up and even chair the Arresting Crime scheme in the first place? Couldn't he see the danger of provoking interest in the subject?'

'I've been thinking about that. Did he want something to liven his later years and took the chance when it came along? How near could he get to being discovered without actually being identified?'

'He's a smart man, Robbie. I don't believe he'd do that.'

'To be honest, neither can I. But I checked back on my notes of what happened at that first pub quiz and I've got a better idea. It could have been a clever defence mechanism.'

'How do you mean?'

'Well, the landlord told me that the table Owen and his pals were sitting was next to the one where the cycle trail idea began. Remember, Owen knew Nathan from twenty years back – he'd been his landlord once. He heard the start of their discussion and realised that they were thinking of something that could lead to the skeleton being found again.'

'You mean the Arresting Crime scheme was a blocking device?'

'No-one knew which scheme would win the quiz, George. If Owen and his pals could come up with a great scheme then the cycle trail would never get beyond a dream. He knew there was at least one old crime waiting because he'd committed it himself half a century earlier – maybe that was what gave him the idea. My guess is he thought that just by raising the prospect he might at least win the quiz. That would make sure the threat of the other scheme, which would lead to a re-examination of the old tunnel, was strangled at birth.'

'So it was the worst of all worlds, from his viewpoint, when both schemes tied in the quiz and both got the green light to continue?'

'I think so. Of course nothing much would happen unless one or other won the Green Tourist Award. It was only Alice

Southgate's organisation which made the cycle trail bid fly. Once the tie had happened Owen must have decided that seizing control of Arresting Crime was the best way of making sure someone else didn't find the old skeleton or ask the wrong questions. He did not want his brother's disappearance to be re-examined.'

There was a roar and a motor bike surged past them. Robbie glanced up and saw that it was Nathan. A passenger was hanging on behind, her auburn hair streaming from under her helmet. She waved to them as she went past.

'That's Rowena with Nathan,' said George in surprise.

And a narrow escape for me, thought Robbie, as he caught George's eye.

As they neared the Southgates' Robbie had one more question. 'I thought it was going to come out this afternoon when we were talking to Miss Trevelyan, but you slid away from it. How did you discover Neville's grave was empty?'

'I persuaded Inspector Lambourn to put a forensic tent over the grave. Given the current interregnum it wasn't difficult to arrange.'

'But it must take ages to get permission to carry out an exhumation?'

'It would. But I managed to persuade him that all he needed to do was to make sure that Owen saw the tent at the edge of the cemetery and understood what it was intending to do.'

'You mean, Lambourn has no proof the grave is empty?'

'Oh he does now. During his interview, Owen Harris was quite happy to admit that Neville's burial was all a fake. In point of fact, the grave never needed to be opened up at all.'

AUTHOR'S NOTES

The real hero of this story is the North Cornwall Railway. Who would have thought that in the last century but one passengers could leave London, travel down to Cornwall and reach Padstow, 260 miles away on the Cornish coast, a mere seven hours later?

The novel is set in a real location but it is only a story. The characters are made up and the suspect Children's Home in St Kew exists only in my imagination. The only exception is the Tourist Visitor Centre lady from Tintagel, Jill Frewer. I appreciate her help in selling my books in Tintagel.

I am grateful to several Delabole locals who have told me how the railway affected their lives, including Sally Holden, who used it to travel to boarding school, and Les Corey, the last stationmaster of Delabole.

The internet has pictures by David Crick, who traversed the Trelill tunnel in 2003. Chris Jennings, on crjennings.com, has other pictures of the tunnel.

Finally I've consulted "An Illustrated history of the North Cornwall Railway" by David Wroe, published by Irwell Press in 1995.

Where source clashed I edged in the direction which most helped my story. This book is not a history: some facts have blurred and operational details are made up. But I hope the result will not be too fanciful to those privileged with first-hand memories; and will give younger readers something fresh to stir their imagination.

Like all authors I would appreciate comments, reviews and suggestions for future Cornish Conundrums.

David Burnell   website: www.davidburnell.info
April 2016

DOOM WATCH describes George Gilbert's first encounter
with crime as she helps Padstow plan an upgrade.
A body is discovered behind the Engine House of the old
quarry at Trewarmett but identification proves tricky.
It takes the combined efforts of George and Police Sergeant
Peter Travers to make sense of a crime which seems, simultaneously, to be spontaneous and pre-planned.

"A well-written novel, cleverly structured, with a nicely-handled sub-plot..."
Rebecca Tope, crime novelist

SLATE EXPECTATIONS begins as George Gilbert buys a cottage overlooking Trebarwith Strand.
The analyst finds herself part of an outdoor drama based on 19th century events in the Delabole Slate Quarry - a drama heightened when one of the cast is found dead, part-way through the opening performance.
The combined resources of George and Police Sergeant Peter Travers are needed to disentangle the past and find out precisely how it relates to the present.

"Slate Expectations combines an interesting view of an often overlooked side of Cornish history with an engaging pair of sleuths who follow the trail from past misdeeds to present murder." Carola Dunn, crime author

LOOE'S CONNECTIONS finds George Gilbert conducting a short study of floods in Looe when, without warning, her colleague disappears.

But without really trying George is drawn into a web of suspense and foul play. But when her personal and professional lives begin to overlap, is she the unwitting suspect or the next victim?

The trail covers various ways of reducing the flooding in the town and events over many centuries. Even the Romans have a part to play.

"History, legend and myth mixed with a modern technical conundrum makes this an intriguing mystery." Carola Dunn, crime author

19239649R00178

Printed in Great Britain
by Amazon